SOFT INHERITANCE

C.E. O'GRADY

Azothwords Publishing

Azothwords Publishing

ISBN 13: 978-0-692-74118-4

Printed In The United States Of America

For Meme, who taught me to love words

CHAPTER 1

I couldn't open my eyes. The sweet protection of the darkness was too addictive. The fear of facing the outside world too great. I tried to ignore the burning in my throat and the sweat collecting at the base of my neck, but it pulled me back into the present, back to my hell on earth.

A voice, high pitched and full of concern shattered my shelter. "Dr. Shay, are you alright?" The impulse to laugh at her question proved difficult to bite back. No, I would never be alright. All my hope, prayers, and murmured deals with devils couldn't possibly save me. Since birth the hands of my illness rested around my neck, but now they were squeezing. The timer on my clock of sanity began to tick.

Sucking in a shallow breath, I slowly opened my eyes. A massive blackboard hung a few feet in front of me, and upon it my own handwriting in chalk. The words read familiar, and to my dismay only half complete. My lecture notes on the Hundred Years' War? Gathering not enough courage, I turned around. Before me sat an immense assemblage of college students, bodies uniformly positioned in the hard chairs, each face portraying a unique shade of shock.

The lapse left me pathetic. Tears raced droplets of sweat down my face. My legs shook so fiercely my slacks quivered. Each breath pushed a wheeze through my scream-scorched throat. The students waited for an explanation. Their eyes held the hope I would somehow spit out words to wipe away what I had done, but those words did not exist. Not knowing which lapse had trapped me, I hadn't a clue as to how I responded to it. As time paused, my reaction could have easily been screaming and crying, though it was just as likely that I beat someone to death.

I could see a proverbial fork in the road open before me. Both paths ending in the same doomed fate, but the journeys to this end differed. My choices were simple. I could run, abandoning my career and the outside world. By locking myself away I could allow the disease to ravage my brain in the comforts of home. In other words, the first path meant giving up and giving in. The second path held blind corners and rocky bottoms. I could take it and fight to continue in my life for as long as possible. The humiliation and dangers I would face would increase by the day, but joy, even in minuscule doses could still be found. Right?

Gazing into the faces of my pupils I debated my roads. Then one thought muted all the others, the thought of my mother.

Having made the decision, I opened my mouth and expected brilliance. "This is exactly what happens when you don't have a balanced breakfast." Brilliance never sounded so ridiculous. In unison the student's expressions creased into skepticism. My choice was made.

"Hopefully you enjoyed class more than I did today. Please don't forget your first exam is on Wednesday. If you have any questions about it, I have office hours tomorrow from eleven until two. Thank you." Most of them left quickly, either pleased by an early release or excited to share the story of their professor's physiological meltdown. I couldn't tell which, but hoped for the former, knowing rumors would soar.

The lingering students approached me tentatively in small groups. Bearing both sincere and grade-grubbing smiles, they told me to get well and offered to escort me to the student health services. I thanked the little groups for their concern and made the false promise I would be fully recovered before our next class.

"I told you he was a freak."

Turning toward the voice, I found Amber spouting to a skinny blonde girl whose cheeks had gone pink. Never breaking our eye contact,

Amber left her friend and marched at me. Her scarlet hair matched the hue of her excessive lipstick. She always reminded me of my great, great grandfather's favorite prostitute, flaunting her low cut blouse and deep, creamy cleavage. As she approached, I dropped my head. The scuffed floor tiles secured a far safer target for my eyes. When the tips of Amber's satin shoes stepped into view, I felt her reach toward me. I tried to lean away, but her fingers were quick and she caught my collar. As she pulled my face up to her own, I heard stitches snapping in my shirt.

"Still too good for me, Dr. Chamberlain Shay?" Her breath smelled like rotten fruit. The closeness of her body forced a gag from the back of my throat. I pried her boney fingers off and told her to leave. Her laughter echoed as she paraded away.

Amber had been aching to destroy me, and my public display of ineptitude gave her the tools to succeed. Had I known she sat among the sea of students witnessing my insanity, I might have turned tail and ran when I had a chance. Ignorance wasn't bliss, but I sure wished for it back.

"Are you alright?" asked a female behind me. This was the second time in ten minutes that the same voice asked the same absurd question.

"Do I look alright?"

"Not even a little," she said.

"Then please, quit asking me that damn question."

Where once singed pain and fear, anger now burned my cheeks. Turning to face the girl, I found a small creature, hands snugly upon her narrow hips. She mirrored a modern image of Anne Boleyn, the second wife of Henry VIII. She held the true face of Anne, not that of the ridiculous paintings created by men born after her death. Her face set my memory ablaze. Four hundred and fifty years stood between their existences, but their resemblance was uncanny. For a moment, I worried I had slipped into another lapse, but the girl's jeans and bobbed haircut hinted her realness. Upon closer observation, I noticed a difference in the eyes. Anne's black opaque stare could have been mistaken for holes in her face. This enchanting girl's eyes shone blue. When she started to fidget, it occurred to me I'd been staring at her for an awkward amount of time.

"Sorry… It's just that… You look familiar. What were you saying?"

"You were biting my head off for being nice to you," she reminded me.

"That's right, I'm sorry, I just... I'm fine OK? And I just want to get back to my office. I don't need any help."

"No, you need help," she declared. "A fine person doesn't roll around on the floor like he's on fire. I thought you were going to bash your head on the ground and kill yourself. Right here, right in front of us! I've never seen anyone freak out like that before." She'd obviously never been to any of my family reunions.

I recalled no memory of my breakdown, but based on the state of my body I figured it had been very bad. Her words stunned me. I felt even more hopeless and wanted to ask her to explain what I had done. A little emotion must have spilled into my expression because she easily read my mind. "You completely blacked out, didn't you? Wow, you're worse off than I thought." I searched the room for eavesdroppers, and found us alone. While I tried explaining I was just having a bad day, she kept shaking her head, refusing to accept any of my excuses. At one point she even stomped her foot. I felt like I was arguing with a toddler, and losing. When I finally realized she clearly wasn't going to listen, I walked to the podium and began packing my briefcase. She followed.

My exasperation released. "Look, if I wanted help I would ask for it OK? But I don't. Thanks for your concern. You did your duty as a nice person. Now please run along and don't waste any more of your time worrying about me. I'm a grown man and I've been taking care of myself for a long time."

"A grown man who can't remember to eat a balanced breakfast, right?" Her frustrated mockery hit me thick.

"Take any health class and you'll learn how dangerous low blood sugar can be. I promise from now on to grab a donut or something." Grabbing up the last of my things from the podium, I brushed past her and staggered for the exit.

"You kept screaming for Da."

Her voice stopped me again. Feigning disinterest with my back to her, I listened. "At first you were speaking in a different language, then you mixed in some English. You said something about animal skulls. And at the end of it you said "blood" and another word, something like fw-ull, I think. You kept saying those words over and over." She wasn't pronouncing it right, but I knew the word she meant. I had been screaming *fuil,* an old Irish word for blood.

She had helped immensely. Not knowing which memory I'd lapsed into would have made tracking the trigger impossible. Thanks to the Anne Boleyn look alike, I could try and prevent this particular memory from coming back to haunt. This softened my attitude about her, but the conversation had gone too far.

Turning to face her, I fought for words to push her away without causing undue hurt. She seemed like a very nice girl. Had I not been her professor or a man on the verge of losing his mind, I would have asked her on a date. As it stood, it was time for the confused gorgeous girl to be on her way.

"My personal problems are just that, personal. While I appreciate your concern, this line of questioning is quite frankly rude. Please mind your own business and leave me alone. If I wanted your help or anyone else's I would ask." I winced inside as the words oozed out, needing to say them, but not wanting to at all. She had done nothing wrong, and she knew it.

Rejection rippled visibly through her shoulders. When she had trampled five or six steps from me I called out, "Wait! What is your name?" I needed to reopen the door I had just slammed in order to properly record our interaction.

"Cara," she replied flatly. Staring down at her shoes, she copied my posture only moments before with Amber. My well of self-loathing gained another drop. She sighed, "I should get going, but... um...." Her goodbye tones made me feel certain a notice would appear in my inbox informing me Cara had un-enrolled from History 201.

"I was going to wish you a happy birthday, but after what happened today maybe I should wish you a *happier* birthday. Either way, I hope you feel better."

"How did you know it was today?" I asked in bewilderment.

"Does it matter?" she deadpanned, stepping through the door, not waiting for a reply.

CHAPTER 2

Nestled amongst traditional wooden decor and oil paintings, a tattered yellow chair lived in front of my immense office window. The ugliness drew the eye like a stain, but its ability to accommodate the sharp angles of my six-foot-three stature made up for its putrid bile color. I rarely sat anywhere else. An upright leather chair throned behind my desk, but it was stiff. The tortuous metal chair intended for student visitors pained too short and cold.

I'd typically spend a few hours each day in my yellow chair, absently staring out my two-story perch. The day's complications disrupted my routine, and I frantically searched for a trigger in the lines of my lecture notes.

Twenty years of tripping over triggers taught me they could be anything; barely detectable landmines buried all around. An image, a smell, a sound, or a simple turn of phrase unleashed profound memories from the dead. Up to this point, I mostly ignored them. When memories ran, I treated them like annoying distractions testing my sanity. Tracking down their triggers seemed as fruitless as tracing the origin of a fallen autumn leaf.

Having spent the morning trapped in a memory had changed my perspective entirely. Triggers could now launch a lapse, therefore, triggers had become the center of my existence.

Thanks to Cara, I knew which memory had taken me, but linking it to my lecture on The Hundred Years' War was difficult. The scene I acted out in class had taken place nearly nine hundred years prior to the war. The blood spilt different, the emotions contrasted; there seemed no common factor. Word by word I searched my tedious outline. As the stack of papers on the arm of the chair diminished, my anxiety and frustration grew. I finished reviewing the final sheet, and smashed it into a ball and threw it and screamed. I brushed the remaining papers off my lap and kicked them away.

It was too soon. I was still a young man in his twenties. Our family history contained a lot of uncertainties, but two facts always remained; lapses wouldn't strike someone so young and lapses were c'est le commencement de la fin, the beginning of the end. Now, only one of these held true. Even with Granddad's attempts to prepare me, I was not ready.

When I was a boy, Granddad devised a game to teach me the art of deception. Promising a candy reward, at random moments he would call out a crazy scenario. "You are crawling around on the floor of a restaurant." To win the game, I had to invent a viable behavior explanation, such as, "I'm looking for my contact lens." As I grew older, the situations he posed grew more complex, but the candy never changed. Thanks to Granddad's game, I developed a stockpile of rehearsed lies and a wicked sweet tooth. Waking from a lapse to an audience of two hundred was finally an opportunity to utilize one of my many practiced fobs, yet I blurted out nonsense and acted the fool. I was not ready.

I drank a glass of water and told myself to calm down. Leaning back and closing my eyes, I focused on my breathing. Muscles unclenched and my pulse stopped throbbing as I drifted slowly away from the lecture and the war. Bit by bit the memory moved into focus. Relaxing and allowing it to build in my head, I lost sight of the world as Dr. Chamberlain Shay. Raw emotions and vivid colors tugged at my brain. I leapt into the mind of one of my most ancient Celtic relatives, a small boy…

Twisting and jerking, Da reminds me of the fish we caught. The four men dragging Da ignore his screams. They disappear into the dark and Ma takes my hand. We follow the path Da's body carves in the mud. My bare feet absorb the cold ground and I know not to complain. We walk through the dark to a group huddled at the center of the Dun. I want to run to the warmth near the lit torches people hold, but Ma stops us short and pulls me into the shadows.

"What is happening Ma?" She does not answer, and holds me more tightly.

The men force Da to stand, and they bind his feet and hands with sinew. The crowd shies away from Da in a wave. Women pull children into their skirt folds and the men force their wives behind them. I am confused and scared. They should be helping Da, not moving from him like he was a sickly stoat! One by one I look at their faces, picking out the ones I know well. Ma helped Ailis bring a babe, and Moire taught me to tan hides. Aodh, Da's best friend is there too, but he is staring at the ground. I can't understand why none of them help Da.

Da is covered in mud, and blood runs from the side of his face down his neck. He cries. Da never cried. He told me many times only women and babes cry. When his eyes find us, shivering in the dark, he cries harder. Ma holds out a hand to him like she is trying to touch his face, even though she is too far away. He nods his head as a secret message passes between them. His expression softens and he tilts his head to the sky, changing the flow of his dripping blood.

The High Elder walks to the center of the mass and stands next to Da. Thick white ceremonial furs still reveal his frailty. "This man is possessed with the daemons of the dead and the whispers of the faeries. Many have come to my council afraid of his behavior. He remembers things he wasn't alive to see. He knows of places only the spirits could have led him to. Are there any among you who can deny this?"

I take a big breath to ensure enough volume for what I have to say, but before the first word is formed Ma covers my mouth with her cold hand and whispers "No."

I know to obey, but I want so badly to explain. They must know that Da isn't bad. He is blessed. We know our ancestor's thoughts, but it isn't from daemons or faeries. We received gifts from the gods. Da said so when I started receiving my gifts.

No one answers the Elder, so he keeps talking. "It is sad when one of our own is taken and we must swiftly protect the rest of the Dun. Woman - bring the boy here."

"No!" yells Da, and The Elder cracks his wooden staff over Da's head. The crowd gasps a loud breath. I feel Ma's body shake, and look up at her to see the moonlight shining through the tears on her cheek.

My terrified knees lock. Ma puts her hands on my shoulders and holds tight to my bare skin. She takes her time pushing me forward and the crowd parts as we near. We stop far from the feet of The Elder and he hisses, "Bring him here woman!" Looking everywhere but at The Elder, I see women weeping and more men with eyes only for the ground. Nudging me forward again we stop when The Elder blocks everything else from view. I have never been this close to him before, and can see what kind of tiny animals' skulls hang on his necklace.

Bending down, he asks, "Do you have the daemons too little one?"

I know this is my chance to explain everything, but Ma's nails bite into my skin. Looking towards Da, I see the word "No" form on his silent lips. I want to sound like a man. I want to sound brave. I weakly say "No." All I hear is the voice of a scared little boy.

"Good!" says The Elder, pulling a bone dagger from one of the many leather thongs around his neck. The handle is made of blue jewels, and hanging from it are wolf teeth linked in chains. He tries to hand it to me, but I refuse to touch it. I have seen it before. He uses its sharp edges to slit the throats of blessed animals during Festival. Seeing the refusal in my eyes, he grows angry and his bald head turns red.

"Take it boy. Prove the seeds of the daemons don't live in you as in your father. Do what needs to be done or share his fate." Ma grabs my hand. She pushes the dagger into my palm and forces me to grasp it.

The men on either side of Da push him to his knees. I hear lots of movement, and looking around I see half the families have left. Da stares straight into me as I look to him for help. His green eyes show none of the fear or pain I know shone in mine. Da looks proud and he whispers, "The blood of my life, the son of my line, you must survive in honor and learn from what has passed." The words are not new. They have been repeated many times from Da to son.

Ma raises our joined hands and presses the dagger below Da's jaw. I see flashes of all of the men. Warm blood flows over my hand and I scream. I fall to the ground...

Impossible not to feel the young boy's pain, I came to shaken by the brutal memory. My teeth chattered and my feet stung with cold. Da's green eyes reminded me of the last time I saw my own father, a birthday years ago...

Curled in my ugly chair, I thought about how the memories, my father, and my birthday could have all worked against me to cause a lapse.

Uncertain how it fit together, but knowing somehow it did. I tried not to think about how someday soon these memories would be my only reality.

I started reorganizing my scattered notes when the door swung open and Briggy flew through. Papers flit as his panicked face alerted there was no time for common courtesies. Being the most polite person I knew, busting in clearly screamed something was horribly wrong. However, he was also Briggy, so I knew best to wait for an explanation before panicking. Collecting his thoughts and breath, I watched silently as he paced, not in straight lines like a normal person, but in random arcs and circles. He held a bright orange piece of paper in his chubby hands, silently reading to himself.

Briggy could have been thirty or he could have been fifty. I couldn't tell and never asked. His dark hair patched with gray curled around his face, caging the black fluffy caterpillars he called eyebrows. He was short and round and jolly.

Briggy's mind burned far more interesting than his appearance. Being a botanist wholly obsessed with the green world also meant he had very little interest in the human world. He typically had no idea what day it was, and a small army of grad students worked around the clock to keep him on schedule. Luckily, being a world-renowned expert on biofuels convinced the school to overlook his oddness and happily stipend his caretakers. Always dressed in a white lab coat stained green with plant blood, typically smelling of fertilizer, and never very observant, Briggy was my best friend.

"The University is promoting blatant discrimination Chamberlain, and I have no idea how to combat it." He held the orange paper in front of my face.

"I found this attached to my car this morning. It is horrendous. Look."

I read it aloud:

In support of a healthy student body and to accommodate dietary diversity on campus, the University is now offering a vegetarian option with all cafeteria meals. We encourage everyone to try this new option and eat more vegetables. - Student Health Services.

Reading the flyer aloud infuriated him even more. He ripped it from my hand and began ranting. "A travesty! Blatant ignorance! What can these people possibly have against plants!?"

I knew my best friend was quite a bit insane, but figured birds of a crazy feather should suffer together. To keep from laughing and smiling too hard, I bit down on my cheek and tried to reason with him.

"Briggy, I have seen you eat a salad. Since when are you against eating veggies? Weren't you lecturing me just the other day about how much nutrition..." He cut me off.

"Yes, I do eat veggies and there is nothing wrong with that, but when I eat I do not discriminate!" Waving the orange paper above his head to demonstrate the extent of his outrage, he yelled, "These people are choosing to target and kill only plants for their dietary needs, and I am *not* OK with that!" I desperately did not want to laugh and hurt his feelings, so I bit down harder on my cheek until I tasted blood.

"It's just a piece of paper. You know how much the students love fast food. I wouldn't worry about it. If you want, I'm sure your grad students would be happy to print and distribute a flyer countering the, um, attack." The suggestion subdued him slightly and he quieted. Watching him ponder his war, I noticed a bit of green popping from his left lab coat pocket. He always had some strange new plant with him, but this looked like a simple weed.

"What have you brought today?" I inquired, gesturing toward the peeking foliage. Completely distracted, he brightened and explained, "This *Taraxacum officinale*, or dandelion as you would call him, was in grave peril, and I plucked him from the jaws of death."

He was excited, and I had never heard him be so dramatic as to use a word like peril. Again I fought back a laugh, noticing my mouth tasted like copper. "What happened?"

"I found him in the parking lot growing between cracks in the blacktop - like he was personally defying the waywardness of society and its artificial ground substances. I worried some vehicle might crush him, so I am going to plant my brave comrade in the greenhouse."

I hadn't the heart to remind him of his research yielding the most effective weed killer on the market. Instead I patted him on the back and told him sincerely, "You are a thoughtful soul." My round friend smiled. I knew I shouldn't have been encouraging his behavior, especially involving saving weeds, but who was I to rob it from him?

Settling down, Briggy and I fell into our normal routine. Over the last few years we'd developed a pleasingly simple pattern of interaction. We spent our time together discussing the weather, our work, and other benign things. Some days we said very little and just enjoyed the physical presence of another person. He did not know about my illness. Like so many other people in my life, I kept him in the dark, although I was sure he would have been very intrigued by its genetic implications. It wasn't that I didn't trust him. History had simply taught me that even knowing about my family illness could be dangerous.

Only fifteen minutes into our visit, a rapid knock tapped at my door. Opening it, I found a small mouse-like student with thick glasses and a book bag so full it forced her into a hunchback. Seeing Briggy, she filled with visible relief.

"There you are Dr. Briggs! I've been looking all over for you. You need to follow me to your Plant Morphology class, the students are waiting." Obviously miffed he'd given her the slip, her glasses twitched on the end of her nose.

"Oh yes! Plant Morphology, the heart of understanding the key differences in the vast flora inhabiting the earth. That's today is it?"

"Yes, sir," replied the hunchbacked mouse. Briggy mustered a knowing nod and followed her down the hallway.

Closing the door behind him, I saw his orange paper thoughtlessly left on the floor. I tossed it in the trash knowing that out of sight was truly out of mind when it came to my friend.

Not long after resettling into my chair, the abrupt sound of high heels echoed loudly through the hallway. The clock on my desk showed it was one minute to eleven, and I knew who motivated those emphatic spikes. It was Libby.

CHAPTER 3

Libby was never late. Libby was never ill prepared, and Libby was never a pleasure to work with. Already at the door by the time she knocked, I swung it open and greeted her as I always did. "Hello Libby, isn't it a beautiful day?" She rolled her eyes at me and crossed the room to take her customary seat in the hard metal chair. She pulled files from her briefcase and arranged them neatly on my desk. As she worked, her long golden hair kept wandering in front of her eyes, and each time she'd violently tuck it behind her ears. Her hair had a mind of its own and did everything it could to hide her worst feature. Twenty years old, she possessed perfect skin and an incredible body, but her face unmistakably resembled a weasel.

Genetic variation is not that vast among humans, and whenever someone new crossed my path, they always looked like someone I remembered.

Everyone except Libby. The first month I knew her all I saw were weasels.

When her files were all laid out, she looked my direction for the first time and unleashed what I expected.

"Why are you all dirty and covered in chalk? You look horrible. Don't you know that appearance is the hallmark of the mental state?" I wondered mockingly if that meant she had the mental state of a weasel. "I can't believe you walk around like that. And what's wrong with your eyes? They're all red," she said putting her hand over her mouth. "If you're sick you should have warned me before I came in here."

"I'm not sick. I had a bad morning. Can't we just get to work?" I could tell she wanted to know why, but apparently didn't care enough to ask. She started sorting through her files instead. Seeing her quick fingers maneuver the large stack of documents, I felt astounded by how much progress had been made since I hired Libby.

She seemed very pleased to work for me, or at least as pleased as Libby could appear. We weren't friends. Libby and I had a very straightforward relationship. She needed my help paying tuition while she finished the graduate program, and I needed her secretary personality. Straightforward, cold, and bright, I depended on her. I knew no one on campus more suited to dig through boring government documents, cut through miles of red tape, and provoke people into submission.

Finding the file she hunted for, she tossed it on top of the others. The burgeoning Colorado file had been causing us issues for over a month. Begging and threatening the Colorado Department of Corrections to give us the current location of one of their inmates, Mr. William C. James, they denied having any record of such a person. In response to their claims of ignorance, we provided documents from Ireland proving a man by that name had been transferred into their custody after extradition. We were sure this hot piece of evidence would loosen their lips, but weeks passed with no reply. Each day it seemed more likely they were just going to ignore us altogether, but as Libby opened the file and handed me a piece of paper, joy spread across her face. At least I thought I was observing joy. When a weasel smiles it looks a lot like they're just trying to show you their teeth.

Sitting, I read the letter to myself first, then out loud. In brief and to the point language, the letter stated the person in question had indeed been housed in the Cañon City facility for two years, but was no longer there. Finally a breakthrough! They were at last communicating with us, but I felt let down.

"They didn't mention why he wasn't there anymore. Or where he went." Her smile vanished and she jumped into silver linings mode. "At least we know he was there and that someone was willing to talk to us."

"Yeah and that person was more than happy to share their name with us too," I said, tossing the paper in her direction.

"I know. There's not even a letterhead or a date marked on it."

I felt bad. I knew it had taken her a great amount of time and effort to get this much, but I still couldn't feel satisfied. Until this point, I searched for him patiently. Patience was a virtue I could no longer maintain. My last and only goal before I went mad was to find this man, and the deadline to meet it felt just around the corner.

"I was just hoping he was still there is all." I could see the question *Why* forming on her lips, but she wisely held it in.

Libby knew we weren't working on a book. I made it very clear in the beginning I wanted her to focus on one task and one task only, to find William C. James. The reason behind finding him was none of her business. I didn't even tell her the C stood for Chamberlain.

She stayed true to her go-getter form. "At least we have a timeline to work with. James spent a year in Ireland after being apprehended there, and then he spent only two years in Cañon City before disappearing. Don't you see? Our focus is narrowed. I'll start checking inmate transfer lists and prison reports from that time. It's possible he had died by this point, so it's vital we track bodies too." I nodded, but her last few words pained me. She was right. He could be dead. In all the years I searched for him, I never wanted to think about finding a body instead of a person. To hear it out loud made it a real possibility, and as much as I despised my father, I needed to find him alive.

Libby outlined her plan of attack and handed me a stack of letters to sign. As a historian I sometimes received extra privileges to information, so she would write the request letters she needed and I'd sign blindly.

She took out a small blue notepad and asked me if I could remember any distinguishing marks William might have had, just in case he ended up a John Doe. I hesitated, and then told her I knew of only two. The first was a tattoo on his forearm, the numbers *1958*, and the other was a scar under his left ear. Pleased with the information, she hastily repacked the folders into her black briefcase.

"Libby, I might have a *new* problem with Amber."

She froze and stared at me hard. "The Amber that accused you of sexual harassment?" I nodded. "If she's bringing that crap back up again you don't need to worry about it. *Everyone* knows she threw herself at you and then got pissed when you rejected her."

I wished Libby were right that everyone believed the truth, but in reality I still had staff members jabbing me disparaging looks in the halls.

"Something happened in my 201 class today and she might have recorded it. I need you to keep an ear out and let me know if you hear anything."

"What happened?" she asked while trying to dust off my chalky slacks and shirt.

I lied. "I don't know, I just freaked out for a few minutes."

"*What do you mean you freaked out?*" She looked at me for an awkwardly quiet moment waiting for a reply I wasn't going to give.

"OK, fine. I'll let you know if I hear anything, but you need to get control of yourself. That girl is out for blood and I can't believe you would give her something to work with. That was stupid professor Shay. I thought you were smarter than that."

The last thing I needed at that moment was a lecture. I hated myself enough for what I let happen. "Just do as I ask, OK?"

"Fine but you don't pay me enough to be a spy, so just be happy I am doing it at all."

She was right. Libby wasn't my slave, so I took a few deep breaths and told her sincerely, "I would appreciate your help. I *need* your help."

"That's better. You should really work on those communication skills. I'll let you know if she starts stirring things up again. I'll be here during your office hours tomorrow." And she was gone.

The door closed and I sunk back into the comfy chair. The events of the day had drained me. With so much to worry about, I kept settling back on one thought, well, less of a thought and more of a face - Cara's face. My brain searched for any distraction, and Cara was the only one who felt safe. Thinking about the shape of her face and the sound of her voice escaped me from the eating stresses. She quieted the loud ticking clock in my head, the one reminding me of how quickly madness marched in my direction.

Reality eventually bit through and I pulled out the small red notebook that always waited in one of my pockets. Flipping through the filled pages, I stopped on the first fresh one and wrote the date, then briefly outlined the good and bad of my birthday. It had been a very long day.

CHAPTER 4

I spent the night subjecting myself to a variety of triggers. War movies, pictures of dead relatives, sniffing bottles of antique perfume, and nothing. Storms of memories flooded my mind, but a lapse never found me. This ought to have brought me joy. I should have dismissed the previous day's misstep as a fluke, but as I pulled into the university parking lot the next morning doubt smothered me.

Lecture notes in hand, I made my way through the classroom door with five minutes to spare. The university decided to offer Historical Writing after gaining me as an instructor: their attempt to squeeze every bit of perk from hiring a bestselling author.

A typical writer might have enjoyed the chance to share his knowledge, but not me. Instructing the class made me feel like a fraud and I hated it. When it came to writing about the past, I was a world-class cheater, and wasn't really sure how normal people did it. While I plucked ancient memories from my mind and jotted down what appeared, the real professionals did painstaking research. I had to steal from several how-to books just to piece together a coherent outline. Many times I'd lazily schedule guest speakers in hopes the students and I could learn something.

An awful way to run a class, the students didn't seem to mind, and I gave most of them A-grades just for showing up.

Turning on the computer, the projector, and lowering the screen, I went about preparing the room as sleepy faced students trickled in listlessly. Once the room mostly filled and the clock indicated time to begin, I reached for my notes.

On the podium waiting for me lay a white sheet of paper. Taped to it were three pieces of hard candy and a juice box. It read:

To: Dr. Shay
Just in case you missed your balanced breakfast.

I had to laugh even though I wasn't certain if this had been left as some kind of mean joke, or if it was actually intended to help. The elegant handwriting gracing it swooped with tails and even pressure, most likely female. My best guess, and the thought that put butterflies in my stomach, was the note came from Cara.

I searched for her face around the room and felt a little shocked how many of the students looked completely unfamiliar. When I first started teaching, I tried to learn most of their names, but after a few years I gave up. Students would have to be very persistent for help, or be exceptionally gifted for me to even recognize them. In this particular class I hadn't gotten to know anyone yet, except for maybe Cara.

Not finding her, I opened my mouth to begin when out of the corner of my eye I glimpsed her walking in. Moving rather quickly, she precociously took the empty seat nearest the door. Before that moment I wasn't sure if I had remembered her correctly. Meeting someone shortly after a mental breakdown imminently caused a little confusion. As she opened her notebook and readied her pencil, I studied her, happy to find my brain hadn't forgotten a single feature of her face.

Figuring she was indeed the one who left the podium gifts, I decided to play along with her little game. Picking up the note, I tore off the juice box and put the candies in my pocket. In exaggerated motions, I poked the straw into the box and took a deep drink. I noticed a smile break across Cara's face as she enjoyed the private joke. Not wanting to make too much of a scene, I set down the juice and turned my attention to the rest of the class.

As I began the lecture, I learned that unless I wanted to lose my place and babble incoherencies I couldn't look at Cara. I couldn't explain it. Four years of being a professor accustomed me to standing and talking to groups, but she made me uncomfortably nervous. To deliver a proper lecture, I spent the majority of class facing the opposite side of the room. The large dose of attention inadvertently landed on one guy in the front row, and on several occasions I saw him wipe sweat off his pencil hand onto his jeans. I felt bad for him, but we both survived the experience, so I figured no real harm had been done.

At the end of class I asked the students to place due papers in a pile on the lectern. One by one they filed down and added their efforts to the stack while I packed up my papers and logged off of the computer.

Always eager to review student work, that day was no different. Grading was an ideal way to discover if they had actually learned anything, or if I had failed miserably. I was also intrigued to see what kind of writer Cara was, but she didn't turn in anything. She waited for everyone else to leave and calmly stood to walk out. I decided to stop her, in case she had forgotten.

"Cara?" I asked, feeling a twitch in my gut.

"Yes?" She turned around.

"You forgot to turn in your paper."

"No I didn't."

I glanced over at the pile wondering how I had missed seeing her. She laughed at my confused expression.

"I didn't forget to turn it in, because I never wrote one."

"Oh, well, you know I don't accept late work," I mentioned in my teacher voice.

"I know," she replied with another heartbreaking smile.

"There are only three papers due in this class," I threatened. "If you receive a zero on this one, I might have to fail you."

"No you won't."

The optimism in her voice was annoying. Did she really think I would pass her just because she was so breathtakingly pretty? I felt angry. I hated being manipulated. "Do not be mistaken young lady, I *will* fail you." She laughed again and paused for only a second before leaving. "No you won't."

I fumed as I walked back to my office. It wasn't like anything could have come of my developing feelings for Cara. After all, she was a student and I was losing my mind, but it would have been nice to have a little crush to feel good about.

Stomping up the tiled stairs to my office, I couldn't help replaying what she said and how she acted. Growing more and more furious, a little voice in the back of my mind spoke up.... *Maybe she's blackmailing you.* I stopped midstride. My sudden halt caused a four-student pile up behind me. I apologized to the disgruntled student mangle, but their scornful looks told me I wasn't forgiven.

Walking faster now, my mind hummed possibilities, all bad. I knew the worst way she could hurt me was to tell the dean what happened in class and convince him I was too unstable to teach. Like Amber, I assumed she might have recorded my lapse. Even if she hadn't, the whole class could stand as witnesses.

I imagined Cara working up fake tears while she retold the story of how her life was in danger. As the betrayal soaked in, I sourly thought of every student as my enemy. If Cara started a spectacle, many would certainly jump on the bandwagon. Who among them wouldn't want to spoil the reputation of a young and brilliant writer turned professor? Random students crisscrossed my path in the hall and I saw each as evil creatures just waiting to go for my throat. In an instant my life returned to the turmoil I thought I had avoided, and just because some ridiculous girl didn't want to complete a silly paper.

Nearing my office, a plan took shape, but the sight of Briggy at my door broke my thought. "There you are my friend," Briggy said with relief. He had obviously been waiting a while. His student helper sat on the floor peering into a very thick textbook.

"Hello Briggy," I managed. Turning to the young man next to him, I let out some of my frustration. "I thought I gave all of you a copy of my class schedule? And I did it for the sole purpose of not making him wait outside my door."

Unfazed, the skinny young man quickly produced a folded piece of paper from his jean pocket and explained with supplicated eyes that he had tried. Taking the paper from him, I held it up in front of Briggy. "It looked old, so I thought it was from last semester," he claimed. "Besides, news this good is worth waiting around to share."

Resigned, I opened the office and led the way in. I turned to Briggy's helper, and he jumped to attention. "I won't keep him long," I promised as charmingly as possible, trying to make up for snapping at him. Unconvinced, he plopped back down and flipped open his giant book with a sigh.

Briggy wasted no time. "I have great news," he beamed. The hot pink flower swaying wildly in his pocket seemed to mimic his enthusiasm. "I got the money to expand the vegetative neurotoxin project."

I had no idea what he was talking about, like usual. I'd given up on following his esoteric work ages ago. Attempting to be polite and stifling my inner rage, I smiled and nodded, trying to project the appropriate amount of excitement.

"That's great," I said unconvincingly.

"Well, I should go. Just thought I'd share. I'll keep you up to date with our progress." Still smiling, Briggy patted me on the shoulder and bounced to the door.

I stopped him. "Wait, there's something I need to tell you."

"Yes?" he asked as if I had good news.

"I think I might be leaving the university, and I wanted you to be the first to know."

The shock impacted so apparent on his face that his fuzzy caterpillar eyebrows leapt halfway up his forehead.

"No, no, no this won't do at all. Not one bit. We are not done with our work yet. We have too much to do here, and with me getting more funding? No, Chamberlain, you have to stay here, you *have* to."

Briggy spoke more to himself than to me, which was a good thing since I felt completely lost by his reasoning. I had no idea he thought my support truly helped in his research. "I'm sorry Briggy, I have to go. But I promise to keep in touch and will come to visit as often as I can." Not happy with my attempt to smooth over the situation, the caterpillars crumpled angrily.

"You are an *oak* Chamberlain Shay, stop trying to pretend you're a tumbleweed. Running away is a weak man's game. I will hear no more of this." He stormed out of the room and slammed the door. I had been called many things in my life, but never an oak, and his words pained me.

Moments after Briggy's abrupt departure, a gaggle of students piled into my office. Until their arrival, I had forgotten my office hours. Normally

I'd only see one or two students during the allotted time, but Wednesday's exam encouraged a rush.

At first I dealt coldly with them, still seeing all students as greedy monsters dooming me to solitude. It felt silly offering help for an exam I didn't plan on being around to give. Not wanting to start rumors before I made the official decision, I focused on the task at hand and shifted into professor mode.

I addressed their issues, answered questions, and made suggestions. Some were the failing types looking for a lifeboat, and the others were overachievers ensuring they overlooked nothing. Eventually the queue trickled until no more questions waited to be answered. A certain adrenaline rush came with teaching, and an hour of one-on-one tutoring pumped me with a strong dose.

Melting again into my ugly yellow chair, I forced myself to think through every aspect of both leaving and staying. The truth blazed apparent. Briggy was right. He might not have had a clue of the circumstances, but he was spot on. Leaving was cowardice. I cowered in the face of many things, like having the family illness exposed and failing to protect Granddad. I feared my impending insanity, but the worst of my fears was becoming like my father. I never wanted to be the kind of man who would run away. Never.

After deciding I needed to stay, despite the sound logic of leaving, I cast the matter aside and thought more about my father. With little difficulty, I pulled his memories into my head and I could see through his eyes as he played joyfully with a weathered softball. His thoughts lit so innocent, so happy, so pure. Feeling his emotions as a child and mixing them with the evil I knew he would later commit was overwhelming. I felt sorry for the little boy he had long since left behind.

"I heard you were leaving." Libby's voice shattered the memory like glass.

"Where did you hear that?" I asked.

"I was driving through the parking lot when that crazy little plant man nearly got killed by jumping in front of my car. When I stopped yelling at him, he demanded that I talk some sense into you."

"Briggy?" I asked, but honestly whom else could she be referring to?

"Is it true?"

Libby's tone demanded, but as she glared at me I couldn't help but laugh at her. Libby's appearance was always near perfect, but at that moment half her hair dripped wet and a large brown stain covered the shoulder of her otherwise pristine pearl silk shirt.

"What happened to you?" I managed between laughs.

"You never answered my question."

"Relax will you? I am not going anywhere."

"Then why did that little plant thing attack me?"

She tried to push the sticky hair back so it wouldn't be so obvious.

"He must have taken something I said wrong." I instantly felt horrible for causing so much turmoil for my friend.

"Well you better go straighten him out before he gets himself killed."

"I'll take care of him, but what happened to your clothes? Don't you know that appearance is the hallmark of the mental state?" I said making cheeky air quotes. She did not find the humor in it, and sneered. I thought she might bite me.

"Some dumb waitress thought it would be funny to dump coffee on me. The joke's on her though. I got her fired and made her pay for my shirt." A smug smile crossed her thin lips.

Eventually our conversation moved to the search for my father. After finding no new developments had been made, I dismissed her. She left half soaked, but in a slightly better mood.

I locked the door behind her. It was time to call home and check on Granddad. Never knowing what direction the call might take, I always locked the door just in case.

The phone was answered after only one ring.

"Hello Doctor Shay. You come home now please." The broken English informed me it was Marisa, Granddad's live-in nurse. She had never made such a serious demand before, so I hopped out of my chair and grabbed my jacket and keys. "I'm on my way."

I hastily scribbled out a note to Briggy explaining I wasn't going anywhere and that I was sorry for causing him so much stress. I begged him to please STAY OUT OF THE PARKING LOT. Dashing out, I saw Libby walking down the hall. I gave her the note and told her where to take it. Begrudgingly she agreed to be my messenger, and I could feel her irked eyes on me as I sprinted away. I jumped in my car and was on the road in seconds.

CHAPTER 5

The miles refused to pass quickly as I raced home. My usually enjoyable two-hour commute debased into two hours of anxious agony. I always enjoyed living tucked away in the folds of a Colorado forest, but as I bottomed out in washouts and fishtailed precarious dirt curves, I questioned if it was still worth it. I banged my hands impatiently on the wheel and sweated profusely. I tried to calm myself and focus on the fact that Marisa was there with him, and I knew she would do everything in her power to keep him safe.

Over a year had passed since I decided to hire live-in help. I put it off until the day I found Granddad shooting a rifle at cottonwood trees screaming, "Them bastards have us surrounded!!" Something had to be done.

It proved a tricky task. I didn't want anyone in the house who would ask too many questions or come to any conclusions. When I made the nervous call to an agency, I had no idea how to request a person fitting our criteria without sounding like I was involved in speciously illegal activities. The agency asked a mountain of questions about salary and expected duties, but near the end of the call they unexpectedly asked a question in my favor.

They asked what kind of priority I placed on English being a first language. It dawned on me that perhaps if the person I hired couldn't understand all of Granddad's ramblings, maybe they couldn't piece together our secret. Hanging up the phone, I had hoped for the best, which was the worst when it came to English skills.

After about a week of waiting, Granddad and I welcomed Marisa into our home. An elderly woman from southern Mexico, she knew better English than I expected. This worried me at first, but as I got to know her all my fears disappeared. I explained that Granddad was mentally ill, and that her primary job was to keep him out of harm's way - or at the very least to contact me if things tornadoed out of hand.

During the last year since her arrival, she had not only taken on her task with astounding proficiency, but she had unpredictably become the driving maternal force of our home. While her manner was sometimes abrupt and no nonsense, it was an easy adjustment when the house looked immaculate, dinner smelled deliciously ready, and Granddad felt safe and relatively happy. Never once did she ask any prying questions or appear to have any curiosity about our family. She was simply too busy.

Marisa dedicated herself to us so fully that I had grown to care for her a great deal. I thought of her as family, and I couldn't imagine our life any other way. Even when Granddad screamed and ripped off all his clothes in the middle of the night, or started hiding all the canned food in potted plants, she seemed eager to set things right and never once complained. Finding her not only aided Granddad, it helped me as well. Seeing her work so patiently with him gave me hope that when I lost my mind someone might be around to make my life bearable.

Trying to reassure myself Marisa could keep them safe until I arrived didn't change the fact they needed me to hurry. I ignored all speed limits. Many a middle finger sprang my way as I blatantly cut off other drivers and tailgated dangerously close. When I finally reached the gated entrance of my home, I mashed my code into the security keypad and waited impatiently for the gate to swing slowly open. I knew the long dirt driveway by heart and pushed to insane speeds blasting through the turns, narrowly missing a couple trees.

Nearing the house, billowing clouds of either dirt or smoke swept across the property from the backyard. Throwing my car in park with a hard transmission thunk, I jumped out and forgot to shut the engine off or close the door. Sprinting around back, I quickly saw the source.

Granddad sat in his old wooden fishing boat, and at the back of the boat sat Marisa. Granddad fiercely gripped oars in his hands, feverishly paddling the dirt with all his strength. He had been at it for a while, as two long holes had been carved out of the ground on either side of the boat. The wind blew in gusts, and each forceful scrape launched another armful of dirt. Unmoved by his efforts, the boat luckily sat anchored, tightly strapped to the ground.

Frozen, for only a moment, I saw myself in Granddad's place. *How long? How long before I was the mad man rowing in the dirt? A week? A month? A year?*

Walking up behind the boat, I saw both of them completely covered in dirt. Granddad paddled as if his life depended on it, drenched in sweat with both hands blistered and bleeding. Marisa held her head down crying. Hoping to free her from the situation immediately, I walked over and placed my hand on hers.

Relief flooded her face as she reached out for me to help her. When she stood, Granddad stopped mid-stroke. He grabbed her shirt with one hand and punched at me with the other. I ducked and he missed, but the maneuver tripped me to land flat on my back. As he pushed her into the seat again, he stared over the boat and in a thick Irish accent yelled, "Do ye have no honor laddie?! Women and children first!!"

Sure of what he saw, his words launched the memory in my own head: the difference being that I knew the memory was not my own, and Granddad thought he was actually living the very moment. He was experiencing the sinking of the legendary HMS Birkenhead in 1852.

After years of watching Granddad degrade, I had learned that extremely traumatic events from our relative's lives left memories of such great detail and emotional intensity that they were almost impossible not to feel. The wreck of The HMS Birkenhead was one of those memories. When it sank outside Danger Point near Cape Town, 450 souls on a troopship of 643 drowned. Many of them were friends and companions of our distant relative, who survived only because he was ordered by his captain to man a lifeboat full of women and children safely ashore.

Experiencing that level of fear, death, helplessness and sorrow left tremendous damaging echoes on our family's collective experiences. For almost a year after I had my first Birkenhead flashback, I couldn't handle being near water, except to shower. I knew helping Granddad would be delicately problematic. He believed he was attempting to save a lifeboat full of women and children, and any men trying to board the boat were endangering his most precious cargo.

I raced through the tactics I had tried over the years to help him. The simple ones were less traumatic but not nearly as effective, and became increasingly useless as time worsened the hallucinations.

Trying to be inventive, I once held a mirror in front of him so he could see he was an old man, and not a ten-year-old boy. It worked, but it failed as the worst idea I ever had. To believe you are young, strong, and just starting out one minute, and then being shown you are actually old and dying delivered a devastatingly painful tremor. He didn't speak for a week. Worried I'd caused permanent damage, I swore to never do it again, no matter how effective. Sadly, even if I were to resort to it, the mirror wouldn't have worked. He had advanced so far into the illness that he believed the memories in his head perceived more real than what his eyes fogged in reality.

I started as I always did of late. Sometimes it worked and sometimes it didn't. "What does that tattoo on your arm say?" No reply. He couldn't see or hear me now. He just kept rowing in the dirt. I switched tactics and decided to pretend to be one of the people in the memory. Maybe I could at least get him to talk to me.

"Please sir, where is my father?" I asked in a child's voice. His rowing slowed, and without looking at me he said exactly what his grandfather had said at the time: "Sorry laddie, t' ocean 'as swallowed 'im up, but 'e was a brave man. Sit wit jer mudder and be quiet."

Answering me meant a small bit of progress, but he still wasn't seeing me. Knowing he thought I was a little boy, I carefully sat in the boat next to Marisa without too much fear of him attacking again.

Scratches and purple bruises covered Marisa's arms. In a murmur I told her, "Sit very still." Taking a moment to run the memory in my head, I dissected it until finding an eventual calmer moment where I could make my move.

After the boat sank, desperate men clung to the wreckage while others fruitlessly swam for the shore two miles away, only to die of exposure and shark attack. Having no other way to help them from his full lifeboat, my great-great grandfather stopped rowing and prayed for the men. Skipping to the end, I adlibbed new words into the memory. "Please sir, can we pray for them?" I asked in my child's voice while pointing to the field where I knew he saw an ocean of dying men.

"Aye son, les pray." He dropped the oars and knelt down. Kneeling behind him, I motioned for Marisa to get out of the boat.

I prayed with Granddad until she walked safely out of arm's reach, then breaking character I asked, "Who is Champ?"

He smiled glowingly. "Champ is my grandson. Chamberlain Shay, one of the most famous writers in the world. He's a bright boy who takes good care of this old man let me tell you." His accent gone, he still didn't see me, so I asked a harder question.

"What's your son's name?"

His joy dissolved quickly into sorrow. "My son is David Shay, though that isn't the name he likes. Changed it he did when he got older to William James or something like that. Said he didn't want anything to do with the history behind the Shay name. Silly kid, always running away from whom we are. I didn't see or hear from him for ten years, and when he came back he made me the happiest man on Earth. He brought me my little Champ." Remembering my father and the day he met me, he began crying.

Wiping tears away, he finally looked up and truly saw me. "Hello Champ, I didn't hear you come in." He looked around and seemed only mildly surprised to find himself boating in the backyard dirt. Noticing the new holes and the dust all over himself, he let out a massive laugh shaking him from head to toe.

"The HMS Birkenhead?"

I nodded.

"That was a terrible thing," he said, lowering his head. "Granny always said it changed Grandpa. She said watching all those people die killed part of him." I knew what he meant as I tried to push the haunting images out of my head.

We talked as he followed me around the house to turn off my still running car. He spoke lucidly, and our conversation turned serious rather fast.

"I wonder if it's time Champ?"

"Time for what?" I asked innocently, even though I knew what he implied.

"Time to lock this crazy guy up. I won't be putting the two of you in danger any longer." He always thought of others over himself, and this was not the first time he had volunteered his incarceration.

"No one is in danger here," I protested. "I am sure if she needed to, Marisa could hogtie you. You know that as well as I do."

It wasn't true. Her being stuck on the boat was proof of that, but we both liked to think of her as being ox strong. He agreed laughingly, but the seriousness of his expression never changed. I started to explain I could quit teaching and come home full time when he stopped me, looked me in the eyes and placed his hands firmly on my shoulders.

"Nope and I won't let you. I love you too much to let you waste your time playing babysitter. You should be out there living your life while you have one. The world is still waiting out there for you to explore. I understand. I was a young man once. Well, you remember don't ya?"

I did remember. The flashbacks I experienced were not limited to deceased family. Granddad misbehaved quite wildly in his youth. He traveled the world and never spent too long in one place. He might have continued that kind of lifestyle if my father hadn't been born. I knew his words were offered up as encouragement, but they pained me. Granddad still believed the world and its adventures awaited me. He didn't know my barrier between memories and lapses had begun to rot.

I knew the day would come when I would have to traverse more extremes to keep Granddad safe, but it would be for his benefit, not because I wanted freedom.

"I was never the free spirit you were," I admitted. "I'm hopelessly boring, and I am happy spending my time hanging out with you. And as far as our safety goes, lucky for you I'm a famous drool writer with lots of money. If need be, I can hire an *armed guard* to follow you around. I can see it now, can't you? A giant man with a big gun and handcuffs being chased down the hall by Marisa, her yelling at him to wipe his boots or taking the broom to him when he finishes the last of the milk."

We both laughed at the thought, but for me certain truth filled my words. I would spend every cent I had to protect Granddad and provide him whatever comfort I could.

"Champ, I am sorry you were born into this family. Mother Nature wasn't fair when she messed with our DNA. Sometimes I wish I could have a talk with that witch. I would ask her straight out why she thought it would do any good to make us inherit all these memories. And if she had a good reason, why the hell not also give us the ability to keep track of'em when we get old?" Heavy tears dripped from his wrinkly cheeks.

I hugged him. "Curse be damned Granddad, I'm just glad to have you, and that's all that matters." Letting him go, I joked, "At least Mother Nature didn't give us the memories of our female relatives." We both laughed raunchily for a moment, and I cringed at the thought of having to know what childbirth felt like.

Walking inside, I asked him if he knew what triggered the Birkenhead lapse, and of course he didn't. He laughed and claimed, "Hell, I can't even remember what I ate for breakfast."

As soon as we walked inside, Marisa awaited us there, armed with a big glass of water and our medical kit. As Granddad drank the entire glass, she went to work bandaging his shredded hands. She worked silently, obviously shaken. She finished quickly, and tired from the physical and emotional strain, Granddad immediately headed to his bedroom for a nap. I took the opportunity to talk to Marisa in private.

As soon as we heard the door close upstairs, Marisa gushed out everything she'd been holding back since we came through the door.

"No more. I do thees no more doctor Shay." A gloomy seriousness in her voice made me doubtful I could change her mind. "Meester Shay eez too strong for me," she said dejectedly, thrusting out her arms to show her darkening bruises.

"I am *soo* sorry Marisa. Are you OK? I promise he didn't mean it. He thought he was saving you. You know how confused he can get."

"Yes, señor. Eet is no heez fault. But he eez too strong. I can no keep heem safe."

She was unfortunately right, and it had been on my mind a lot. In his ever-declining state Granddad not only endangered himself, but endangered her too. Being pragmatic, I also had to face the fact that I would be needing help as well. Our current situation couldn't last

I pleaded, "Instead of leaving, what if I got you more help?"

She thought about my question for nearly a minute, and then requested that the person would have to listen to her and be very strong. I agreed with everything she said, and to make her point, Granddad ironically yelled something from upstairs about a chicken.

The only question left for now: how to find the perfect person. The agency was an option, but that was like drawing a number out of a hat, and we had too many issues to take any chances. While talking with Marisa, I could tell she hid a suggestion she bashfully held back. After begging her to share, she beat around the bush a bit and then explained she had a nephew who recently lost his landscaping job. I told her to have him come start right away.

"You no want to meet heem?"

"Nope, I trust you. If you think he will work out, I am sure he will. Not only that, but you will be here to keep him in line right?"

"Gracias!" she agreed beaming ear to ear. She happily skipped from the room to make the call.

I did trust her and it was nice. I could confide in so few people. I'd been given proof of that earlier, and as my thoughts drifted to Cara and her blackmail an ache squeezed my chest.

After Granddad's nap he made a heartfelt apology to Marisa, which she humbly accepted, and we settled into our normal nightly routine. We set the table and sat together to enjoy dinner and each other's company. I asked about the rest of their day. Marisa filled in the parts Granddad couldn't remember, or when he answered in Gaelic, which she took as gibberish. She started explaining about watching a movie when she jumped from her chair and marched over to the large poster board hanging on the wall. Pulling a pencil from her calico apron she wrote, *Ship Recks* under a long list of banned items.

The list was her idea and it was a great one. When she started working for us, I racked my brain to tell her everything that might trigger Granddad's episodes. For the first few months she kept encountering things I'd forgotten, so she made a big list and hung it in the wall - a great idea we both knew could only help to a certain point. Even without triggers, Granddad had serious problems.

Finishing his dinner, Granddad ignored Marisa's list addition and turned the conversation to me. "So how's work Champ?"

I instantly felt all my new fears creep in and pile onto the old ones. A few years earlier I would've told him how I had my first lapse, how scared I was, and about how little time I had left to find my father, but anymore it just felt cruel to subject him, so I lied, sort of.

"Things are great. Briggy scored a new grant he's very excited about." Granddad liked Briggy a lot. "I'm glad to hear it. That man is very smart." Briggy was the only outsider I had allowed into the house in the last year. He visited for dinner during summer break, and he and Granddad hit it off right away. I kept waiting the whole visit for Briggy to notice something odd about Granddad, but he never seemed to. Even when Granddad slipped into a memory and began talking about harvesting potato crops in Scotland, Briggy got nerdily excited and started taking notes.

As the evening progressed, Granddad's lucidity began to slip as he spoke wobbly about how prohibition was causing more death than drinking ever had. By the time he went to bed he was calling me *Sir* and tried to tip Marisa with a crinkled dollar. It was so hard missing someone who was still half there, and when he was around and normal it only made watching him slip back that much harder. Feeling tired myself, but too distracted to sleep, I went to my library.

Unlike most libraries, my books were not stored in shelves; they lived in fireproof, museum quality safes. My books were the most important items in the house, and I protected them like precious jewels. The collection began in the 15th century when a relative mustered the bright idea to write down the details of his life in a diary. His intention? To remember what memories belonged to him. What began as a personal tool for him became significant peace of mind for all of us, and in a life bound by insanity, even small pieces of help felt huge. He taught his own son to do the same, and the tradition carried all the way down to me.

The diaries of each individual were bound into books and preserved from generation to generation, collected not out of nostalgia, but out of need. It was reassuring to be able to re-read what life was your own, and they were effective tools for looking back to figure out the context and origin of a certain memory.

I first learned their value at eleven years old, plagued daily for weeks with the memory of someone shooting a horse. I was terrified by what I saw repeated, convinced one of my relatives was a brutal animal killer. The flashbacks distracted so badly I eventually went to Granddad for help, and he showed me how to use the books.

We learned the horse was very dearly loved by the owner, and put down out of compassion when severely maimed. This changed my whole perspective of the incident, and I was able to let it go. The books remained our only anchors in a turbulent sea of jumbled memories.

I added Granddad's edition to the collection when I noticed he was just rewriting the memories of others. I opened each safe to obsessively check on them, running my fingers along their spines, hundreds of years of history stacked in front of me. They didn't smell like other old books. Absent the mustiness of aging paper, the books smelled like blood and sweat.

Often I thought I could feel the spirit of each man as I touched his book. It always astounded me that each volume had been preserved for so long. The one glaring exception was my father's. His book's empty slot matched the hollowness in my chest.

I retired to my bedroom, where the pages of my journal still required text. I never carried it with me on the off chance prying eyes might find it, so I hid it under my bed and carried a small notebook around with me instead.

Settling myself, I pulled my little notebook from my pocket and placed it next to the large journal labeled Chamberlain Shay 1987 --. Flipping through the pages, I saw glimpses of old photos, crayon drawings and chocolate, all reminders of my youth. Having handled it daily for years and years, so memorized was the weight and feel of the book in my hands that I could close my eyes and find the next blank page.

I copied my notes from the night before. I stared at the page.

Met Cara - the girl with the most beautiful face.

My feelings for her had changed so abruptly from when I initially wrote it, it was difficult to copy. I still believed her to be the most astoundingly beautiful person I had ever seen, but now her beauty had faded under the ugliness I knew existed within. It made my first entry feel tainted with blind ignorance, and that irritated me. I copied it anyway, a memory was a memory after all, no matter how misjudged. I quickly moved to writing the current day's events. Some days I wrote long entries detailing minutia. Other days when I didn't feel inspired, I just made lists. This was an uninspired night.

- *Found Granddad in the backyard reliving HMS Birkenhead.*
- *Hired Marisa's nephew to help with Granddad.*
- *Lost control of the memories in class.*
- *Believe Cara is trying to blackmail me and decided to confront her about it!*

I slammed the book closed and made my way to bed. I wasn't sure how I'd do it, but somehow I'd find a way. I stood helpless against many of the trials I faced, but for those which I could confront I would. Confronting Cara would be a great start.

CHAPTER 6

I clutched the note in my hand as I walked to class, worried that if I put it in my pocket or briefcase I'd postpone giving it to her. I could see myself waiting until the end of class and then waiting until the following class, until finally I would keep putting it off until wimping out altogether. I couldn't let myself do that. I had to stick to the plan. I purposely walked into the room a few minutes late. I wanted to be sure she'd be seated and wouldn't have a chance to question me. I enjoyed a sigh of immense relief in finding I had timed my arrival perfectly.

Cara sat in the front row. She had pinned back her jaw length black hair, allowing full visibility of the long line of her neck. She wore a silk red blouse matching the hue of her lips, and on them a massive smile. She looked amazing. Too amazing. How could I be so attracted to someone who was out to destroy me? Wavering for what seemed like only a second, I swallowed a deep breath and walked straight up to her and handed her my note. I watched her face intently as she read it. The very straightforward content merely said, "*See me after class.*" She looked up, biting her lip slightly, and nodded in agreement.

While handing out the exams, I glanced around the room trying to gauge the atmosphere. I studied the faces of the students to discern if any were still thinking about my breakdown. Thankfully, their expressions staled no different than any other set of anxious pupils preparing to take a test. Walking back to my seat, I realized Amber's face was not among them. Double-checking, I glanced furtively around the room again. Either good or bad news, I exhaled pleasantly to have her gone. One evil female in the room was enough.

After briefly explaining testing procedures, I took the seat at the front of the room and turned my attention to grading the stack of papers from my Historical Writing class. Typically in a one-hour period I could grade nine or ten papers coherently, but distractedly sneaking peeks at Cara, I barely finished two.

I had memorized what I was going to say to her once she entered my office. I stayed up half the night torturously thinking it through. I had no idea how she'd respond. Different scenarios crept in, spreading the gamut from her slapping me, to my favorite, and the one least likely to occur, where she tearfully apologized, and while comforting her, we kissed. I lingered on that thought for far too long, and before I knew it students were walking up to my desk.

Some eager and some reluctant, each student walked over and placed an exam facedown on my desk. I eventually announced time was up, and waited for the last few stragglers. Cara purposefully walked up last to add to the pile.

"Did you want to talk in your office?" she asked nonchalantly, almost like a dare.

"I believe that would be best."

Gathering up my things, I led the way as she followed silently. Nervous energy pulsed through me. I had to focus on keeping a normal pace. My feet wanted to run. Following me into my office, Cara suddenly gasped loudly. Startled, I nearly dropped everything in my hands as I jumped away from her.

"Is that THE Lamarck?" she asked, gazing in astonishment at the large oil painting on the wall across from my desk. "Why do you have a painting of him? You're not that into science are you?"

I stood stunned.

No one had ever recognized who was in the painting before. Jean-Baptiste Lamarck was well known in the world of science by name for his incredible works around the turn of the 19th century, but typically not by appearance. His efforts were studied and critiqued in many science classes, but not for typical reasons. What made Mr. Lamarck worth studying was that he was wrong, or at least the world *thought* he was wrong. Ridiculed, Lamarck went down in history as the father of *soft inheritance*, a theory he developed about genetics. A theory he developed around my family.

Being a nice man very interested in plants, he had quickly become very close friends with one of my relatives. A genuine man of science, our condition fascinated him, and he pitied how we had to hide it. A proactive type, he proposed a way to present our condition to the world. It was his belief that my family held all the keys to humanity's many genetic doors, and if we no longer needed to be secretive, we might be able to find help for the devastatingly negative symptoms we carried.

Lamarck knew he couldn't expose us directly, at least not at first. He instead developed his evolutionary theory of acquired characteristics explaining our situation. Using vague examples, mostly involving animals, he theorized how *learned traits* could indeed be passed from one generation to the next. He believed a bird did not learn to fly, but was born knowing how, and if that could occur for a bird, why not a man? Pleased with how his theory came together, Lamarck evangelized his knowledge with other scientists. He assumed they would be open to his incredible idea and help him research it further.

Unfortunately, he was wrong. No part of the cemented scientific world felt readily flexible for a new genetic theory. Lacking the ability to see beyond their noses - coupled with vehement anti-evolution rhetoric from Georges Cuvier - the entire scientific community rejected his idea outright. Shortly thereafter, the Church excommunicated him for blasphemy. Soft inheritance ruined poor Lamarck's life. He might have even saved himself some grief by naming us as the specimens upon whom his theory was based, but he died a man of honor. Even in his darkest hour, dying poor and blind, he kept our secret. The Shay family owed an eternal debt to Lamarck for his kindness.

My relatives were sadly unsurprised by the public's reaction. He had simply proven further what we had known for hundreds of years. We were not only ill; we were indeed cursed.

Feeling bad Lamarck had been sucked into our suffering, I gladly bought the very expensive portrait of him at an auction, figuring it should belong to someone who truly respected him and knew his legacy. Still, choosing to hang the painting in my office was not primarily out of respect. I hung it there as a constant reminder. Every time I looked into his face, I felt the memory of his awful funeral. He died in 1829, and my relative had to stand there in the cold and endure Lamarck's horrific eulogy. In front of Lamarck's ashamed family, a sodden priest raged for an hour, vehemently preaching about blasphemy and the evils of evolutionary ideas, and how Jean-Baptiste Lamarck's soul charred endlessly in the hungry fires of Hell. It was a disgusting memory, but it served me well. This painting of him reminded me to keep our secret because it was not just me that it could hurt, but everyone it touched.

Forgetting my prepared words, Cara caught me off guard and I had to ask, "How do you know who he is?"

"I always thought he was an interesting character, and his ideas were cool."

We had ventured way off topic and I had to rope things in.

"Please Cara, have a seat."

She obeyed, but instead of sitting in the hard metal seat in front of me like I expected, she moseyed over to my comfy chair and plopped down like she owned the place. This reignited my resolve.

"What you are doing is wrong and I won't allow it. How dare you try this with me." Anger soaked my words.

"What?!" she asked confused.

Obviously she expected me to kowtow to her blackmail without a fight. She must have expected this meeting would be about negotiations and not a refusal.

"You know I'm right, and if you are determined to pursue this I will take action against you."

I did it. I said my entire speech. Now the ball was in her court. The relief I felt was instantly trumped as I watched her do what I so completely believed to be the most unlikely outcome. Cara dropped her head and burst into tears. Dark, teary spots dripped on her sheer red blouse.

"I'm... so sorry. I didn't think I was... hurting anyone." She barely pushed the words out.

Looking much like a kicked puppy, I couldn't help but feel remorseful. I had never hurt someone this way, and while wanting to stand my ground, I also had the deepest desire to comfort her.

"You seem like a very smart girl, I don't see why you resorted to this. There are so many ways you could have gotten help. Hell, I would've helped you if you would've just asked." She still wouldn't look up.

"I did try everything! You think I like doing this? Sneaking around, always feeling like an outsider, a mutant. I didn't think it mattered really if I stayed out of the way and never took advantage of it." I was so confused by her response I couldn't find the words to ask for clarification.

"How did you think you could blackmail someone and still not take advantage of them?" Looking up with tears streaking her cheeks and red forming around her eyes, she stared at me like I had just hit her.

"Blackmail?"

"Yes, that's what your doing isn't it? Using my little breakdown in class to try and get grades you haven't earned?" It felt strange explaining Cara's own plan to her.

She took a long pause, her face a mangle of hesitation.

"Is that what this is about? Well then fine. If you believe I deserve a zero on the paper give me an F right now. I'll watch, and don't worry, I won't let anything stop you."

Her tone demanded with an uncomfortable certitude. I ground my teeth. Was this a dare? Did she think I was too much of a pushover to do it?

"Alright let's do this," I said angrily. "I can't believe I waited to talk to you first."

I yanked my chair under me and pulled up the class grade book on my computer. I typed *Cara* into the search bar.

No results found.

"What is your full name?" I barked.

"Cara Gentry."

Jamming the letters into the keyboard, I searched again. Zero matches. "Is this some kind of a game?" I asked, glaring at her.

She had stood up to stare out the window. Looking up at her outline, I tried to ignore how her stunning figure made my body stir.

"No more games," she said somberly. "I told you before that you wouldn't have to fail me, and I was right. You can't fail me, because I am not enrolled in the class." I ran frantically through all the things she had said to me since we met, and staring at my computer screen with *zero results found* staring at me I knew I had messed up.

Sometimes the right words just won't come out, and this was one of those times. What I should have said was sorry, but I was still mad, and those weren't the words that left my lips. "You are supposed to ask before you sit in on a class."

Still gazing out the window, she handled the criticism well. "I know, but I guess I didn't want to have to explain why I needed to sit in. I know you don't have to deal with this kind of thing being a millionaire and all, but telling someone you're too poor to pay for a stupid class is a little embarrassing." Her eyes never left the window.

"Do you even go to school here?" I wasn't accusing anymore. I was simply curious. Her gaze shifted to the floor.

"No, I go to the community college, for now."

When she said *for now,* she clearly held an expiration date on her attendance. Feeling embarrassed, my anger fading, I tried to patch things. "I hear the history department is pretty good there." I had never actually heard that before, but I feigned to turn the subject in a positive direction.

"I wouldn't know. I'm not a history student. I'm actually studying psychology." I felt more puzzled by her every minute.

"So, why are you sitting in on history lectures?"

She blushed and chewed on her bottom lip. "I have to admit, I've been a fan of the famous Dr. Chamberlin Shay for quite a while. Well," she teased, "until recently I guess."

Her simple words nearly dissolved me into the floor. Unable to respond, she thought I required more explanation. "Your writing has always fascinated me. You seem to really *understand* the people you write about. Almost every history writer barely feels beyond the cold facts and dates, but when you write about something, it's like, well, *it's like you were there*. You somehow know not only what the people are seeing and experiencing, but what they're feeling too. I love it."

The conversation leapt into dangerous territory. She wasn't the first to say such things about my writing. But very few fans held an interest in psychology, saw me have a mental break down, and had a fascination with Lamarck. All the pieces of my hidden puzzle sat right in front of her. I relinquished.

"Thank you so much Cara. Can you please forgive me?"

Even though I couldn't let her get to really know me or allow myself to have deep feelings for her, I could at least ensure she wouldn't walk around hating me.

"Please," I begged, rising from my chair and walking around the desk toward her. Offering me absolution, she extended her hand.

Her hand felt so tiny and fragile in mine. She smiled warmly as we shook. It felt so right touching her. I lost myself in a romantically happy place reminding me of something... Some time... The memory rose slowly in my head...

I stood in front of a sopping hut. A woman riding bareback trotted up to me. She dismounted swiftly. I stared as the wind blew her long blonde hair around her face. Walking hurriedly toward one another we extended arms and at last embraced. She clung to me so tightly I could feel her heart beating and the warmness of her cheek pressed against my neck. Warmth radiated through her. Not saying anything, I simply breathed her in and sighed. Completeness and peace overfilled me.

Rallying all my will, I walked behind the safety of my desk. Love threatened a very addictive emotion, and I didn't want to test my ability to kick it. I decided it was time Cara Gentry left me for the day. I gave her permission to attend my classes, and even offered to help find scholarships. She thanked me too much, turning to leave when she blurted out a request.

"Promise me you won't let the dead destroy your life."

What did she know? Was her question based on the fact I screamed "Da" during my lapse, or had she figured out more? I didn't want to jump to conclusions. I had already done that with her once.

"What do you mean?"

"After the breakdown in class, and the way you always look so sad, I just figured something from your past is haunting you. I don't want you to live your life being held prisoner by things that don't matter anymore. I've been there and done that and I know how badly it sucks."

"Yeah it sucks big time," I admitted. "Honestly though, I'm not able to let it go. Thanks for caring, but I can't make this promise." Every word was the truth.

I wanted to ask more about her pain, her life, everything. But I withheld, knowing that if I pried and she opened up, I'd be expected to reciprocate. Instead, we stood there in silence reflecting on our scars.

Looking down at the stack of papers on my desk, I recalled she was the last to hand in the exam. "So would you have taken it even if I hadn't asked you to see me?" I asked, grinning as I reached over to pluck it from the pile.

"Nope, and now that we're all good you don't get to grade it."

"You wanna bet?" I challenged playfully, and as my fingers wrestled free her paper she placed her hand on top of mine and whispered softly, "Please don't it's awful."

I quivered like she had some kind of mind control over me when she looked in my eyes. I left my hand where it was and savored the feeling of our contact, the same hypnotizing warmness as the handshake we shared. Her slender fingers grazed the full length of mine as she removed her hand. The sensation sent shockwaves across my entire body. Once all contact between us broke, I stared at my hand, secretly wishing to have the feeling back. I shook my head and tried to push the emotions out. Lifting her paper, I tore it in two and tossed it in the trash.

I wasn't completely without experiences with women. But as I sat there staring at her, I knew I would have traded all of those cheap meaningless experiences for a simple touch of her hand. My feelings for her weren't the side effects of peer pressure or the animalistic need to alleviate sexual tension like the others. I was drawn to her in a deep, deep way, far beyond reason.

"You look like you're having a bad day Chamberlain, let's go for a walk and I can show you my favorite spot on campus." Cara's bright suggestion sounded pleasant, but I knew what would come of it. This was the point of no return. If we had a great time enjoying each other's company, I would have no way to pull away from her. I would want her always, and that meant condemning her to a very bleak future. A future I promised to never inflict on anyone… Ever.

"Thanks for the offer, but I better stay here. These papers aren't going to grade themselves. Unless you think I could just tear these up too." We laughed, but true to her dogged nature I was quickly learning of, Cara didn't give up.

"Okey dokey," she tempted, tauntingly kicking her hips back and forth. "I guess I'll just go see the most amazing thing on campus all by myself."

"The most amazing thing on campus? How is that possible? I'm standing right here." Her laughter filled the entire room, a gentle, high-pitched wind chime chortle. She reminded me of my mother.

"OK, maybe the second most amazing thing on campus," she said staring at the floor and blushing a little pink. "Please come with me. It's the least you can do after accusing me of being an evil blackmailer."

She had me there. I did owe her. I had just made her cry and felt horribly ashamed. "OK let's go. But I only have half an hour." She was already making me weak.

I followed behind her as she led me to the most amazing place on campus. While we walked, someone else's memory buzzed strongly in my head. I relived being one of two lovers running away from a harvest festival. Not yet betrothed and unable to touch when other people could see them, they snuck away to find privacy. Like Cara and I, the lovers walked in silence, but their silence was due to the anticipation of being alone. Ours was a product of awkwardness. As we walked passed the chemistry building I sunk deeper into the memory. By the time Cara and I reached the middle of campus, the lovers' world became so vivid I could smell freshly turned dirt from their fields, tasting the tangy sweat clinging to my relative's body.

As the lovers reached the safety of the trees and embraced, I struggled to block them out and focus solely on where Cara led. I assumed I knew where we were going. There was only one really amazing place I could think of on campus, and that was Briggy's greenhouse. Double the size of the entire history building, it towered as the largest, most elaborate building in the entire city.

The greenhouse, nicknamed The Green by students, comprised of several levels, and each held a specific purpose. The top floor was dedicated to lab research, and the rest of the floors were divided up as different regions of the Earth. It housed a wondrous collection of specimens from environs tropical, grassland, high altitude and swamp. Even the basement was filled with massive tanks to host rare aquatic plants. If Briggy were to design heaven, it would look a lot like his greenhouse, only bigger.

Since I knew where we were going, I took an easy slight lead, as my stride kicked much longer than Cara's. Strolling along, I turned in surprise to hear Cara shout my name. Looking back, I found her standing at the doors to the Library. Befuddled, I turned around and followed her inside.

"Where did you think I was taking you?" she asked, obviously happy she had surprised me. I told her I thought we were headed for the greenhouse, and while she agreed with me that it was a great place, she insisted she knew a better one.

Entering the elevator, she pushed the button marked B. A little panic ran though me as I thought about how no one would be down there, unless they were repairing something or cleaning. The likelihood that we would be alone together was very high, and it would be a different kind of alone than we experienced in my office. Within my four walls there always existed the possibility someone would walk in at any moment. In the basement of the Library, that wasn't the case.

As we stepped out of the elevator, I watched Cara produce a key from the front pocket of her tight jeans. Winking at me, she explained she had very powerful friends, specifically Carl the janitor. She sashayed down the dimly lit hallway with a confidence indicating she had been there many times before. Stopping at an unmarked door, she unlocked it and we stepped inside.

Many blinks later my eyes adjusted to the dark room, and I was stunned by what I saw. Covered in a fine layer of dust sat rows and rows of red velvet seats. The walls draped with time-dulled colorful murals, and spider webs hung heavily in every corner. The standout feature of the very large room was the antique wooden stage protruding from the back wall.

"Isn't it wonderful?" Cara asked as she sauntered through the room taking it all in like she had never been there before. I followed her down to the front of the stage, trying not to sneeze and cough on the clouds of dust we kicked up. Stopping, she turned and sat on the one chair that had been recently cleaned. She sat down comfortably as if she sat there a lot.

Cara motioned to the chair next to her and apologized for the dust. The grime from the chair stuck to my dress pants, but I pretended not to be bothered. I waited patiently for her to explain the history of the room or how she found it, but it was as if she had forgotten my presence. Cara sat entranced, staring at the empty stage. I tried asking her what she liked most about the room and why it was her favorite place on campus, but she only offered vague responses that never really answered the questions. All of a sudden she seemed not in the mood to talk, so I let it go.

Sitting in silence, my mind wandered as I remembered a different theater that existed long before either of us.

"Would you like to hear a story about a theater?" I asked, planning to regale her with the swirling memory. She nodded, still never looking in my direction. I stared into space as I conjured old ghosts and told her a small tale from my family history.

"Once there lived a boy, who like most boys had a huge crush on a girl. The girl, however, never noticed him. He attempted many things to catch her eye, but nothing succeeded. Then, one summer day he overheard her mention she enjoyed the theater. Now, keep in mind this boy was dirt poor, and the theater back then was expensive. Undaunted, he knew that if he could somehow get her tickets she would eventually fall in love with him. The boy started tucking away every extra cent. He skipped meals and gave up on all his pleasures, and with holes in his soles he remained happy knowing each saved bit brought him closer to spending an evening with the girl of his dreams.

"After a month or so, he finally had enough in his pocket to buy their tickets. He felt madly nervous to ask her to go, but he managed, and she accepted.

"When the night of the show arrived, he looked in the mirror and saw a boy he didn't recognize. Having borrowed several pieces of nice clothing and taken extra care in combing his hair, he could almost pass as a gentleman. Walking to the theater an hour early, he struggled to remember all the things gentlemen did, like opening doors and holding out his arm to accompany her.

"It took him twenty minutes to walk there, but he was glad, for it helped him work off some of the nerves shaking his bone marrow. After pacing around the front area for a spell, he eventually settled into the one spot where he knew he could easily see her arrive no matter what direction. The butterflies in his gut threatened wildly to escape as their meeting time grew nearer and nearer.

"Then their time passed, and she hadn't arrived.

"He waited and waited, and a few times thought he spotted her amongst the crowd, only to be disappointed. When the doors opened and everyone piled inside, he just stood there. When it was finally apparent she wasn't coming, he sat down on the sidewalk and stared out into the empty street, cursing himself for getting his hopes up.

"Not feeling like watching the show by himself, the boy stood up and decided to go home. Passing by the box office he couldn't help hearing an argument. A pretty, curly haired blonde girl dressed in white fur jockeyed for admittance. The man behind the counter argued with her, insisting something livid about her father. After several minutes of bickering, the girl shrugged and gave up.

"Feeling bad for her and having just had his night open up, the boy rushed to her and volunteered to take her inside. Without any hesitation, the girl grabbed his arm and marched him to the entrance. When he handed over the tickets, the girl stuck out her tongue at the greasy fat man behind the counter, but he let them go inside anyway.

"The play had already started and they hurried to find their seats. The first half of the show must have been very good and very funny because the blonde beauty beside the boy never let her eyes stray from the stage. Her laughter ejected loud and sincere. The boy knew all these things, but he couldn't have told you what the play was about, for the whole time his eyes never strayed from the girls face. He was smitten.

"During the intermission they made small talk. She asked him why he had an extra ticket, and when he told her he'd been stood up, she squeezed his arm and told him the other girl was a fool. The time they had to talk fell short, and before he knew it the curtain was drawn. The second act must have been dreadfully sad, but again the boy never bothered to look at the actors on stage. He watched as tear after tear fell from the girl's face, quickly patted away with a lace handkerchief. When the show ended in rousing applause, he offered to walk her home and she accepted.

"During their walk, he discovered she came from a very wealthy family, and that her father had forbidden her from attending the theater. Her father claimed plays were a wicked waste of time, and put her in the circles of bad company. Still, the headstrong girl attended whenever she could sneak away.

"When they reached her home, a palace compared to the loft he lived in, the boy panicked. He suddenly realized he would most likely never see her again, and the thought hurt unbearably. He had only known her for a short time, and he loved her, even though he started the night thinking he loved another. Desperately young and deeply hoping to see her again, without thinking he offered to take her to the theater again the following week. Letting out a little squeal, the girl threw her arms around him and kissed him on the cheek.

"Walking home, the boy rattled and racked his brain trying to think up ways to find the money for the next show, and as luck would have it, a thought occurred to him as he passed the theater. Finding the doors unlocked, he peeked his head inside and saw what he expected to see: a group of young men hard at work cleaning the theater. Watching them, he easily determined who was in charge, and bolstering his courage he walked over to the plump man planning to make a deal.

"The boy explained that all he wanted were tickets for the shows, and he wouldn't need to be paid. The boss bulked a hard man, and demanded the boy not only come in and clean after every show, but also stay as watchman every night. Happy to have some kind of resolution to his dilemma, the boy agreed right away.

"The entire week was hell on the poor lad. He worked all day and kept watch almost all night, nabbing only a few hours of sleep in the wee hours of each morning. When the week finally passed and the beautiful girl in the white furs arrived, he knew it had been worth it. Same as the first night, she watched the actors and he watched her. They shared tidbits of titillating chatter during intermission, and a slightly longer conversation on the walk home.

"For many months they met for theater dates, and the sleep-deprived boy worked tenaciously, deliriously in love. He tried a few times to convince her to go other places with him, like the park or dinner, but her only interest lie in the theater. After running out of patience, and hoping to move their relationship a step further, the boy scraped up enough money to buy a simple, tiny, gold ring. He planned on giving it to her as a token of courting.

"As he sat alone in the theater waiting, thinking he had been alone since the end of evening rehearsals, he turned the ring over and over in his hands, so excited and nervous to give it to her. Consumed with thinking about what her reaction would be, he heard a loud sound from behind the stage. He felt certain someone had broken in the back door.

"Walking as quietly as possible through the dark, he snuck around the side and made his way through backstage. The sound grew louder as he neared the green room. Putting his ear to the door, he could make out whispered voices and quiet laughing. Pushing the door open in one swift motion, the boy was almost knocked to the floor by what he saw.

"Embraced in a passionate kiss, his girl wrapped herself around an actor. Hearing him enter, she turned around and smiled at him like she had done nothing wrong. The actor walked over and offered the boy his hand, thanking him for making sure his girlfriend got home safe after every show. A loud ringing ping overtook the boy's ears, and he wanted to punch the man in the face. The girl, seeing the confusion and pain in the boy's expression, explained that her father did not approve of her relationship with the actor, and that's why he had banned her from the theater. Crippled by the betrayal, the boy threw the ring onto the stage and vowed to never fall in love again or ever attend another play. He ran out of the theater and never went back."

Completing my tale, I refocused on the room in front of me and pulled myself back into the present. I noticed Cara staring at me with her mouth slightly open.

"That was a terrible story," she said, irritated I had soiled her special place with it.

"I'm sorry, it's just the first theater story I remembered."

"So what happened to him? Did he really never fall in love again?"

"Not to worry," I assured. I know for certain he went on to marry, and that he even had a son." That appeased her slightly.

"There is a moral to this story. Can you guess what it is?" I asked.

"That women are evil?"

"No, Miss Negative."

"That men are naïve?" she said, grinning at me.

"Not even close."

"OK then mister, err, doctor know-it-all, what is the moral?"

Using my most pretentious voice, I explained, "The moral of the story is simple. If you are busy falling in love with someone, you better damn well make sure they're not busy falling in love with someone else."

I expected some kind of quick-witted comeback, but instead she looked away.

"Are you alright?" I asked. She answered with a question.

"Who are you busy falling in love with Dr. Shay?"

CHAPTER 7

Her question stole the breath from my lungs. The sound of Cara's voice absorbed into the walls while conflicting memories burned through my neurons. Soft movements beneath silky sheets fell to shreds under the screams of heart break. Joyous girls in white gowns wasted away in grief and grew cold and cruel. The Shay family illness set fire to even the purest of love, and I remember it all.

Where lies failed me the day of my classroom lapse, a million brewed forth. Simple ones, honorable ones, waited for a simple wag of the tongue, but there they sat. The full force of my will could not unravel my feelings for a woman I barely knew. And in the most selfish act of my entire life I said nothing.

I waited for her to break the tension, for her to crack a joke and momentarily offer release from my turmoil, but as the seconds ground into minutes, the torture remained. Eventually, I thanked her for sharing her amazing place, and left. She didn't speak, and shook her head slowly as I fled.

I ran from the room straight into the elevator. I needed to be away from her and shut out the feelings overwhelming me. The elevator ride felt as if it lasted forever, lurching its short journey back up to the ground floor. The doors chimed open to a crowd of students blocking the exit path. It required all my restraint not to plow through them and shove their bodies aside. After agonizing minutes of slow maneuvering, I made my way outside and began running again with no clear direction or destination. I just needed to get away from her smell, her face, her eyes, her wit, her fire.

Completely out of breath and my throat burning, I eventually stopped randomly at my favorite place on campus, The Green.

I drank deeply from the water fountain right inside the front door. The cold water shocked coughs from me all the way to the elevator. Stepping inside, I had a better idea of where I wanted to go and pushed number three.

The third level housed the desert flora. It was hot, dry, and sterile. Having always preferred cool and damp, I wasn't drawn to the room by its heat. It was the unfamiliarity of it I desired, a region in which I had no concrete family memories. My relatives always settled in wet, verdant climes, with histories in Scotland, Ireland, France, and lastly the greener regions of the United States. I came to level three often, and seldom did a foreign memory interrupt without intention. Standing in a virtual desert, I could be alone with my thoughts. It was also very quiet and empty most of the time, as typical greenhouse sightseers preferred the exotic and colorful tropical plants in the hot house. I was pleased to see that once again I was the only visitor.

One spacious room encompassed the entire floor. It had two levels of ground, a tiled path where visitors walked, and a natural habitat of mostly sand and rocks banked up two feet higher. As I wandered the maze of pastel tiles the dazzling yellow flowers of prickly pear cacti dotted my vision and tall Saguaros waved subtly all around.

My legs ran on autopilot as I paced the path and spoke three words aloud, "oxytocin, dopamine, vasopressin." The knot in my brain only tightened, and so I tried screaming the words, over and over. They were the only defense against what I felt, and they were failing me miserably.

For most of my adult life I suffered with the realization that I could never allow myself to be in love, so, to cope with the crushing loneliness, I decided to destroy the myth of love with a bit of research. Science, in its cold and calculating way, deduced what causes people to feel love, and it boiled down to three neurochemicals; oxytocin, dopamine, and vasopressin. Once upon a time this fact comforted me. When I crossed the path of love birds nuzzling one another, to numb my jealousy and pain, I would imagine those chemicals wreaking havoc on their behavior. The trick helped. It never cured, but it took the edge off, and as I walked the artificial desert, not even my magical three words would hold my pieces together.

It wasn't a scuffle inside me, but a full out war. My attraction to Cara ran deeper than any chemical. The essence of my being reached for her, craved her, and yet for her wellbeing I had to find the strength to push her away.

My thoughts were busy tearing away at me when the elevator doors swooshed open. The couple stumbling in had also assumed it a typically empty room, already entwined in a very intense kiss. The girl had her legs completely wrapped around her beau's waist, his mouth busily at work on her neck and chest. Neither saw me, and before I could make a noise to alert them, the girl looked straight at me and smiled.

It was Amber, and her sly expression evidenced she was very excited I had caught them. Clearing my throat, the man almost let her fall to the ground in his attempt to be free. Turning toward me, I recognized the distinct ponytail and strong jaw line of Dr. Edmund Kaliska, my boss. Amber's plan was at last revealed.

I stood there in familiar shock. This was not the first time I'd caught him with a student, but it sickened me he had unknowingly become a pawn in Amber's revenge.

"Hey Chamberlain, didn't see you there," he said grinningly proud to show off his newest conquest.

"I was just leaving," I said coldly.

"You weren't up here with anyone were you?" he asked, pretending to look around the room. Amber murmured a sinister laugh. He always enjoyed teasing me for being a prude, but I wasn't dumb. I knew it made him nervous that I stuck to the code of conduct. He hoped that if he teased me enough I would eventually give in and take up a student lover, relieving some of his guilt. A tiny voice in my head cheered as I remembered Cara was not, officially, a student.

"Nope, totally alone," I said while walking away.

"Wait!" called out Amber. "I think there is something Dr. Kaliska wanted to talk to you about first."

I stopped but did not turn to face them. This wasn't going to be pretty, and Amber had no idea what kind of mood she had caught me in.

"What?" I demanded. Steaming fury crept into my voice. Kaliska shakily stuttered, unsure how to start. Amber had put him in a difficult spot, having most certainly made him promise to confront me. He probably hadn't planned on doing it at all, and surely not seconds after I'd caught him fondling her. I walked over and got up in his face.

"Just spit it out!" My hands clinched into fists at my sides.

A hundred fistfights flashed before me. Grown men, school boys, and drunken brawls where the memories blurred from intoxication. Some of the fights ended in pain. Others closed with the singular satisfaction of feeling another man's nose crunch against a well-flung fist. I was never a violent man, but being called out because of a girl like Amber, and by a man as slimy as Kaliska, was all I could bear.

"You OK there Chamberlain? I heard you had a little *breakdown* in class and I wanted to make sure everything is alright." His words sounded concerned, but I knew him too well to believe he felt those emotions. Kaliska didn't care about me. He only worried about the stellar reputation I gave the University, and the long list of evil things I knew about him.

"I'm great. Thanks for asking. How about you? I haven't seen *your wife* in a while?" My teeth clenched as tightly as my fists.

"I'm good," he said looking at his shoes. "I'm good."

I had blackmailed him and he knew it. Amber, seeing the conversation not going at all in the direction she had planned, tried to push him.

"This man is a lunatic and a danger to the entire campus! You can't just let him get away with this. You need to place him on permanent leave until there is an investigation!" I ignored her and never let my gaze shift from Kaliska's squirming face, daring him to talk.

"He's fine. Let's just go." Kaliska wanted Amber to shut up even more than I did.

Even though I'd been anxious about this conversation since my classroom collapse, I wasn't troubled anymore. His own demons had left him incapable of confronting me on mine. Our relationship would never be the same after that moment, and I was so glad. He truly saw how much I despised his behavior, and he knew I wasn't afraid of him. He could never again confront me on anything.

Struggling to lead Amber out of the room, he said obligatorily, "Good to catch up as always Chamberlain. We'll have to go for a beer some time." I waved him away and watched Amber tearing at her hair.

"You ball-less son of a bitch! What are you scared of him for? You are his boss remember? Are you freaked out he might tell your wife what you're up to? Oh gimme a break, like she doesn't already know. And you!" she barked, pointing a shaking finger at me."You disgust me and I will make you pay for… for..."

She couldn't even finish her sentence; unable to voice she hated me because I rejected her. When words failed her, she tried to spit on me. Her phlegm fell short by a foot and stuck mainly to her chin.

"Quite a lady you've got there boss. I hope it's worth it."

Wiping her chin and flinging her dribble into the sand, Amber leapt at me to scratch out my eyes and screeched,"You bastard!!" Kaliska quickly wrapped his arms around her waist and pulled her back. She clawed at his hands yelling,"Let me go let me go let me go!"

Seeing them in that position and hearing Amber's shrieks, I started being pulled uncontrollably into the memory of Mom's death. I tried to push it away. It would undo everything I had just accomplished if they saw me lapse. Losing control second by second, time slowed as I watched Kaliska yell his apologies and pull raging Amber onto the elevator. Just as the doors closed, I lost all control and collapsed into my worst personal memory…

Birthday cake and blood covered the floor. Only moments before I was blowing out my nine candles and Mom and Dad were singing to me. I thought about my birthday wish - the dog I'd been begging for since my last birthday - when Dad suddenly snapped. It happened so fast. One minute he playfully ruffled my hair, and the next he raged a mindless monster. He walked over to the trash to throw away burnt candles, and when he turned back around he was someone else.

Mom never saw him coming. She was too busy cutting the cake. Before I could let out a peep, Dad ran over and grabbed her by the wrist. She dropped the knife on the table. Using his arms like ropes, he entangled her and locked her against his chest. She struggled against him and reached for the knife. He screamed, "No Cake! NO CAKE!!" He screamed it over and over again. My ears rang and I covered them with my hands. Mom started screaming, "Let me go let me go let me go!" Dad did not hear her pleas, even though her lips were only inches from his face. He just held onto her, blanking into space like she wasn't there.

Wrestling with all her strength, Mom leaned over the table and used her elbow to nudge the cake a couple inches in my direction. Tears cascading down her pale face, she looked me in the eyes and said in a very determined, but tired voice, "Son, eat your birthday cake." Her persistence snapped Dad out of his blankness and he forcefully used their interlocked bodies to knock the cake off the table. It slid across the pale tile floor, leaving a smeary chocolate wake.

Seeing her beautiful cake ruined, Mom erupted. Like a ferocious animal, she began hitting him in the chest with her tiny fists. Dad barely flinched, so she scratched and bit at him. She dug long pink gashes into his face, arms, and neck, and a steady flow of blood dripped from his right hand where her teeth had cut through. Despite the pain, he held tight and never slackened his hold.

Watching the two people I loved most in the world commit such violence on each other shocked my little system, but I couldn't look away. Somewhat fortunately, it became harder and harder to see them as tears filled my eyes, and soon they were no more than loud blurs. I wanted to make it stop. I felt compelled to rescue Mom, but I couldn't move. Frozen to my chair, prisoner of my fear, I regressed into a human statue unable to do anything but endure the bleary horror.

Blinking away some of the tears, I caught a glimpse of Mom pulling out handfuls of Dad's hair, but still he held tight. Then she kicked him squarely in the knee and he buckled to the floor. She freed herself, and sprinting to my side she half carried me out of my chair and ran us toward the second floor balcony. She flung open the French doors. Hobbled and infuriated, Dad lunged at us and grabbed Mom by the ankle. Trying to keep me out of his reach, she pushed me through the doors onto the patio.

Frozen night air burned the tearstreaks on my face. Turning around, I saw they had made it back onto their feet. Giving up on fighting him, Mom clawed at empty air to reach me, but I was too far away. I took one small step toward her when Dad yelled "Stop!!" It was the first time he'd spoke to me since the episode began and his fierce tone froze me.

Seeing his attention now on me, Mom elbowed Dad in the face and blood exploded from his nose. Dad raised his blood soaked hand, and in one powerful motion brought it across Mom's cheek. I shrieked. His mighty hit threw her off balance and she careened into the wall. She toppled over in slow motion as her head fell closer and closer to the floor until the sickening sound of her skull smashing on stone tiles silenced every other sound.

Father jumped to her side and screamed something, but I couldn't understand the words. The spreading crimson puddle transfixed me. Mom's blood mixed with chocolate frosting... and I thought about how only moments earlier Mom and Dad were singing to me, and I was blowing out my nine candles...

I awoke on the tile floor covered in sweat. Picking myself up, I walked shakily to the nearest bench and sat. I fought the tears for a while, but the image of Mom on the floor forced too much sorrow and I started to cry. I hated the feeling. I felt weak, helpless, alone. Always alone.

Many times I asked Granddad why Father had killed her, but he always refused to tell. Watching Granddad deteriorate, I figured my father must have lapsed into a memory. After years and years of searching my memories and rereading the family books, I still couldn't figure out the mystery of what made him act that way. I had obsessed to solve it for years, but the only person with the answer had disappeared. The night he killed Mom, my father dropped me off at Granddad's and I never saw him again.

Drying my eyes and sitting up straight, I tried to pull myself together. Quickly my thoughts drifted to Cara. Reliving my mother's death refreshed my determination to never put someone I loved in danger. I knew how dangerous the curse could be for others, and I knew how painful it would be to watch someone degenerate. I had to quit playing with Cara in grey areas. It was the only way to keep her safe.

The drive home passed quickly as scenic vistas did nothing to distract me from Cara. Now and then, small glimpses of Granddad's youth in the backwoods of Tennessee forced their way in; images of opossum traps and Copperheads and turtles in an impossible rainbow of deciduous trees.

But always back to Cara. Her face. Her laugh. I tried to focus on a plan to cut her from my life, but the more I thought of her, the more my 25-year-old hormones interfered. I imagined kissing her and running my hands through her hair and over her shoulders, feeling her pressed up against my chest as I pulled my hands down the length of her thin back. My heart raced and my eyes glazed over.

A huge brown mule deer jumped into the road ahead of me and I slammed on the brakes. Yanking the wheel to the left, I spun 180 degrees into the shoulder and heard a sharp squealing sound as a tree scratched the side of my black, 1970 Z28 Camaro.

Stepping dizzily out of the car to inspect the damage, I marveled as the deer paused a moment from the trees to look at me. I could almost hear her say "Human fool, watch where you're going!"

Angry at the deer and furious at myself, I climbed back in my car and belched a string of fiery obscenities that lasted for miles. I felt much calmer by the time I pulled up to the house.

In my driveway I found a vehicle I didn't recognize, an older green Ford truck. Having so many other things on my mind, I had forgotten Marisa's nephew would be waiting to meet me.

I could smell dinner and felt unusually hungry, as I'd forgotten to eat all day, so I walked straight into the kitchen. Marisa was busy checking on rolls in the oven, while Granddad sat at the table watching her.

"Hi Granddad!" I chimed as I crossed the room and patted him on the shoulder. Marisa jumped, having not heard me come in.

"Don talk to heem señor Shay. He no say peep all day," she said wiping her hands on a dishrag and turning to stir the stew.

Mostly ignoring her, I bent down level with Granddad and looked him straight in the eyes. "You OK Granddad?" He could see me, but he only replied with a slow head shake. He looked terribly frightened.

"What happened today?"

"I don know señor Shay. He jus stop talking."

I grabbed a pen and sticky pad from the counter. Handing it to him, I hoped if he wouldn't speak perhaps he'd write. He took the pen and removed one small neon yellow sheet from the pad. Then he very slowly and deliberately scanned the room for several minutes.

Satisfied that whatever or whoever he was afraid of wasn't present, Granddad quickly scribbled on the paper. In a smooth, sleight of hand motion Granddad flashed the writing in my direction and then stuck it in his mouth and swallowed it whole.

CHAPTER 8

I didn't respond to his odd behavior. I didn't know how. What he had written didn't make any sense. It simply said "Shhh."

At supper, Granddad grabbed his bowl of stew from Marisa quite barbarously and began devouring it like he had never eaten. He was recalling someone starving, but as Irishmen, this didn't offer me much of a clue. Marisa reprimanded him mildly in Spanish for his brash behavior while she carefully placed a cream colored napkin in his lap. He didn't hear her and just kept shoveling it in. Settling into my own bowl of stew, I savored the warmth it brought to my stomach. The carrots and hunks of meat were so tender they melted. Only three bites in, Marisa's nephew walked through the back door.

Wiping my face, I stood to properly meet our new household member. As he stepped into the dining room light, I nearly sunk to my knees in awe. Granddad jumped from his chair and ran up the stairs to his room. I had to force myself to stand in one place and fight the urge to run as well. As he neared, my knees rattled. Standing before me offering me his hand mirrored an image of one of the most feared men in our collective history.

The Boss.

The height, the build, the facial structure - all a perfect, frightening match. Just like The Boss, this young man looked aged and beaten down by life, but still held all of his whippersnapper strength and power. His thick, protruding brow deceived a handful of folks into believing he lacked intelligence. However, looking into his eyes revealed a sharpness observing and absorbing everything around him. His darker complexion helped me keep a more stable foot in reality than Granddad, but I couldn't have spoken if I wanted to. The haunt of a personal hell had returned to live in my home.

While the memory of The Boss was old, it could never be old enough. During the 1600s, the English imprisoned and sold hundreds of thousands of Irish slaves, and killed even more, decimating the Irish population. My family had the unfortunate experience of being owned for a brief time by a man known only as The Boss.

A large rock made contact with the back of my head, forcing me to the ground. Within seconds three men had me pinned and tied my hands. Before long, they shackled me to two others. We tried desperately to pull free and fight off our guards, but they countered every attempt with brutal punches to our sides and faces.

The village burned in chaos. Young men were captured and beaten, while the women and children were slaughtered where they stood. My only blessing was the ringing in my ears drowned out the sounds of misery. I searched in vain for the faces of my wife and child but never saw them. I knew every dead body that lay upon ground, and each one I would have died myself to defend. The piles of gore made me vomit where I stood. Heaving brown and grey bits onto the ground, I caught the attention of The Boss, a dangerous mistake.

He was not difficult to spot. His shouted commands and vicious behavior made it clear who was in charge. From his perch on a pristine white horse, he urged his men to herd the women and children toward him so he could personally impale them one by one with his broadsword. When tired of that murderous game, he ordered his guards to wipe off the blood so as to not ruin his blade.

He leapt from his steed in a bright burgundy tunic and shiny gold leggings, obviously fancying himself some kind of English king. Walking over to us, he gingerly stepped over my vomit and said a few words to one of the more decorated guards. He spoke in a foreign tongue, but by the way he pointed it was clear he spoke about me. The guard asked me if I was ill, because if I so, The Boss wanted to burn me so I wouldn't infect the others. Although I wished for death, the idea of arriving there by being burned alive still seemed disturbing. With all my might I explained and begged that I was indeed well. After inspecting my mouth and skin, the man in charge forgot about me and moved to other torturous tasks.

After the carnage, they pulled all the captured men into a group. Looking around at whom they had spared, the massacre's purpose evidenced itself. Only young, strong males had been left alive to be sold as slaves. While most had given up, some still fought even though they were tied and helpless. I watched as my brother spit in The Boss's face, and then promptly had his left ear cut off. Everywhere I looked begat a new torment, so I closed my eyes.

They moved us like cattle. We were forced to walk while they rode horses on all sides. The terrain was arduous, and when we were too slow or when someone lagged, The Boss promptly rode his horse to the line and whipped at random. His whip cracks sliced deeply into our skin, but we trudged on.

During the journey, we learned The Boss's biggest annoyance. He hated noise. Even the guards spoke in whispers. Once, two fellow slaves were caught talking. Without warning, and with incredible swiftness, The Boss cut out their tongues. Another man cried out when whipped for falling behind, and his rope bound hands were set ablaze. The blood from our backs and mouths, and the steady dripping from The Boss's whip and blade created an obvious vermillion trail behind us.

The night watch changed as we ventured further from our homes. We were surrounded the first night, with fewer the next. On night three only a handful stood watch. They figured we were beaten, and they were right. Already dead inside, I waited until my outsides matched.

Only two men guarded on the fourth night, but we were too weak and scared to do anything. We stared into nothingness, exactly what I was doing when something glinted in the moonlight - a small shadow no one else seemed to notice. I watched the same spot for so long that I thought my mind had gone. Then I saw it again, this time clearer. The outline of a child appeared, and as it moved slightly out of shadow I recognized my seven-year-old daughter, Alana. I had no idea how she had lived or found the strength to follow, but seeing her gave me reason to live again, and more importantly, someone to fight for.

She remained in the shadows, crossing silently back and forth to catch my attention. Sick with fear the guards would see her, I wanted badly to swoop her into my arms and run. She moved closer, staying in the protection of the brush, but the whites of her eyes gleamed in the darkness. The guards devoured their dinners and didn't lift eyes to notice me. The other prisoners slept, or seemed oblivious to my discovery. I motioned for her to crawl to me, which she did hurriedly. Once in my arms, I could feel her galloping heartbeat through her skinny chest. I didn't want to let go, but she would be killed instantly if seen. Instructing her to follow the creek downstream and find people to help, I felt a hand on my arm.

I looked back to see a frowning visage of evil. With all my might I pushed my daughter as far away as possible. The Boss had a hold of me, and calmly called the guards for help. With no time to react, I knew the price I must pay.

"Run Alana! Run downstream!" I screamed, tackling The Boss's legs and dropping him in the dirt. I screamed it over and over until the guards had me by the arms and The Boss had my tongue. They beat me until all went dark.

I awoke with so much blood in my mouth I thought I was drowning. The pain from the beating numbed compared to the burning in my face. Slowly rolling off my back, I spit out as much as I could and realized several of my bones were broken, especially my right arm. Wondering how I'd be able to walk any further, I looked around to see everyone gone. Beaten too badly to be sold, they left me behind. Too broken to care for myself, I would die in that field alone, and I was happy. I would die a free man.

Resigned and waiting for death, I suddenly tasted wetness on my lips. Opening my swollen eyes, I beheld my sweet beautiful daughter holding a clay cup to my lips. Behind her stood a throng of men I had never seen. Despite the pain, I drank every drop.

The memory replayed fuzzily behind my eyes as the young man smiled and held out his hand to shake. Looking into a carbon copy of The Boss's face, I could taste blood filling the place where a tongue should be. Forcing myself to act slightly more normal, I faked a smile and shook his hand.

"Mucho gusto señor Shay, my name eez Geraldo. Or joo can call me Gerald." His big honest grin stretched his assimilated name out to sound like *Jay rolled*. His warm and happy tone encouraged me to relax. I told him how grateful we all felt for his willingness to help. In order to maintain a coherent conversation about his pay and duties, I stared at the wall behind him.

If he noticed my odd behavior, Gerald was polite enough not to say anything. After our conversation petered out, Marisa gave Gerald his bowl of stew and I was free to finish my own. To my dismay, the harrowing memory of The Boss built a knot in my stomach and I couldn't take another bite. Handing the remains to Marisa, I saw the disappointment on her face. I lied about a late lunch and asked her to save the leftovers, which seemed to placate her a bit. As I walked upstairs to check on Granddad, my head threatened to explode under the stress of so much to figure out. Adding Gerald and his affect on Granddad threatened to push me over the edge.

I found Granddad happily reading the newspaper in his room. He loved reading the newspaper, and since I was a child it was tradition for him to read it out loud when I joined him. As he aged and the sickness worsened, the stories he read were no longer current, but memorized tales of mainly World War II. Still I found comfort in hearing them, so I took my seat to the left of him and he began to read aloud. He spoke in his familiar, grandfatherly voice containing the magic of instant ease.

Granddad orated halfway through an article about the death of a woman at the hands of her husband. A few sentences in, I realized he was reciting the story published about my parents. I knew it by heart, and kept a copy of it in my personal journal tucked under my bed. It was a sad thing to read. In a cold, matter of fact way it described how my mother's body was found, and blamed domestic abuse for her death. For being such a major part of my life, the article was very small and pathetic. They didn't mention how wonderful and beautiful my mother was, nor did it say anything about the expensive funeral Granddad arranged for her.

Finishing the last line, Granddad folded up the newspaper, wiped his tears, and patted the top of my head like he did the first time he read it to me.

"It's going to be OK Champ. You're never going to be alone. There will always be someone around who loves you." An echo from the past, I believed him the first time he said it. Now I wasn't so sure. Granddad seemed invincible in my youth, but as time slowed him, the curse stole more of his mind each day.

"Granddad, we need to talk about Gerald." I said it softly, hoping he'd come around long enough to help me find a solution. "Who's Gerald?" he asked, somewhat clear and back in the moment. I explained who he was, and whom he resembled, and Granddad listened quietly, nodding in an understanding way. "The Boss was a horrible man. It's a pity our young Gerald looks like him. Can't imagine the kid would be comfortable wearing a ski mask or heavy beard."

A keen beard suggestion, but I just wasn't sure what kind of crazy story I could come up with to convince Gerald. Growing facial hair wasn't a typical request from an employer, and the last thing I wanted to do was scare him away. Tucking Granddad in, I told him goodnight and made my way downstairs to talk to Marisa.

Gerald sat in a chair, and he and Marisa practiced English phrases while she tidied the kitchen. He was facing away from me, giving me time to prepare myself for the images sure to surge when he turned around. They stopped talking, obviously waiting for me to join the conversation.

"So, we have a little bit of an issue. Gerald, you remind Granddad of someone from his past, someone who scares the hell out of him."

"Oh no señor, I am sorry," he said with serious feeling, turning towards Marisa in confusion. "Está bien su abuelo?" I assured him it was not his fault, and Marisa nodded, confirming she knew something was wrong since Gerald arrived. I felt pleased they responded more concerned than angry.

"I think I have a way to deal with it, but it's totally up to you Gerald. Would you mind... growing a beard?" I hadn't planned on giving him an option, but it was his face. I didn't have to wait long for his answer.

"¡No problema! Siempre quería llevar la barba." I raised my eyebrows like I understood what he'd said, but he knew I was lost. "Si señor Shay. I like de beard." His contagious smile relieved me and we all laughed hard for a minute. I hugged Marisa, and shook Gerald's hand and wished them both goodnight. As I dragged myself upstairs, I silently prayed the beard would work. I hated the idea of firing Gerald. We needed help.

CHAPTER 9

Retiring to my room, I retrieved my book from under my bed and updated the newest highs and lows. Reading my words, I realized that in the same day I had finally admitted my feelings for Cara, and only moments later resigned myself to cutting all ties with her. Life is never promised to be fair, but I couldn't help but curse my dilemma.

Lying in bed and staring at the boring ceiling, I thought about how my father's life had turned out, and what he might be doing at that very moment. Wasting away in a cell? Crazy and on the run living under a railroad bridge? All were possible, yet I couldn't imagine any as reality.

He seemed so joyful before he killed Mom. He enjoyed being funny and always knew a good joke or outrageous story. Wading through his memories and seeing his perspective, I knew how much he loved my mother. He had never been serious about any other women until she came along, and like myself he had decided at an early age not to spread the disease to the next generation. If he'd had his way, I would have never been born.

Unfortunately, Mom had no knowledge of our illness until after I was born. Many days my father lied or faked headaches to keep her from the truth. How he ended up breaking it to her and how she took the news was unavailable to me in his database of memories. However it happened, she must have looked past it, because she stuck around. Granddad's wife bolted the moment my father started having the memories. Her abandonment caused serious hurt to both my father and Granddad, but how she reacted was sadly not a surprise. An exhaustively long list of women had run away or suicided because they couldn't handle it. How could we blame them at all? The brave ones who stayed subjected themselves to years of hardship, and some went crazy once they realized the future that had been passed to their own children.

Drifting to sleep, I relived the first time my parents met, seeing it through my father's eyes and feeling it from his heart:

The party could be heard from a mile down the road. Someone had brought a guitar, and group singing filled the mountain air. Reaching a long line of vehicles parked on the side of the dirt road, I pulled in behind the last. I left my flashlight, but grabbed my coat. Firelight beckoned through the trees. Tripping over downed branches and loose rocks, I worried about breaking my ankle, but arrived safely. An amazing amount of people had already gathered, as the news had been hyping the appearance of Halley's Comet for weeks. Finding the moment a perfect excuse to party, young people romped in force.

Most of the girls perched on giant logs circling the dangerously large bonfire, happy to be talking amongst themselves. The guys indulged their primal urges, finding new objects to toss into the blazing heap. Scanning the myriad faces, it seemed comical no one bothered to look up at the sky. Bending my head back, I realized the light from the fire made comet watching impossible.

I decided to walk away from the central group to find a better look at the stars, or hopefully run into someone I knew. On my way out, a skinny drunk kid claiming he was The Beer Fairy ran up and offered me a beer. I gladly accepted and watched him stagger away, spinning clumsy pirouettes. I took a swig and decided to find a place to sit.

Leaving the partygoers behind, I walked a long while until the sky shimmered brightly with stars again. I found a large, flat rock positioned ideally for a person to recline and enjoy a cozy view of the sky. Even though no one was around, I felt an urgency to claim it as my own and climbed atop it quickly. To my great surprise, that very same moment someone else approached from the opposite side. Suddenly face to face, the lightning surprise of seeing another person shone both ways.

She was a very pretty girl with long blonde hair and dangling feather earrings. We stared at one another for a moment, and I started to back away to let her have the spot when the most beautiful sound filled my ears. She laughed. Despite my resistance, she pulled me up on the rock with her, insisting sweetly, "There's plenty of room for two."

I introduced myself, and conversation flowed easily as we lost ourselves in the sky's milky wash. Her name was Nichole Sile. She said she'd been looking for the comet for days and was very disappointed.

"We just got unlucky," I joked. "If we had been born a hundred years ago, we would be witness to a most excellent show." Intrigued, she enthusiastically asked me to share what I knew about the comet. She was so excited to learn, it was a pleasure to talk with her.

Like most people, Nichole knew Halley's Comet passed the Earth every 75 or 76 years. She showed more interest in the composition of the tail, the comet's size, its elliptical orbit, but most especially, its impact on humans.

"Did you know many believe Genghis Khan chose the path of his reign of terror based on the comet's westward trajectory?"

"Seriously?" she asked, scooting in a bit closer with interest.

"It's true. For thousands of years the comet has always been both feared and admired as either a good or bad omen, depending what side of history's favor you've fallen. Mark Twain was born two weeks before the comet's 1835 appearance, and he knew for certain he would die when it reappeared in 1910."

"Was he right?"

"He was indeed. He died one day after its zenith."

We talked for over an hour until I finally ran out of comet knowledge. When she realized I had no more to offer, she laid back and watched the sky. I kept waiting for her to ask how or why I knew such things, but she never did.

We lay next to each other until night allowed early morning and a cold crispness settled the air. Without a word or warning, Nicole shifted toward me and settled herself in the crook under my arm, resting her head just under my chin. The sweetness of her hair as it blew around my face intoxicated me, blending beautifully with the surrounding pines as if she were meant to be a part of the forest. The closeness of our bodies kept February's cold at bay, and I could feel myself falling asleep when the sound of loud footsteps broke my doze. Trying to ignore them, I kept my eyes closed.

Nichole was suddenly torn off of me with a yelp. Sitting up to see what happened, I found her on the ground with a well-dressed woman clutching her arm. The woman looked older than the typical comet partier, and her matching blonde hair hinted her as Nichole's mom. She was furious.

The enraged woman held Nichole to the ground and accused her of being a whore. Nichole instantly began crying and pleading, "Please Mother, nothing happened I swear. Nothing happened!"

Backing up Nichole's word, I stood up on the rock and promised nothing had occurred, but the mother never acknowledged me and continued berating Nichole, dragging her away. Nichole's patience burst. She yanked her arm back and stood up.

"Let go of me Mother! You have no control over me anymore. I am 19 years old and I can do whatever the hell I want! And what I want is to be away from you forever! I hate you!"

Mother did not take the news well and slapped Nichole hard to the ground. I rushed to her aid, but an icy glare warded me off. Crying hysterically, Nichole jumped up and ran off path into the deep forest. Mother followed hot on her trail, threatening to take her daughter out of this world the same way she'd brought her in, whatever that meant.

I decided to call it a night. Walking back to my car, I couldn't help but think about Nichole. I hoped she was all right, and that I might see her again.

Most of the partiers had left, and only a handful of cars remained. A small layer of ice had formed on my windshield, so I let the car warm up a few minutes while searching for a tolerable song on the radio. Heater blowing warm air, I put my car in drive, and before I could lift my foot off the brake Nichole opened my passenger door and jumped in.

"What in the world do you think you're doing?" I asked annoyed.

"I have no idea," she said.

Looking at her swollen red cheek and her gorgeous smile, I smiled and took my foot off the brake. We pulled away.

That night, all night long, my father's memories of Mom controlled my dreams.

CHAPTER 10

My success was measured in time, for one month and seventeen days I had been lapse free. This was also how long I had avoided all non-professional interaction with Cara. Each day I carefully planned a list of excuses to free myself if we ended up alone or if she suggested another trip to the library. I never went to class early, and I never stayed late. But most importantly, I controlled my desire to look into her eyes.

Smiles still passed between us, and many a casual "Hello" or "Have a good weekend," but that's where it ended. Determined to keep her on the outside boundaries of my life, I had yet to find an antidote for the affection rooted in my soul.

Cara began turning in the assigned homework for her classes. The professor in me believed she did it to improve her history knowledge. The romantic in me eagerly hoped she did it as a secret communication tool. She remained focused on the scholastic topics and didn't sway to anything personal, but her conversational writing read like she wrote directly to me. Regardless of why she turned in papers, their content brimmed with her unique feistiness. I came to understand that not only was Cara bright, but also witty and sarcastic, even acerbic at times. She had the charmingly irritating habit of inventing words, and refused to use commas in the correct places. Most of all, I was impressed by her desire for truth, a feeling I understood well.

I never put a grade on her papers. What was the point? Instead I filled the margins with comments requiring a great deal of time to compose, imagining she might be searching for the same hidden meanings I scoured her writings for.

I made photocopies of each of her assignments, for reasons I couldn't truly rationalize, and kept them at home in a safe. I was so addicted to this demented form of vicarious contact that the other students in her classes suffered. I assigned twice as many essays in my 201 class, as well as a handful of extra credit papers. I even went so far as to make daily journal entries mandatory in Historical Writing. Reading her words satiated like wearing a nicotine patch while trying to quit smoking. It wasn't satisfying the relationship I desired, but it gave me a taste of the fix.

In those 47 days I also began obsessively staring out my office window to guiltily feed my affections from afar. Like a love-struck stalker, it occurred to me that in order to reach the history building, Cara had to pass by the plaza fountain below my perch. The first time I waited, I held my breath as she walked by, striding with attractive, nonchalant confidence. A few times on exceptionally warm days I watched her studying at the fountain. She liked to lie on the grey cement bench holding her book above her head. I dreamed of being with her, imagining her hair spread across my lap as she read out loud, both of us laughing at her zesty commentaries. At first I believed my fantasies could do no harm. I figured that if I couldn't live it in real life, at least I could live it in my head. I was wrong. Pretending only made clearer what I denied myself, and left me aching for her even more.

As I commuted to school contemplating successes and woes, foreboding storm clouds claimed the sky. By the time I reached the parking lot, snow started to fall, forming wispy whirls across the blacktop. A handful of half-frozen studentcicles sluggishly climbed from the warmth of their cars. I groaned in acknowledgement that very little learning would be achieved that day.

The cold chewed at my neck and face during my walk and dissipated in pins and needles as I stepped into the history building. By the time I reached my office, I was burning up. The campus buildings never failed in being uncomfortable. Overzealous air conditioning forced students to wear coats during summer, and in the winter, dry heat suffocated every room.

A fervent bureaucratic desire to provide thermostatic comfort somehow produced the opposite effect no matter how much everyone complained.

I pulled off my coat and sweater and checked my email. My inbox burst with messages from students who didn't want to face the cold but refused to cop to it, feigning illnesses instead. To my happy surprise, I also received notice that Amber had officially withdrawn from History 201. I nearly kissed the computer screen. I hoped it was a definitive sign she had finally given up on exacting revenge and had become Kaliska's problem. I tried to pity him, but the thought of him getting what he deserved was far too sweet.

On my way to class I ran into Briggy. Two glass test tubes clanked precariously about in his breast pocket, a green moss-looking substance swimming around in each as he gesticulated in jolts. Staring at the ground while he spoke as if he was thinking of something else entirely, he babbled about the future using long textbook words. I could only understand about one in five phrases, so I just patted him on the shoulder.

"Good morning Briggy. Good to see you as always."

He was still talking to himself when without a goodbye he spun around and left. Watching him, I amazed how many people had to stop in their tracks or jump out of the way to avoid colliding with him. I could hear the test tube mosses screaming for help as he recklessly zagged through the hall.

Once in the room, I prepared the board with notes and waited while students trickled in. Wearing the same tired expressions as their parking lot counterparts, several would surely fall asleep while I lectured. As I ran out of things to organize, I kept catching myself eyeing the door in anticipation of Cara's arrival.

She shuffled in wearing a light blue hoodie and jeans, both dotted in snowy wet spots. Instead of taking her typical seat near the door, she passed it and headed my direction. I pretended to be reading my notes while I listened to her footsteps clop closer and closer. My heart sped up, and when she stopped a few feet in front of me, I took a deep breath before looking up. It was the closest we had been to each other since the day I ran out of the library.

Still pink from the cold, her fingers curled around a small book. She held it out to me and I took it, examining the cover. In gilded lettering on the leather cover read the title, *The Stage Of Love*.

"What's this?"

"A present," she said coquettishly, like she knew something I didn't. I thanked her and tucked the book into my bag as she stepped away to her customary seat.

As expected, only half the class had shown up, and many slept the full hour. I avoided looking at Cara while I delivered a flawlessly mediocre lecture to a scattering of attentive faces. When they gladly filed out in the same zonked mosey they had arrived, Cara merely waved as she disappeared out the door.

The little book she had gifted me burned a hole in my bag as I hustled to my office. I wanted so badly to scour the pages for a message or meaning, but it had to wait. Libby had arranged to meet me right after class, and she didn't tolerate distractions.

Again armed with her ever-growing briefcase of files, Libby arrived right on time. We skipped formalities and went straight to discussing her newest developments. "After five disgusting hours of pouring over descriptions of dead bodies," Libby said with a shiver, "I am certain William James did not die at the Cañon City facility."

No proof that he was dead made me hopeful, but I could tell this disappointed Libby. She only half said it, but I could glean from her demeanor she sickened of the manhunt and wanted to move on to work that interested her.

Trying not to insult her, I inquired what type of pressure she had put on the prison. I knew she was doing her best, but after so many years of fruitless searching for my father, impatience itched my every word.

"I threatened to sue them on behalf of William James," Libby said proudly.

"On what grounds?"

"*Habeas corpus* of course. While imprisoned it was his right to be brought in front of a judge. He didn't even get an arraignment hearing. The system swallowed him with no regard to due process, ergo, we've got them by the balls." It was so brilliantly Libby. She went straight for blood and I loved it.

"How long should we give them before we hire a lawyer?" I asked, eager to attack.

"At least a month, if ever."

This was not the answer I wanted. I was ready to start making appointments that day. "Why so long? I want to move on this now."

Like she was explaining to a child, she answered slowly, "We don't want to hire a lawyer because we are just using it as a threat. We want to scare them into telling us what happened. If we did try to sue them, their lawyers would come up with a bunch of privacy issue crap. And since we are not his official representatives, nor are we related to him, we technically can't demand to know his whereabouts."

I almost told her I was William James' son. It took everything not to blurt it out, but I had to wait and see if her scare tactics worked. Being a well-known writer made privacy difficult enough, and the public eye would scrutinize me if it got out that I witnessed my father killing my mother. I had no desire to be pitied, and valued my privacy far too much to shout to the world that I am the spawn of wicked blood. With Granddad's protection to consider as well, I agreed to wait the recommended month. I graciously thanked Libby for coming, and we agreed to our next appointment.

Once alone, I hastily retrieved the little book. On the inside cover Cara had written an endearing inscription:

"Chamberlain, Thank you for sharing a little time at the theater. May we find another special time to share the stage."

I reread it over and over until memorized.

Turning to the actual text of the book, I found it was the same story I had told Cara that day in the basement. *She sure is good with search engines* I thought. I had no clue the story had ever been published, and flipping back to look at the author and contributors I didn't recognize any names. This wouldn't have been the first time someone ripped off one of our stories, but it was the first revealed to me by an outsider.

I tucked the book back into my bag and moved to the window to check on the storm's progress. The combination of rain and snow always made for interesting days on campus. Slick spots in the history building's halls were almost impossible to avoid. All day long the janitors toiled in vain to contain the puddles amidst the continual echo of slipping bodies slapping the floor. Most students carelessly walked in without attempting to stomp off their shoes. Even those who made some effort still ended up shaking their accumulated snowflakes all over the floor; feeling entitled their mess was someone else's job.

Before I left the university, I called and booked my normal room at a local hotel. As the snow accumulated heavily on campus, it would be much worse on the way home. I had no desire to spend hours in the car fighting icy roads, only to face the same treacherous drive in the morning. Heather, the front desk girl, sounded rather bored when I called. Having booked the room many times before, it seemed like she sat waiting around for my call since the last time. "Your regular room is waiting for you professor."

After laying out my lecture notes for the next day and making a quick call to Marisa to check in, I locked my office and headed for the car. The weather canceled the later classes, and reaching the parking lot I noticed only one other car. The flakes grew exponentially in size with each step, and by the time I started my car I was covered in white wetness. Letting the engine warm, I rubbed my hands together hoping I wouldn't have to get back out and wipe off the completely whited out windows.

An abrupt knock at my window scared me so badly I screamed like a victim in a horror film. Not wanting to unroll the window and spill more snow into the car, I swung the door open and heard something hit the ground a few feet away. To my astonishment Cara lay sprawled on her back in the snow. I quickly scrambled out of the car and crouched at her side, horrified I had seriously injured her.

"Ohmygosh Cara! Are you OK? Can you move? No wait, don't move! Stay still. Just stay right there. OK, maybe I should get an ambulance. Umm, holy shit. Do you think you need an ambulance?"

She lay there, wide-eyed, losing herself in the deluge of flakes. I had just pulled out my cell phone when she began to giggle.

"Why on Earth did you open your door?" she laughed, sitting up.

"You're OK! Oh thank goodness! I am sooo sorry Cara. I can't believe I did that." Explaining the whole no snow in the car thing, I helped her up.

"I assumed you were going to roll down the window, and when the door came at me I stepped back and slipped."

"I am so sorry. Are you sure you're OK?"

"I'm fine, really. Just a little bruised and wet." She wiped the snow from her clothes, but the snow fell fast enough to cover us anew immediately. "Crazily, this is the least of my worries right now. I've been sitting out here trying to get my stupid car started since class ended," she said, motioning to the lone car on the other side of the lot. "So when I saw you walking to your car, I thought I'd come ask for some help."

"Yeah, umm, no problem," I stammered. "Now that I've given you a concussion, the very least I can do is loan you my cell phone."

She bit her lip and shook her head.

"You know, I can't afford a mechanic right now, and no one's coming out to rescue me in this storm anyway. I don't want to be a pain, but, would you mind giving me a ride?"

I knew driving her somewhere would break my no-Cara streak, so I offered an alternative that didn't involve us being together in my car. "Let me go take a look at it. I'm definitely no mechanic, but maybe it might just need a jump."

I walked toward her primer colored late model hatchback, but she didn't follow. She said, "I know what's wrong with it."

"What?!" I yelled, already closer to her car than my own. Cara gestured for me to walk back to her, like what was wrong with her car was a secret and I needed to be closer so no one else would hear.

"It doesn't need a jump, and it's technically not broken," she said.

"OK then. Why do you need a ride?"

"It's out of gas and my money is at home," she admitted. I felt bad she was embarrassed, but also saw her predicament working to my advantage.

"Well that's an easy fix. I'll just go get some gas and bring it right back. You can pay me back next time I see you in class." I liked my idea. She wouldn't be stranded too much longer, and I wouldn't damage my streak.

Cara didn't like my plan.

"Thanks so much, but I really just want to get home. I've already been out here for over an hour and I'm freezing cold and wet. I can get a friend to drop me off with gas tomorrow. Please, do you think you could just take me home?" I tried to conjure an excuse from my prepared list, but her request was so simple. I gave in.

I unlocked and opened the passenger door for her.

"What happened to the side of your car?" she asked, pointing at the long gash left by the tree.

"That's your fault actually." I shouldn't have said it.

She stood there mute and confused for a few seconds.

"Don't worry about it," I assured. "Let's get going. It's freezing out here."

I decided it wasn't a great idea for her to know that I almost killed myself while fantasizing about making love to her.

Walking back to my side of the car, nervous excitement and gut wrenching regret churned inside. My hands shook intensely as I buckled my seat belt, and I pretended it was the cold. Some of the snow had melted off the partly warmed windshield, and I flicked on the wipers to clear the rest without hassle.

"So, where are we headed?" I asked, forcing a casual cool tone into my nervous voice.

"Home."

I laughed. "You gotta give me more than that."

"My home."

I smiled and started to pull away, planning to ask for instructions as we went. After five minutes of small talk about the weather and school, we ran out of chatter, so I switched on the radio to avoid the silence. The volume was low, but it really didn't matter because even if it were all the way up, I wouldn't have heard it. I drove far too focused on her presence. She emanated a mix of coconut and mint, and having nothing to say, Cara started singing along with the radio. She did so absently; out of habit was my guess. She knew all the words to the song, but her tone was off. And as quietly as she sang, her voice stood out. High and breathy, it hit my ears familiar, so familiar it eventually carried me into a memory, one so fortunately mellow I had little difficulty running it through my head while I drove.

I could hear her voice in distant Vienna… in the late 1700s…

A private concert in the home of wealthy friends. Well-fed and rounded buttocks filled every richly curved parlor seat. The women wore sparkling jewelry and long gowns. At the piano, a young Franz Schubert played, his fingers tickling deftly over the ivories. A pretty young woman sat next to him, and the contrast between the two was vast. The girl's swan like neck and high aristocratic cheekbones towered over the short and squat Franz. The party had been gathered so the young woman could present Franz with a gift. He had been giving her music lessons, and to show her appreciation she had written lyrics to one of his songs.

Her words swelled dark and beautiful, very fitting for the tune he wove delicately behind her. Love and desperation burned in her eyes as she sang, and who that love directed toward could not have been more clear, for her eyes never left Franz while she performed for a room full of people. The awkwardness of the situation made guests shift in their seats. Franz was deeply in love with the girl, but could never act on it. Unknown to her, but common knowledge among the crowd around them, Franz had contracted an illness in the seediness of a brothel. If he were to love her in a physical way, it would ruin her.

When at last the song subsided and the girl belted out the last high note, Franz rose from his seat and hastened from the room, wiping away the incendiary tears of a man doomed to the loneliness of a shameful death.

Cara directed me to park in front of a large brick building. "Want to come inside and meet the family?" she asked while gathering her book bag and pulling the light blue hood over her head. This was the last thing I wanted to do. I had already crossed too many lines and I knew I couldn't cross more.

"Thanks for the offer, but I really need to get going before the roads get worse." She insisted she owed me hot coffee for my troubles, and I felt hypnotized by her smile. Before I knew it, I was climbing the creaking wooden stairs up to her apartment.

I wasn't sure what to expect when we went inside. While making our way up, I imagined walking through the door and being bombarded with small children and an aunt or grandmother who'd pinch my cheek and ask cooingly when I planned on marrying Cara. We stepped inside her apartment to darkness and silence.

CHAPTER 11

Cara skipped around the tiny studio space flicking on lights. The entire apartment could be seen from the front door. Stepping into the closet that doubled as a kitchen, she yelled, "Make yourself comfortable!" I wasn't exactly sure what she meant, but assumed it involved finding a place to sit. The main room contained way too much stuff, but very little recognizable furniture. In the corner sat her desk and a twin-sized bed. Not wanting to trespass onto her bed, I took the sole chair at the desk.

Similar to my office, her home contained an insane number of books, all piled along the walls. Perusing the titles, there seemed little method behind their arrangement. A turn of the century hardback French novel sat right underneath a paperback pulp title. The only stack all containing the same author was the stack I couldn't help but notice. Next to Cara's bed sat everything I had ever published. Her collection even contained papers I wrote during my undergrad work. Pretending I hadn't noticed my bibliography, I switched my eyes to her walls.

Erratic bits of torn paper and napkins of all shades splattered the walls. Standing for a closer look, I found each piece of paper had a name and date scribbled on it. Some dated from the 1800s, and others were as recent as that year. The names appeared random. None of the names belonged to famous people, at least not any I could recognize, and none shared her last name. Her entire apartment collaged in obscure encyclopedic vomit.

After loud cabinet banging and a few less than ladylike words, Cara came into the main room and handed me a chipped mug. With a bit of embarrassment she explained that she would have offered cream and sugar, but she was out of both.

"I like my coffee black anyhow. Thanks very much." The first swig I took filled my head with memories. Coffee ignited a common trigger for me, as was milk, or any other traditional flavor that hadn't changed in a hundred or more years. Morning breakfasts, and men by campfires late at night flickered in my mind, but they were easily pushed aside.

"Do you live here alone?" I asked.

"Yep."

"Where is this family you insisted I meet?"

Grabbing me by the hand, Cara pulled me into her bathroom. Once inside I saw nothing but a toilet, sink, and toothbrush.

"She's in the tub," Cara said, putting her hands on her hips.

"Who is?"

"Just pull back the curtain."

"No thanks," I said taking a half step back.

Cara rolled her eyes and yanked back the purple shower curtain, exposing a dry tub and a seriously irritated ferret. "Rosa likes to sleep in here because it's cool," Cara said, picking up the white haired, red-eyed rat-looking varmint. "She's four years old, and she's nice. See?" Rosa looked intimidated, so I reached out and scratched her behind the ears. Taking this as a signal of interest, Cara held her out for me to hold.

Pulling my sleeves back to my elbows, I reached out and gently cradled Rosa in my arms. Cara backed out of the bathroom and pulled her hoodie up over her head, tossing it onto a pile of magazines. She wore a sheer white v-neck, just short enough in all the right places to make me force myself to look away. I turned to sit again at the desk chair, but Cara led me by my elbow to her bed. The ferret climbed up the front of my shirt and settled herself on my neck as I sat down. Clearly not proper ferret etiquette, Cara grabbed Rosa off of me and put her on the floor. Embarrassed by what she had done, she hopped back to the bathroom. Cara began to apologize, but I waved her off, and she noticed my tattoo.

She boldly grabbed my arm and turned it palm up so she could see the design more clearly. "I didn't know you had a tattoo. Is this the only one you have?" I nodded and swallowed hard in dread of the next question bound to follow.

"Why your birth year?" she asked, delicately tracing the numbers with her fingertips.

"In my family, we have a tradition that on a boy's thirteenth birthday, the year of his birth is tattooed on his forearm. It's a family tradition dating back to the 16th century. After I got mine, I showed it off to everybody I knew and didn't know. I spent three Colorado winters in short sleeves to make sure everyone saw it."

I had said more than I had wanted, and as her hand caressed the inner crook of my elbow I lost control over what fumbled out of my mouth. I barely maintained the wherewithal to shut up before I explained the tattoo would help me know whom I was when my mind left.

She giggled adorably. Not looking up, she said, "It's nice to have family traditions." Regarding my arm, she sat beautifully and contemplatively like a model in a historical painting. Her shadowy veil of hair draped her cheek, hiding most of her face, but her jaw and graceful neck glowed open and exposed. Unable to control myself, I reached over and softly pushed her hair behind her ear. She closed her eyes and sighed gently as she parted her lips. My desire exploded out of my chest with the urge to pull her down to the bed and kiss her.

"Tell me more about your family," she said in a slow, dreamy entice. Her expression changed as she felt my whole body tense. I pulled my arm away from her grasp.

"I should get going," I said standing up.

"Please don't. It's nice to have company. Please stay a little longer. Please."

Her tone wasn't begging, but it tugged at me. My resolve melted into puddles around me, and I sat down next to her again.

"Just hang out long enough to tell me about your family," she implored.

"My family is pretty boring," I lied. "Why don't you tell me about yours?" She hesitated for several deep breaths.

"Well, Rosa is sweet. I got her from a friend who moved into a pet-free place." She sidestepped the real question, and a polite person would've taken it as a hint. I pushed for more.

"As much as I want to hear all about your rodent, I'm curious about your human family."

"Ferrets are weasels," she said, rolling her eyes. She lay down on her stomach and stretched out, resting her face right next to my arm. Her warm breath on my arm made my legs shake. I didn't say anything else. I knew she was deciding if she would open up or not.

"Fine, I'll tell you. But I have one rule, and if you break this rule I'll..." She trailed off, unsure what she wanted to put on the table.

"I'll *bite* you!" she said, placing her teeth on my arm in a threatening way.

"All right all right, what is your rule?" I asked, feigning fear for my life.

She took a deep breath."Don't say you're sorry after I'm done. OK?"

This obviously meant the story would be painful and sad."You have my word. I promise."

"I don't have a family. When I was five, my mother signed me over to the state. I assume she was into drugs or something. I don't know. Most people who adopt kids want babies, so I was kinda screwed. I was moved around a lot from one foster family to the next, and some were friendly, but most were really horrible. Most of the families thought of me as a paycheck.

"But I did have one good place when I was fourteen. The family already had a lot of their own biological children, and they really seemed to care. I was with them for almost a year when they decided to move to Africa to do some kind of mission work. I begged them to keep me, but I was tossed to another place again.

"When I got older, I tried to find my biological mother. It wasn't hard because she hadn't moved from the town where I was born, and the first thing I found online was her obituary. I was able to get ahold of her parents though. I was too scared to call them - just worried they'd hang up on me. So instead I went to their house thinking maybe if they saw me they would have to like me. I borrowed a nice churchy dress from a friend and tried extra hard to make my hair look the way I thought they might like. I took a bus and then had to walk a really long way, but I eventually found my way to their beautiful blue house, all clean and trimmed in white like a magazine house. I was so nervous I thought I was gonna hurl on their rose bushes. But I forced my way up the steps and rang the doorbell.

"A grey-haired woman answered the door with a sweet smile. I told her who I was, and said I had come to meet her. In just a few sentences, her whole demeanor changed. At first she looked sad, and then angry, and before I could get my story out she cut me off.

"She yelled, 'I don't have a granddaughter! Now get off my property!'

"She slammed the door in my face. But I didn't cry. I just walked back to the bus stop and waited." Her voice fell small and quiet.

"I'm sorry Chamberlain, but I can't tell you about my family. At least not the kind of family you're thinking of."

I felt terrible for asking her any more questions, but at the same time I yearned to know more about her life, even if it was tragic.

"What about your father?"

"Dead."

Cara stared at my face, I assumed in an attempt to guess what I was thinking, and I did my best to keep the pity I was feeling from touching my eyes.

"Well, if they weren't smart enough to keep you then they didn't deserve to have you. Trust me when I say it was their loss. Morons all of them!"

I jumped off the bed. How anyone could ever treat Cara in that way was beyond me. I wanted to go back in time and wring all of their necks. Surprised by my reaction, Cara watched me. She didn't say a word to calm me. She just sat and watched while I continued my rant until I realized I was the only upset one in the room. Still pacing, one of the napkins on the wall grabbed my eye. I stopped to study it.

The blue pen writing on the white napkin said Jonathan Mincer, 1943. "Who is this?" I asked. Cara jumped up and joined me at the napkin.

"I read a lot of non-fiction history stuff. That's how I came to know about you. Anyways, when I learn about someone I like, I worry that I might forget them later. I feel like everyone deserves to be remembered, so I write down their names and birthdates so I can remember not to forget."

Cara gave me a short tour of the people on the wall. She knew a little bit of information about each soul. We laughed as we came to Lamarck's name, remembering the awful day I accused her of blackmail. As I neared her headboard, Cara stepped in front of me, blocking my way.

"This one is a little embarrassing," she said. I laughed and playfully pushed her aside. On a crumpled tan napkin she had written my name and birthday.

"So you worry I might be forgotten?" I asked, completely confused.

"I've been reading your work for a long time," Cara said staring at her shoes I walked over and placed my hands on her shoulders. "I'm flattered."

Like wind stripping branches from an ancient tree, my resolve and restraint snapped and plummeted to the ground.

I slowly leaned down and placed my hand under her chin. I held her still as our lips lightly touched. My conscience screamed at me, but the devastatingly soft and warm sensation drowned out the warning. All nervousness, fear and doubts slipped away. I wanted so badly to sweep her up and crush her to my chest, but the very impulse was overridden by a need to gently relish every second. I am not sure how long we stood there with our lips touching, but as she slowly leaned away, I knew it wasn't long enough. She stood on her tiptoes and wrapped her arms around my neck.

I stared into her deep eyes, awed by the love and desire reflected back at me. Never in my life could I have imagined someone could look at me that way. I whispered what I had known since the first time I saw her.

"I need you."

Not quite understanding my meaning, she pulled my face to hers and kissed me passionately as if she were trying to eat my mouth in the best possible way. I responded in kind, and before I knew it we were entwined around each other, ensuring every bit of our bodies touched.

I did need Cara, as selfish as it was, but for much more than physical pleasure. Terrified by what kind of harm I would bring to her, I needed love, affection, and someone to share my secrets with. I had tired of fighting my needs, and in her arms I let myself slip, breaking the oath I had carried for years.

We stood in that same spot feeling, tasting, and breathing each other in. When our legs tired, we fell to her bed. I lay on my back and she positioned herself above me. She touched my face and neck as her eyes inquisitively took me in, almost like she was observing a new creature for the first time. It had been so long since either of us spoke, that when she did, her voice cracked.

"Tell me more about you. I know you are brilliant, funny, strong, and sad, but I don't know little things. Like what type of food you like to eat or what your favorite movie is. I want to know all about you." Normally these types of questions would send me into a panic, but the time fast approached when I would have to explain the darkness of my future and let her choose for herself if she should be part of it.

"I hate tomatoes and I like mustard. I'm a sucker for zombie movies and I can't stand romantic comedies. Watching college football dominates my Saturdays, and I hit a tree and scratched my car while imagining what it would be like to kiss you."

"That's what I'm talking about," she beamed. "The *important* stuff. What else?"

"My best friend is Professor Briggs."

She made a sour face. "Um.... Does he know you're not a plant?"

I laughed so hard it shook both of us and the entire bed.

"I'm not entirely sure. He did tell me that I'm an oak tree!" I laughed even harder, realizing I felt happier than I could ever remember.

"Well, let's see. I live with my grandfather. I call him Granddad and I adore him."

"I would love to meet him," said Cara with a slight squeal. I nodded silently, trying to ignore the panic that came with her request.

"So what are your worst flaws Chamberlain? You know the deal breakers? Most guys your age are either married or on their way to being." Her very appropriate question instantly vaulted me into reality. My deal breaker was not a cute little quirk that she would laugh off. Mine was indeed a real deal breaker.

Would she laugh? Would she think I was making it up? Would she push me out the door and call me a lunatic? My head buzzed as I considered telling her the truth. What was I thinking? What if she believed me? What if she accepted me?

"Just spit it out. I know you're hiding something major. You think you act normal, but you don't. I see how your eyes glaze over and you go somewhere else. I also watched you freak out in class, remember? I promise whatever it is I won't run away screaming." She took my hands and looked up mischievously. "Unless you're an alien or something gross. Then we might have some issues, because to be honest, I am not that into Sci-Fi."

Laughing at her uncanny way of lightening the mood, I made up my mind, and for the first time in my life decided to explain my condition to an outsider.

CHAPTER 12

A lifetime spent hiding my secret had mentally and physically trained me not to tell it, and I could feel my throat shake as I fumbled for a way to start. Forming the words to explain the curse fumbled like trying to spontaneously speak a new language, knowing one error could result in brutal loneliness. So I just blurted it out.

"I am not normal. I have memories from the past - things I can remember that happened hundreds of years ago."

It was a blunt start, and I would have kept going but Cara interrupted.

"Are you immortal?"

I added *slightly naïve* to the list of things I assumed about her, and then quickly replaced it with *trusting*.

"No, of course not. And I didn't fall from heaven, nor do I drink blood."

She smacked my arm playfully, but it stung enough to make me feel I unnecessarily protected myself with sarcasm. I had to restart my courage, so I took her hands in mine. When I started again, I wasn't alone. Memories of the same speech being given a dozen times filled my head in several different languages and circumstances as I could see the men of my line spilling the truth, anxiously waiting for reactions. I tried to ignore the bad and focus on the good.

"I have a genetic illness."

Cara's tiny squeak of concern broke my focus. I closed my eyes and started again.

"While normal families pass down hair color and hooked noses, mine passes down more. You see, we pass down memories. Thanks to some random mutation in our DNA, every male in the Shay line, from ancient times until now, inherit all of the memories of every man before him."

"Does that mean..."

I gathered Cara's hands and kissed them.

"There is more," I whispered. "My entire life I have been distracted by the memories, but their power over me is changing. They are starting to cripple me."

"What do you mean?" Her words were equally soaked with concern and curiosity.

"How many memories have you made in your life?" I asked.

"I don't know, a million, maybe more," she said.

"Imagine multiplying all of those memories by the lives of hundreds. A brain simply cannot keep all that information straight. As the men in my family age, the memories take over. We forget where our lives begin and our ancestors' stop. We call it lapsing, but basically we are sucked into memories and relive them. Over time we are no longer ourselves and are trapped in the events and minds of other men."

The explanation felt so short compared to the enormity of the content, but I had done it. I had told her the truth and I didn't pretty it up. Peeking up to see her reaction, I expected panic or disgust, but neither graced her calm and relaxed face.

"So, soft inheritance is real? Lamarck was right?" she asked, pointing to his scribbled name on her chaotic note wall.

"Yes indeed, and my family knew Lamarck. He tried to help us by explaining our condition to the world. You know how that turned out though. The poor guy was persecuted because of us, and ever since then we've tried to tell as few people as possible."

She sat there fixed on me with utmost understanding and acceptance. I thought, *Why is this so easy?*

"Aren't you skeptical at all? I mean, don't you wonder if I'm making all this up? For all you know this could just be some really strange sweet talk," I said waving my arms in the air like a carnival barker. "Swooning you with a history-laden mystery illness so you fall helplessly in love with a sad mutant."

She laughed a little scoff that said *Don't be ridiculous.*

"I knew there was something very unique about you, but I just couldn't put it together. And as far as believability, I know you're a great writer and all, but not even you could make this up. Truth is always *way* stranger than fiction, and..." She stopped short of whatever else she planned to say.

"And how dare you accuse me of loving someone I don't trust?"

She did it. She had accidently said she loved me and I caught it. Like a coward, I wasn't ready to say it back, so I quickly asked if she had any more questions about my condition. She did.

Cara asked about the lapse in class, and I explained. She actually seemed to be excited, pelting me with more and more questions about how far back I could remember specific historical events. I could see small revelations collect in her mind as she pieced it all together. She inquired about every detail except for the most important - my impending insanity.

"So that's how you're able to write about history the way you do. I always wondered how you could research so much detail and seem to know exactly what the people were feeling. But isn't that kinda cheating?"

"Yep," I answered without thinking about it. "I always feel a bit ashamed when I receive awards and special praise for my writings. I can't shake the feeling that I'm fraudulently taking credit for the lives of others, but it's truly the best way to share our history without repercussions."

Her questions then turned to my parents, and my automatic impulse to lie returned. Almost like she read my mind, Cara leaned up and placed her lips on mine to silence me. When she released me from our kiss, she didn't pull her face away and rested her forehead against mine. We touched noses and she whispered, "It's OK Chamberlain." She looked directly into my eyes to make sure I understood her seriousness. She said a bit sadly, "If life has taught me anything, it's that our parent's sins are their own - not ours."

That was all I needed to hear. I let go and told her all about my father killing my mom.

I was not a man who cried often, and never in front of other people, but I did in that moment. Tears slipped from my eyes and mixed with hers on our cheeks. Locked in her attentive gaze, I explained my obsession with finding my father and how I had acquired Libby to aid the search. Saying Libby's name forced a surprise face from Cara, and I asked if she knew her.

"All too well."

Feeling sore and drained from hours of intense emotions, I didn't pursue her comment and pulled away from her. Sensing my fatigue, Cara got up and poured a glass of water from the kitchen sink. I gulped it down. She refilled it, and returned to lie down next to me, staring at the ceiling, or just beyond the ceiling.

"I would understand if you never wanted to see me again," I implored.

She grabbed my hand and placed it on her cheek.

"I could hurt you someday," I said. "Even kill you. I know how much my father loved my mom and it didn't stop him… And at the very least I will get sucked into the memories like Granddad and won't be able to take care of myself, and I can't put you through that. I can't even give you a timeline. My lapses started earlier than normal, the illness might progress quicker too. I don't know. I might be gone by next month." Another wave of tears rushed in.

"It's my choice," she said firmly, almost motherly like I didn't have a choice.

"You have explained exactly what will happen and I honestly don't know if I can stand by and watch you lose your mind and become other people. But I do know how much I care about you right now, so I have an idea. What if we just take things one day at a time? I'm not perfect either, I promise, so this works both ways. I think people feel this need to jump into *forever* when they don't need to. I'm not saying I'll run for the hills at the first hint of trouble, I just mean let's choose to be together for now. Right now. What do you think?"

"I like it," I admitted, relaxing several tons of pressure from my shoulders. "I'm always so stressed about the future that maybe if we can manage the proverbial day by day I'll worry less."

Leaning over the top of her, I pushed her hair behind her ears and asked, "Are you sure? You have no idea the type of memories that are in here." The faces of evil and virtuous men doing wicked things rushed into my head. I took my hands away from her face and smashed my palms on the sides of my head trying to squeeze them out of my brain. She sat up and pulled my hands from my face.

"You will be in there somewhere, and no matter what I will always remember that. It doesn't matter what kind of memories you have. To me you are Chamberlain, for the good and the bad."

We didn't talk much more that night. I had already confessed more than I ever had to anyone. We kissed and writhed and caressed for hours, and in the short breaks between we stared and breathed in each other's warm exhales. We shared the most romantic moment of my own life, and the most romantic of *any* life I could remember. I never wanted it to end, and, of course, the sun inevitably rose.

Acting like Romeo and Juliet, we pretended the shafts of light through her small window were street lamps until her pre-set alarm clock blared and we knew it meant time to face the real world. Stretching asleep and atrophied muscles and limbs, we slowly leaned out of her bed, both hesitant to leave our joined warmth. Being in close physical contact with another person for that long altered my brain, and when she walked into the other room I instantly felt like an amputee. It was as if she had walked away with both of my arms when she left to start coffee. I searched my pockets for my phone.

I was halfway through a conversation with a tow truck company when Cara returned. Hearing what I said, she grabbed my arm and emphatically shook her head no. Dismissingly pushing her aside as nicely as possible, I finished my call and turned to find her growling.

"What?" I asked, oozing innocence.

"I told you my car was just out of gas," she fibbed.

"And that was a lie because you didn't want me to know it was broken."

"Maybe..." she said looking away. "But how did you know?"

"You're way too responsible to just run out of gas. You've been on your own for so long that after I thought about it, I realized it just wasn't something you'd let happen."

It felt good to understand another person so well, and I was gloating a bit much by explaining my rationale.

"Wow, let a boy spend the night, and suddenly he thinks he can read your mind. Very impressive professor." Her mischievous smile cut through her rascally sarcasm. "You caught me, but in all honesty I can't pay a tow truck or a mechanic to fix my car. I just started my new job on campus and I won't get my first check for at least a few weeks."

Wrapping her in my arms again, I insisted, "Well, I do have the money, and I can't have my Cara walking the winter streets now can I? How can you keep me this warm if you're frozen? Face it, you're going to have to suck it up and let me help you." She thought about this for a moment and pulled away.

As I watched her walk to the front door my heart plummeted, fearing I had gone too far and she was going to kick me out. Instead, she grabbed her black school bag and dumped its contents all over the floor without thought to the mess she made or damage to the books inside.

"What are you doing?" I asked. She bustled by me and grabbed a large notebook from her desk. She said adamantly, "You're right, but if you're allowed to help *me*, I get to help *you*."

Help me? I wondered. She had accepted me despite my flaws. She had given me happiness and hope for the future, and changed my outlook on life completely. I was puzzled what more she believed she could do.

"Don't be so daft smarty pants. I'm gonna help you find your father."

Seeing that she had made her mind up completely, I shrugged and hugged her.

"Thank you Cara. This means the world to me."

She grabbed my hand and pulled me to the desk to get started right away. Her enthusiasm was refreshing, but I felt a little more practical.

"We haven't slept in over twenty-four hours. Aren't you tired?" I asked, hoping to stop her momentum.

"Kinda, but I want to solve this for you right away," she said tugging my hand.

"Well, the tow truck company said that many of the roads are closed due to the storm. Why don't we check and see if school is cancelled for the day?" Agreeing, Cara opened her laptop and pulled up a list of closings. Our university claimed the top of the list. Looking like she didn't quite know what to do next, I suggested, "I have an idea. Why don't we get cleaned up, have a decent nap and then go get something to eat? Then we can work on finding my father with fresh heads."

She stretched her thin arms above her head as the suggestion of a nap snuck in and made her yawn. She agreed and kissed me. She grabbed a couple towels out of the overstuffed closet and headed for the bathroom. Pausing at the door, she turned and seduced a bashful smile.

"Would you like to join me?"

I really wanted to, and I almost collapsed when she asked. I felt immensely attracted to her, but I politely declined. She seemed to have accepted me entirely, but I felt betrayed by my lust and wanted more time to give her a chance to get away when she saw how bad it could be.

Cara obviously didn't see it that way. "Your loss," she said as she slowly teased off all of her clothing as she walked into the bathroom. I ground my teeth as the door closed behind her and a memory launched in my head.

"The need for satisfaction boiled inside me. As I sat and watched the performers, I was annoyed the displays were more circus-like than flesh filled. The Moulin Rouge promised some of the best courtesans in Paris. It was my first time paying for a girl, and I hoped she would be very professional to put me at ease. With each new performance I mentally chose a new girl to be mine at the end of the night, but there were so many of them, I couldn't keep track of my favorite. When the final cancan commenced, a man approached discreetly asking if I planned to stay for the after hours show. Holding out the requested sum of coins, I could only respond with a silent nod as my throat had dried with anticipation.

The usher led me through a dimly lit corridor into a warm crimson room. Several other men joined me as we awkwardly shifted in place, distracting our nervousness with the garishly decorated floors and walls, doing everything we could not to make eye contact. After a five-minute eternity, the sound of giggling, high-pitched voices began gathering behind a partition of red silks. A stream of astonishing girls paraded into the room, dressed in the same loudly colored outfits they flirted on stage. It felt like being surrounded by a rabble of naughty butterflies.

Each girl had a slightly different look. Some were tall and thin with willowy arms and legs, and some were very exotic, as if they came from places imaginary. I had expected the girls to be shy and quiet, scared of what the men might do, but instead their relaxed and good-spirited mood instantly lightened the atmosphere of the uncomfortably tense room. The party had started, and as if there was nothing strange at all about the situation, the girls instantly mingled about talking to each other and the men, cooing and taunting their barely covered bodies.

Observing all this from a corner I had unconsciously backed into, I realized the number of men in the room quickly declined. Paying closer attention, I observed a short man and a very tall girl pair ever so smoothly and disappear behind the same red partition through which the girls had arrived. I wondered in frustration how it was done. Starting to feel like the merchandise instead of the buyer, I felt rejected.

Standing to leave, a redhead in a very revealing corset blocked me. By far the prettiest girl in the room, her fiery hair hung loose and long to her waist, and the peppering of freckles dotted atop her creamy cleavage made me realize my mouth hung agape. She smiled broadly at me, exposing a set of slightly crooked teeth. Before I knew it, we were walking through the silken partition. Even though I was never asked who would be my choice, I knew as we walked arm in arm that I would have chosen her from the very beginning.

Following her to a small room off a long hallway, I mustered the courage to speak. "How did you know that you were the only one I desired?" She laughed in a thick Irish accent, "Ye didn't. Yer Willie did." Taken aback by her crass observation, I was too intrigued to stop her explanation.

She removed her stockings as I listened how the process worked. She explained that some "dir'y dick places" lined up the girls like sheep at slaughter, but the Rouge was a little different. She made it seem like the girls simply walked around until they found a fellow they excited. Embarrassed my body had so visibly betrayed me, by the time she finished stripping, I had forgotten my own body and was lost in hers. The redheaded enchantress seemed to be reading my mind as she led me over to a small wooden-framed, straw bed.

It was over in minutes... Which she neither complained about nor seemed a bit surprised by. I simply dressed, thanked her, and walked out. I was happy the physical pressure had released, and my mind felt clear.

As I made my way home, a nagging feeling consumed me - the sensation that the experience wasn't complete. A critical aspect unfulfilled, I had never felt so lonely.

Shaking off the hollow residuals from the memory, Cara strutted back into the room, wrapped in a white towel. Her wet hair dripped onto her shoulders as she walked to the dark wooden dresser to pluck out clothes. Her back turned to me, I gawked unashamedly at her elegance. The first time I'd seen her legs exposed, droplets slowly coursed down her long, taut calves, begging to be touched. I stood up and walked over to her. I kissed her shoulders and back as she exhaled deeply and sunk into me.

"As much as I would love to stand here all day and watch you undress, it's my turn to get cleaned up. Where are your towels?"

She spun around, yanked off her towel and stood there naked without one bit of shyness.

"Just use mine."

I grabbed the towel and quickly made for the bathroom. Hearing her giggle through the door, I felt proud of my restraint, but knew the shower would need a cold finish to dissuade my impulses.

"Watch out for Rosa!" she yelled. Trying to be delicate, I used my foot to push Rosa out the bathroom door. She shot me a gnarly look, but I ignored her.

The shower felt amazing. I lingered a bit as I smelled her shampoo and thought about how only moments before she had stood naked in that same spot. Drying off, I cursed myself for not grabbing my overnight bag from the car. Putting on dirty clothes after a shower felt like a violation. Finishing my last shirt buttons, a small knock rapped at the door.

Remembering the parking lot, I opened the door slowly to find Cara smiling. Dressed in blue jeans and a soft black sweater, the skin of her chest glowed in contrast.

I reached out and placed my hand on her neck and slid my palm down over the top of her chest, letting it rest at the base of the V in her sweater. Her eyes closed, and as I leaned in to kiss her it occurred to me she must have gone down to the car to get my bag because she was hiding it behind her back.

"How did you get that?" I asked, a little baffled.

"I just grabbed your keys from the desk and went and got it," she replied while handing me the bag.

"Yeah, but how did you know I needed it, or even had it?"

"You're not the only one who knows everything professor. I saw it in the car last night, and I just assumed it had clothes in it. Was I wrong?" It wasn't a question. It was a challenge. I laughed and closed the bathroom door.

CHAPTER 13

Falling asleep in each other's arms, we didn't stir for several hours. First to come to, I listened to Cara breathe and make little moaning sounds as she slept curled up on my chest. Her eyes looked even larger when closed, and the slight purple hue on her eyelids gave her the appearance of a porcelain doll. For nearly an hour I watched her, admiring her, adoring her. Her breath heaved evenly, and the rhythm helped me meditate on what the last twenty-four hours had brought. Conflicting feelings ran through me as I replayed the events. Remembering I had confessed my curse brought an icy chill to my bones, but it was quickly dismissed and warmed by the affections we had shared.

Carefully reaching for my crumpled jacket on the floor next to me, I retrieved my little notebook and pen from the front pocket. Without disturbing Cara's slumber, I transcribed the day's events.

I always tried to be completely honest in my updates, knowing that lies would not help track the past accurately. However, it was often difficult to determine exactly what was the truth. Writing that Cara loved me would be an example of this. Even though she said it, there was absolutely no way of knowing for sure, so instead I scribbled *Cara told me she loved me*. The same applied to her reaction to my confessions. Surprisingly she took it in stride, but I didn't know exactly what was she was thinking, so I wrote *Cara didn't have any adverse reaction to the news and agreed to take it day by day.*

What was the absolute truth, and what I could put in my book with all certainty, was that I felt a deep affection for her. And I felt happy, genuinely happy.

When at last Cara opened her startling blue eyes, we agreed we were beyond hungry. Deciding where to eat was not a question of what we were in the mood for, but more of what would be open, as well as our safety getting there. Looking out her little window, the sun had broken the clouds, shining through to turn the blanketed snow into a blinding slush.

"There's a diner with crappy coffee and cheap grub about ten blocks from here," she said. "They never close."

I asked her to wait inside while I warmed up the car and cleaned the windows. She rolled her eyes at me, but I insisted, "Let a fella enjoy a chivalrous moment every now and again, all right?"

She relented and plopped down on the bed. "You've got five minutes, and then I'm coming down to help."

Keys in hand, I headed for the car. Before leaving, I took one last look around. So many unforgettable memories had just been formed in those little rooms. Leaving was like walking away from a magical realm that might never reappear.

After starting the car, Cara came skipping down to help. She had not waited the full five minutes, not even two. This time she saw my eyes roll as she cinched her sleeve and started wiping off the passenger side windows. Almost immediately her sleeve hung heavily wet as the snow completely soaked her hoodie from wrist to elbow. I knew it was useless to fight her, so I moved double speed to finish the job quickly.

We buckled into our frigid seats and I immediately took Cara's hands in mine to warm them. After a few meaningful gazes and kisses, we drove. With a mutual sigh of relief we found the open sign blinking. The diner appeared a timeless hole in the wall, with Café painted in white on a red brick front.

Inside, the smell of hot coffee was so overwhelming it was difficult to discern if the odor emanated from a fresh pot, or if the essence had cooked into the walls and fixtures over the decades. After a second sniff, it was obviously both. A classic, long counter with stainless steel trim and swivel stools dominated the center of the room.

A middle-aged waitress with an old school jeweled turtle broach met us at the front. "Just the two of ya?" she asked grinning, leading the way to a booth. Cara and I held hands as we followed her. Not wanting to let go, we opted to sit on the same side.

"Ohhh, young love," joshed the waitress in a half-mutter. I expected Cara to blush at the comment, but she didn't, and agreed, "Yep." She kissed me on the cheek. I had never felt more normal, so close to mimicking typical human behavior. "Two coffees please," I smiled.

In our quiet discussion over which looked better, the biscuits and gravy or the blueberry pancakes, an angry voice arose from the far end of the counter. So transfixed on Cara, I hadn't seen the man when we entered, and I actually thought we were the only customers in the whole place. Draped in a filthy plaid coat, and jeans that were more stained than blue, he was obviously homeless. His reddish beard hung greasily, and he kept most of his messy long hair pushed up under a ball cap. A cup of coffee and an empty plate sat in front of him. He sat alone talking to himself, or all of us, very loudly.

Seeing our attentions drawn to the man, the waitress hurried over. "Sorry about that folks, I hope he's not disturbing you two." She leaned in a bit and hushed her voice, "We call him Bible Bob, and we let him sit there a spell if there aren't too many customers. Do you mind?"

Cara and I looked at each other, and then back at her and shrugged approvingly. I noticed her nametag said Vera. She bowed a grateful smile and took our order.

Cara and I began chatting to ignore Bible Bob's ever-increasing volume, but his rant quickly hijacked the entire diner. The longer we listened, the more I recognized certain phrases. Cara heard the same enlightenment because she turned to me and asked, "He's quoting Bible verses, right?" Listening a few seconds longer, I agreed. "He's not just spouting random scriptures either. He's all about Hellfire."

The more brutal the passage, the quicker he spoke and the more violent his tone enraged. The tenor of his words mixed an ancient memory in my head... a frightened boy's first encounter with the famed St. Patrick.

Hiding my face in the coarse brown wool of Ma's skirt, I peeked out to see the stranger standing by the fire. I could tell his eyes burned in the smoke, but still he stood there. He wasn't like any storyteller I had seen before. Not from our people, he talked like us but in a funny way. Some of the words came out weird and some of the older kids kept laughing at him. The man was skinny, and his clothes were ragged. He held a long stick in his right hand, and when his words excited him, he waved it around like he was trying to kill a flying bug. Smokey tears running down his red checks, he held his stead by the large fire. I was glad he didn't move because it was the best place for me to see him.

We had all come to listen to the storyteller. At first he told a story about creation. It wasn't one I had heard before. In his story the creator was a man, which was odd because everyone knew that women were the creators. How come he didn't know this? I wondered. He kept talking about a god, but never said which one. There were so many gods I wanted to ask which one he was talking about. Luckily, I wasn't the only one who wondered this. Erias, the elder who taught us about the gods, asked him the same question. As soon as the words left Erias' mouth, a change happened in the man. He suddenly angered and screamed, "There is only ONE god!!" He was so loud and so scary that I climbed into Ma's lap and wrapped my arms around her neck.

From this vantage point, I could see Da standing close behind us. He had one hand on Ma's shoulder and the other on the hilt of his dagger. He didn't look scared at all. Even though he was looking at the storyteller, it was like he didn't see him. I had seen Da look that way before. Ma said he was having an awake dream. "Someday soon," she said, "you will see them too." I felt excited by her prophecy because I wanted to be just like Da.

The stranger started screaming words I didn't understand. Many people were leaving, and this made him even angrier. "You will all burn forever in the fires of Hell's dark breath if you deny God now!! Accept the ONE TRUE GOD and bow before his mercy!" I took my hands off Ma's neck and covered my ears. He was a bad man. I wanted to leave, and I started to cry. Da put his hand on top of my head and turned to Ma. He said, "Take him home my love." As she carried me back, I hoped to never again see that scary storyteller.

It was a familiar reminiscence, one I had pulled up many times to use for book content. Ancient scenery melting from my head, I realized how tightly Cara pressed against me. It felt so nice despite her wet sleeve. Even the thickness of her jeans could not block the heat of her leg snugly fitted next to mine.

The waitress arrived with our food expertly balanced on her shoulder. "Let me know if you'd like any more butter for those pancakes," she said light and airily, refilling our coffees. I noticed the tight set of her jaw. Vera was stressed out. Every time Bible Bob's craziness climaxed, visible fear shuddered through her.

"Would you like me to speak to him Vera?" I asked, ready to do anything to resolve the stress clouding our divine moment. "If you don't mind," she whispered. "I mean, he doesn't have to leave, I just need him to calm down some."

"No problem. I'll see what I can do." Somewhat relieved, she slinked away. Placing my red napkin on the table, I starting getting up when Cara grabbed my arm and shook her head. I could see her plea and her fear, and I should have felt grateful she would worry about me, but that's not what I felt. I was repulsed.

That raving lunatic at that end of the counter could have easily been Granddad. If I weren't there to look after him, he would either be locked up, or like this poor soul, out wandering the streets. "Let go of me." I gritted as my irritation bled out.

"No, I am going with you," she said adamantly, sliding out of the booth and clenching my hand. I tried to relax her grip on my hand, but she wouldn't let go.

Bible Bob sat with his back toward us on a red stool at the end of the counter. As we approached, his smell stuck out as apparently as the dirt and debris clinging to his shaggy hair and clothing. I didn't want to surprise him, so I first spoke about ten feet from him.

"Hello, friend." I called. He either didn't hear me or didn't care because his recitation of Revelations continued forcefully. "But the fearful, and unbelieving, and the abominable, and murderers, and whoremongers, and sorcerers, and idolaters, and all liars, shall have their part in the lake which burneth with fire and brimstone…." I wasn't sure how to proceed next.

Cara stepped in and placed her dainty soft white hand on the back of his filthy shirt. "Excuse me sir. What is your name?"

I wasn't sure if it was her touch, her sweet voice, or the question, but whatever it was, it worked. In an instant he snapped out of it and turned to look at us, and what I saw almost caused me to faint.

Bible Bob was like looking into a distorted mirror. My age, he had my nose and eyes, and could have easily been my twin. The only differences between us were dirt and hair. I pulled at Cara's hand, wondering if she saw the same resemblance, but she acted oblivious.

"My name is Simon," he rasped in the same hoarse voice he had been yelling in moments before.

"That's a great name," she said. "So, isn't this a wonderful diner Simon? I just love it here. How about you?"

She distracted him easily with casual conversation, and I stood unable to speak, in awe of his too familiar mannerisms and hand gestures.

As their exchange waned, I realized I couldn't bring myself to ask him to leave like I had planned. All I felt was a burning desire to help him. I offered to buy him some food. He accepted, but never looked at me, and with Cara in the same room I couldn't blame him. Leaving them, I retrieved the eavesdropping waitress by the kitchen door. She never looked at the man as she took his order, but she was polite. After she walked away, I mentioned to Cara that our food was getting cold. We hadn't walked ten steps when his Bible reciting resumed, this time at a more civil volume.

I could tell Cara wanted to talk about our interaction with Bible Bob, but I wasn't ready. I was in action mode. "Why don't you eat while I make some quick phone calls?"

She grabbed her fork like a starving person. I called the hotel where I had my standing arrangements, and told the eternally bored desk girl that I needed my normal room for the next two weeks. I explained I wouldn't be staying there, but would be paying for someone else. Cara's eyes rose over her pancakes. The desk girl reminded me I'd be responsible for any damages caused by the other person, and I agreed to keep my credit card on file. Then, trying to act like it was standard practice, she asked the gender and age of the person staying in my place. I wasn't deceived; I knew her curiosity drove the questions. Wanting to return to my food as quickly as possible, I just answered.

I ended the call and dialed again, this time with a mouthful of food that Cara had shoved into me. Muffled by pancakes, I gave the cab company the address of the café. Swallowing a gulp of coffee, I glanced back at Bible Bob, or Simon. Even though he was eating, memorized bible passages still formed across his ketchup covered lips.

"Do you take care of every homeless person you meet?" asked Cara as I put away my phone. "I'm just saying, I could talk to myself a *lot* more if you want to pay my rent." Even though she was laughing while she said it, I took her seriously.

"You won't need to pay rent anymore."

"Yeah right," she dismissed while kicking back the last of her coffee.

"I want you to meet Granddad, and if you aren't scared away by him, I want you to live with me."

I couldn't believe I had just said it, and while I wasn't ever going to take it back, it surprised me. I hadn't thought it out at all. I didn't know where she wanted to live, if we would get married, or what she had planned for her future. It was too late to think about those things now. I had said it, and I meant it.

A long, awkward silence stole the booth. Had I moved to fast? Was her silence a reflection of her fear of meeting Granddad? Tornadoes of questions swirled my mind while I waited for her reply.

Never looking at me, and in no hurry at all, Cara wiped her mouth on her napkin and turned to look at me. With her beautiful blue eyes boring into me, she reached out and put her hand under my chin. "Well, we should get on the road then. And don't forget, I need to pick up Rosa."

"Alright," I said more confident than I felt. "But first let's take care of Bob, er, Simon."

I paid the waitress for the three meals, and asked Cara to talk to our new homeless friend and direct him outside. I watched as he quietly obeyed, and once outside my eyes dazed for a moment in the melting snow's brilliance until the bright yellow cab parked behind my car was impossible to miss. I explained to Simon that I had paid for a hotel room for him, and that the cab would take him there. I gave him two hundred dollars, all the cash I had on me. He was very confused, but willing to go. I tried not to look him in the face as he climbed into the cab. Seeing a disheveled version of me looking back at me was too freaky. I paid the driver and gave him specific directions about what to do with Simon.

As the cab pulled away, I wondered why I felt so compelled to involve myself with Simon. Did he really look that much like me, or was that just what I had chosen to see?

CHAPTER 14

My left leg shook nervously, uncontrollably. Cara, on the other hand, seemed not the least bit concerned about what was about to happen. She occupied our time in the car asking questions about my life and the lives of others, periodically checking on Rosa, who unhappily scratched at her temporary box. I told her all about Granddad, Marisa, and our newest edition, Gerald. I even told her the beard story, and most of our conversation was refreshingly light and full of laughter.

"So, who is the most beautiful woman in your memory?" she asked.

I pretended to ponder on it for a long time. "Hmmm." I started and stopped a couple times like I was having a hard time deciding, the whole time watching Cara out of the corner of my eye as she blushed and stared out the window. When the torture had lasted long enough, I told her, "The most beautiful girl in my memory is a girl named Cara Gentry."

She laughed and punched me in the arm. "Tell me the truth!"

As we pulled to a stoplight, I took her face in my hands. "You are the most beautiful woman to grace the Earth in thousands of years. And I should know, I am an expert." This ignited a rather intense kiss, which quickly ended with repeated honking when I missed the light change.

Resigning to the fact I wouldn't change my mind on the subject, she altered her question and asked who was the second most beautiful. I knew right away who it was, but allowed a few seconds to pass before I answered, not wanting Cara to feel too jealous.

"Let's test your knowledge of history, shall we?" I said, starting the game.

"Oh, but professor, I'm not prepared for a test," she said in a girly voice while twirling her hair.

"Too bad." I took her hand, "This woman was *very* beautiful," I said seriously.

"That is not a hint," Cara reprimanded.

"OK, this woman seduced a king," I said, squeezing her thigh when I said the word *seduced*.

"Seduction... Ooh I like it," Cara said, squeezing me back, almost sending us over the snowy shoulder as my leg tensed for a second and punched the gas pedal.

"Ahem. This woman had an older sister."

"That's not much of a hint."

"You're right. Here's an easy one. She became Queen of England, but not for too long." I knew I had given too much away, but I was ready to end the game and focus on driving.

"Anne Boleyn!? You guys knew her?" Cara squealed with joy, "How?"

"Anne was supposed to marry an Irish guy who just happened to be a relative of yours truly."

"Wow, that is amazing," said Cara like she had just seen a unicorn. "Was she really that beautiful?"

"Yes she was, but of course you know how I feel about brunettes." As I said it, I gently pulled at the ends of her hair. She smiled enchantingly, and I lost myself long enough to remember I had forgotten I was driving.

"Didn't she have almost black colored eyes?" she asked.

"Yep, not blue. Hence her being in spot number two."

"If only Anne knew that she missed the title by this much," Cara giggled, holding her thumb and index finger an inch apart.

The Anne Boleyn conversation led to a whole new round of questions, all centered on famous people I remembered. It was fun watching her face light up every time I dropped a name, but the entire time I felt distracted. The responsible side of me debated calling home to warn

Marisa. She needed to know I was about to add a woman and a ferret to our household; I just couldn't bring myself to call. I worried it would lead to a conversation about Granddad's latest episode and remind me what I was dragging Cara into. Emotionally on the edge, I didn't want anything to weaken my resolve, so I just kept driving and talking and before I knew it we were pulling up to the house.

"Wow!!" exclaimed Cara as we pulled into the yard. "That is one of the most beautiful houses I have ever seen! I've always loved castles. Do you really live here?" We stepped out of the car and I walked over to put my arms around her. "It's hardly a castle, but one day I promise to take you to Scotland and show you real castles."

Shivers of excitement ran through her. "I would like that."

Cara had only packed one change of clothes, and everything she needed fit easily into her backpack that I took out of the back seat and slung over my shoulder. She carried Rosa, and the sound of hissing and scratching reverberated from inside the box as we made our way to the front door.

Everything sounded quiet, eerily so. Calling to Granddad and Marisa, I was surprised they weren't there. I certainly didn't expect we would have the house to ourselves. I knew Marisa took Granddad to town for grocery shopping sometimes, but those occasions had become less frequent as his condition worsened. This was a positive sign he must have been having a good day. Enormously relieved, I hoped he'd stay that way for a while.

Cara hadn't moved from her spot just inside the door, and looked around a bit strangely. I went to her side and retrieved Rosa from her. "Should I take off my shoes?" she asked timidly.

"Well that depends. Do you think we should?" She shook her head no with a tinge of uncertainty. "Well then, how about a tour?" I suggested.

"How about we set up Rosa first?" I agreed, and took her to the nearest bathroom, knowing how much she liked them. We set up food, water, and a litter box for the little red-eyed devil, and left her to explore her new surroundings.

Taking Cara by the hand, I walked her through the house, opening and closing doors as we went. Every several minutes I strained to hear if the rest of the household had arrived. Many of the artifacts and heirlooms littering the house triggered memories, and Cara insisted on hearing them all. It was fulfilling and cathartic talking about what I was seeing in my head instead of trying to hide it.

The room that took the longest was the library. I opened each safe and showed Cara the family books, explaining their purpose. She looked vitalized to see copies of her school papers there, and enjoyed watching me squirm as I tried to explain why I had them. "I forgive you for stealing my work," she taunted.

I watched her meaningfully stroke the ancient leather bindings of the books as if she fully grasped their importance. "Where is yours?"

"In our room under the bed," I said without thinking. *Our* came out a little weird and I hoped she hadn't noticed. She did of course.

"And when will I be seeing this room of *ours*?"

"That would be the next stop on the tour. Right this way my lady."

I placed her backpack on the edge of the canopy bed and sat down while she explored the room. Making a circle and touching each of the four burgundy walls, she stopped at the heavy drapes covering a very large window. My bedroom had been just that, a place to sleep and store my current work projects, nothing more. As she pulled back the curtains and soft warm light filled the room, I felt like I had been depriving myself for years. The wooden floor lit up and the paintings on the walls fluoresced with colors. The entire room looked and felt wonderfully different with one wave of her hand.

Cara sighed sounds of awe as she gazed out the window. The light enveloped her, and highlighted strands of her black hair glistened silver. I climbed off the bed and embraced her from behind. Looking over her head, which was easy to do since I stood more than a foot taller than her, I gaped, awestruck by an impossibly pink and orange sunset over an endless mountain range.

"Have you ever seen anything so amazing?" she whispered.

"Let me see," I said, spinning her around to face me. "Nope, never have."

She blushed and looked away.

"What a beautiful painting," she said, distracted, looking next to the bed. Without looking, I knew which one she referred to. My family had come to call it "Nameless Lady". A small but captivating portrait of a girl's face, the painter had somehow perfected the spark of life in her green eyes. Cara had good taste, even if she didn't know anything about art. That particular painting was by far the most expensive item in the house, and besides some of the journals, one of the oldest.

"Who is she?" Cara asked.

"Would you like the long story or the short?"

She opted for the long story, as I knew she would. Removing her shoes, she jumped into the bed and made herself comfortable to listen, just like a kid preparing for a bedtime story. I carefully removed the painting from the wall and joined her. Both of us staring into the girl's face, I conjured up the two memories of its tale.

"This face has haunted us for centuries. It consumed and almost killed one of my relatives. We have no idea who she is, so we just call the painting The Nameless Lady. The original memory belonged to an obsessed young man, one who had just started noticing girls. One day while far from his home, this man-child saw a girl and was instantly taken by her beauty. He watched her for an hour as she laughed and talked to friends, but he never worked up the courage to approach her. Many years later, that boy went on to marry someone else and never really thought about the girl again.

"Almost a hundred and fifty years later, that image of the girl would reappear in a different mind and cause a world of havoc. It was during the 1700s, and couldn't have happened to a nicer man. With a wife and two children whom he loved dearly, that man thought he was invincible. He had survived famine and dysentery. Had been forced to eat grass, rats, and insects, but they survived. With a changing Ireland, *hope* was spreading and the man had found a patriotic dose of it. Until he saw that face.

"It came on suddenly. Leaving the market one day, for no particular reason, the nameless girl popped into his head. Being of the Shay line and having the curse, he knew what the memory was, and just like all the others he shook it off and moved onto the next. But it kept coming back, like an echo that doesn't stop. Her face kept reappearing in his head and each time it arrived feelings of lust seized him. For weeks he was plagued. He knew by her clothing that it was a memory from long before he was born, and he knew she was dead, but it never stopped his obsession. Pouring over the books night after night, he could not find a single mention of her, not even a name.

"The man's life began to fall apart and he couldn't tell anyone about what was happening. Looking at his once adored wife was painful. Overcome with guilt, when she smiled at him or spoke, guilt chewed at his bones. So, the once devoted man started avoiding his family, and his family fell apart and his wife worried. He started drinking heavily and stopped eating and sleeping, knowing he couldn't remove the images, hoping to numb the feelings. It didn't work. The obsession with the dead woman drove him crazy. He needed her and it was impossible.

"Seeing no way out, the man desperately considered suicide. He thought that perhaps by being dead he could finally be in the presence of the unnamed lady. Twice he put a rope around his neck, and twice he clutched poison in his hand, but at the last moment his lack of faith stopped him each time. He was not sure if he would truly be with her, or if he would die and never see her face again. He couldn't take that chance.

Very aware her husband was in trouble, but unsure how to help, his wife reached out to a friend, Francis Bindon. He was one of the few who knew the secret of the curse. After hearing the wife's pleas, Francis tracked down her spouse and found him in a deplorable state. Dirty and skinny, he had taken to wandering without purpose, and didn't recognize his friend Francis. With much persuasion and physical force, Francis transported his friend to his home where he could look after him daily.

"After a week the obsessed man suffered in even worse shape. He had to be force fed, and he refused to wash. One minute he'd silently stare at the walls, and the next he'd fill the halls with insane screaming. In calmer moments he subjected Francis to hours of hyper descriptive essays and rambling poems about the girl's face.

Unable to help his friend, Francis grew frustrated, and to calm himself he painted for hours each day. He worked as an architect, but spent his earlier life as a famed painter, and many times returned to the brush to relax. Having had the intimate details of the girl's face freshly repeated to him several times a day, she had become his muse. He developed several different portraits, and after each retelling of her features he found intricacies to improve upon.

"When at last Francis thought he had correctly depicted the woman, he couldn't wait to reveal the painting. He found his friend blankly staring at a white wall, and he walked over and placed the painting in front on him. Francis waited a minute.

"Please tell me. Did I portray her as you remember?"

The ill man responded mystically. His unseeing eyes cleared as he reached out for the painting and embraced it. Sobbing and cradling like a child, he thanked Francis again and again.

He eventually healed and returned home to his wife. All he needed was to be near the unnamed lady in real life, in some form, and to know that no matter what he would never forget her face. Knowing his love for his family transcended the haunting visions, his wife forgave him for his deadly behavior, and learned to accept that wherever he went he carried a painting of another woman. What a saint she must have been, right?"

Cara nodded. "Are all your memories that detailed?" she asked, never letting her eyes stray from the painting.

"Are yours?"

"No, some are so real I can almost transport myself into the memory, but others are just blurring flashes."

"Ours are the same way, except I found a pattern. The more emotion involved in the memory, the more about it I can remember. The story of the Nameless Girl isn't just memory, I also researched the family books to find out more about it."

"But you never wrote about him? So why the extra work?" she inquired while tucking her feet between my calves.

"I was named after the guy, which in my family is huge because double naming is a great way to start the confusion early."

I took the painting from her and set it against the nightstand. I pulled her fully into my arms. As she leaned into me, Cara stopped abruptly as a question formed on her face. "Why did they name you Chamberlain then?"

"My father apparently thought the painting represented hope. He believed we might be able to find ways to solve some of the side effects, if not find a cure."

"I hope so." Cara said brightly, but her words pained me. If she had hopes of me getting better, she'd spend the rest of her life being let down.

I begged her, "Be honest with me Cara, and be honest to yourself. How can you love me when you know there is no hope for me - for us?"

I expected a long moment of contemplation on her behalf, but I was learning to have no expectations when it came to Cara.

"You can be so pessimistic! Do you also believe that cancer will never be cured? So what if there's no proof that you'll get better? There is also no proof that I won't drop dead right here. So no! I will not give up hope, and no I won't be let down. This curse, if that's what it is, is who you are. You are the most unique human I have ever met, and every day I get to be with you will be a joy, not a letdown, so kiss me and quit being all doom and gloom."

Honoring her request, I started kissing her. Not the peck her mouth was positioned for, but a deep, long, singes your toes type of kiss. My hands worked their way down her long silky neck. She breathed heavy sighs into my mouth, encouraging me further as her hands pushed under my shirt to pull at my chest.

I was so consumed that I didn't hear the door open and close downstairs, but Cara did. Pulling away, she smiled at me, her lips slightly swollen from kissing.

She said, "It's time."

CHAPTER 15

Straightening my clothing, I escorted Cara to the bathroom to freshen up. While inside, I paced the hallway. My most critical sink or swim moment imminent, I hadn't a clue how it would go down.

Not looking a bit nervous, Cara exited the bathroom with a little skip and grabbed my hand. As we neared the front room, I could hear Granddad talking in Gaelic while Marisa put things away in the kitchen. Squeezing Cara's hand and holding my breath, we made the last few steps.

What we walked into shocked even me, but Cara handled it with grace. In the middle of the front room wearing only his underwear stood Granddad holding a rotting squirrel. When he saw us he rushed over, swinging the maggoty corpse inches from Cara's face. He exclaimed something in Gaelic as if he was proud of his capture. Cara smiled and nodded even though she had had no clue what he said.

"He peeckt eet up in de parking lot!" Marisa yelled from the kitchen, still unaware we had a guest.

The putrid rot overwhelmed the room, and I urged him to please take it outside before the clinging maggots fell on the floor. Cara on one side and me on the other, we gently corralled him outside. One step out the door, we were all startled by a scream in the kitchen.

Running inside, I found Marisa bearing down on Rosa with a frying pan.

"No!!!" screamed Cara.

Looking up, Marisa saw Cara for the first time. Freezing with the pan still held above her head, she looked from Cara to me and back again. Terrified Rosa decided to run right up to Granddad and climb him, clawing her way up to his neck. He stood there barely moving as the tubular rascal made her way to the back of his neck where she curled over his shoulders. Everybody held their breath waiting for his reaction. I grit my teeth knowing there was a strong possibility he might snap and beat Cara's only family to death.

Taking a moment to sort out what was happening, he dropped the dead squirrel, and reaching slowly around removed Rosa from his neck to cradle in his arms. The room exhaled in audible relief, and the unpleasantly intrusive smell of dead animal filled our lungs again. Springing into action, Marisa grabbed the nasty thing and tossed it out the door. Granddad had made his way into a chair, and softly sung a lullaby to Rosa, totally unaware of our presence. It was a lullaby I knew well, and listening to him took me back to when I was a little boy on the receiving end of the song.

Moving to the kitchen, Cara and I followed Marisa as she rushed to wash her hands. "Marisa, this is Cara. She is my..." I stopped not knowing how to label the relationship. So many words came to mind but none fit, so Cara filled in. "I'm his soul mate," she said shamelessly. She nailed it, but instead of thanking her for filling in where I failed, I continued to stare into Marisa's face waiting for the reaction. Until that moment I had been so busy worrying about how Cara and Granddad would get along that I didn't realize how much Marisa's approval meant. In so many ways she had become a stand-in mom, a matriarch to our broken family.

She left me waiting only seconds for her reaction. Running to Cara, she scooped her up in a big hug. "Ooooohhhhh señor Shay. She is sooo beyooteeful. You better be nice to thees one." Cara's face lit up and she smiled huge at me as Marisa began her barrage of personal questions. Listening, I was pleased to find I already knew all the answers. Our romance had happened so quickly that it was reassuring to feel like I knew so much about her. Marisa asked only one question that neither of us knew the answer to.

"So, when you get married?"

Blushing a bit, Cara turned the full force of her eyes on me and said, "For now, we're just enjoying one day at a time." Her blush made me wonder if she was also still thinking about what we had been enjoying before the family came home.

Changing the topic, I asked Marisa where Gerald was, and if the beard was still working out. She explained that Gerald went to a cousin's wedding out of town, and would be gone a few days. She happily reported that the beard had worked wonders. Granddad now referenced Gerald as Carter, and frequently talked Carter's ear off. I remembered Carter was the name of my great grandfather's best friend who also wore a beard.

After Cara volunteered to help Marisa with dinner, I left them to check on Granddad. He had fallen fast asleep in the chair with Rosa curled up in his lap. I stood there watching him and wishing so badly he would be himself in the morning. I wanted Cara to experience the Granddad I knew and loved, not some stranger in his head.

Taking the seat next to him, I started thinking about the future and the logistics of it all now that I had allowed a new person into the circle. Then I realized I had never spoken to Cara about having children. I had drawn that line for myself a long time ago, and I didn't think I had too many sane years left. Even adoption was a liberty I wouldn't be willing to take. The idea of subjecting a small child to the madness just seemed cruel. The more I thought about it, the more panic I felt. This could be the dividing point between us. Absolute fear set in at the idea of only having one day with her. I needed to find out at that moment.

Jumping up, I spirited into the kitchen. The ladies laughed together about something while Cara dredged chicken breasts in flour. Her hands coated in floury gunk, it didn't stop me from grabbing ahold of one and marching her to the back deck. Once out there, I had a hard time speaking, fearful of the outcome.

Only the slightest bit of light lingered as the sun had completely disappeared behind the mountains. The backyard's clearing tinted bluish in a way only that time of day could produce.

"That's a neat boat," Cara said, breaking the silence.

"Thanks, Granddad likes it," I said, enjoying a private joke.

"Did animals do that?" she asked, nodding toward the large furrows in the ground on either side of it.

"No, Granddad was having a bad day and..." Preparing to tell her the story, she cut me off before I could continue with, "Nuff said."

"Speaking of bad days, there's something we never talked about that I need to know right away. I never asked you if you wanted to have children. I forgot to ask before. I'm sorry."

I kept my eyes on the yard as I spoke. If things were about to come to an end, I didn't want to see the expression on her face when it happened.

"Chamberlain, I've already thought about that, and the truth is that I *have* imagined myself as a mom from time to time." Her words were killing me, but I let her continue. "I thought about how cool it would be to give a kid the life and family that I never had. But falling for you has changed that completely. We couldn't give a kid a normal life, and like hell am I going to let them suffer the pain you've gone through, so to answer your question, no."

It was the answer I hoped for, and though it was wrong, I decided to test her. "What if I told you I always wanted kids?"

Her response came lightning fast. "Then I would tell you that goodbyes were in order. As much as I love you, I couldn't hurt a kid that way."

Turning to face her, I grabbed her into a huge hug and apologized. "I feel the same way you do Cara." I felt like a horse's ass to test her as our embrace dissolved the very last of my reticence to fully accept her love. It did still worry me that she would miss out on something she wanted because of me.

"Are you absolutely sure? This is a huge decision, and I'd hate for you to one day think you missed your chance..." She put her hand over my mouth and put my mind to rest.

"Don't you see? I have it all now. The fantasies I had about being a mother were only because I craved a family so bad, but look around. I have one now. It's a little different than most."

"You think?" I joked.

"Yeah, but I love it. You know how I feel, and if I could have just one more day exactly like today I would have my happily ever after."

Her speech filled me with the optimism and hope she always emanated. My need for her washed over me again, and we quickly lost ourselves in another heated kiss. The sky bent from blue to pitch black as we kissed, forgetting the world until Marisa beckoned us to come in and eat. Walking hand in hand back into the house, we found a wonderful repose. Inspired by our new guest, Marisa had outdone herself. She'd set the dining room table with the good china and crystal, with tall white candles as centerpieces. The room glowed yellow and warm. Marisa was still bringing the food to the table when I pulled out the chair for Cara. "Everything looks absolutely divine Marisa. Muchas gracias." I left to wake Granddad.

He wasn't in the chair anymore, but Rosa was. She had tucked her head underneath her butt to form a furry white donut. Leaving her to snooze, I walked upstairs to track down the old man. Passing through the hallway I had walked hundreds of times, I realized the whole house felt different now. It felt *alive*. I wasn't sure if it was Cara's mere presence, or if my attitude had changed. Everything felt so different.

I knocked at the door, knowing the likelihood of a response was slim, and I was surprised when he told me to come in. I found Granddad standing there in a very old tux, admiring himself in the mirror. It was his wedding tux, and it sparked the memory in my head. It was a beautiful memory, and made me wish I could have been there.

"Why so dressed up?"

"For Robert Kennedy's stag party. Aren't you going?" He was somewhere in 1950, as he knew Kennedy from a brief stint in the Naval Reserve. At least he was remembering one of his own memories. Having immediately forgotten my entrance, he continued to preen in front of the mirror, laughing and pretending to smoke a cigar, cracking ball and chain jokes. Telling him the rest of the party was waiting for us to eat, I led Granddad downstairs by the arm.

Seeing us step in, Cara popped out of her chair and stood by the table waiting for me to make the introduction.

"Granddad, this is Cara," I said, enjoying her name on my lips.

She reached out her hand, and instead of shaking it, Granddad took it, made a slight bow, and kissed it. He held onto it waiting for her reciprocation. Having never had her hand kissed like that before, Cara looked at me for what to do next. I made a quick, subtle curtsy, which must have looked hilarious, and Cara followed in kind.

"It is wonderful to meet you," said Granddad, "I am truly sorry you have to go. This is a boy's night after all," he said ribbing me and winking.

"It's my pleasure," smiled Cara. She whispered to me, "Do I need to leave?" I shook my head.

With introductions complete, or, at least as close as we were going to get that night, we all made our way to the table to dive into our feast. Marisa reached to pass the mashed potatoes when Granddad stood up and bolted from the room. Irritated and hangry, I followed him and encouraged Marisa and Cara to eat. I didn't have to go far because he was already on his way back - carrying Rosa. "What is a wedding party without the best man?" Granddad asked, as if I had tried to stop him.

Laughing, I held out my hand to indicate he should lead the way. Reaching the table, the looks on Marisa and Cara's faces couldn't have been more disparate. Pleased Granddad and Rosa were getting along so well, Cara grinned happily. Marisa looked more like she wanted her frying pan to keep the creature at bay.

Granddad sat Rosa on a chair and grabbed a plate for her. Loading it up with more food than even I could eat, he sat it down in front of her and returned to his seat. Not entertained at all by our formal dining situation, Rosa jumped down and hopped out of the room.

Over dinner, I explained to Marisa where Rosa would live and how to maintain her food and water. "She likes to steal things, especially shiny things," warned Cara. "But she always puts her treasures in one place." Oblivious to our conversation, every now and then Granddad would refer to Cara as Joe, and then make a toast full of suggestive one-liners. Trying to spare Cara and Marisa, I stopped him only once when I knew the embarrassingly raunchy end of a joke he wanted to tell.

When dinner ended, I helped Granddad upstairs where he forced me to drink scotch with him, which I substituted with water, and smoke cigars, which were actually markers. He chewed mightily on the end of his marker, talking and reminiscing about the Navy, and it took close to an hour for him to settle down. As fatigue set in, his mind began to clear.

"How was school today Champ?" he asked, though I wasn't sure if he was in the present or thinking I was a little boy.

"No school today. They closed because of the snow."

"I am sure your students were very disappointed," he laughed. I breathed a sigh of relief knowing I actually had him there with me, and didn't waste one second asking him for advice.

"Granddad, I am in love. She is a great woman, and I know she is the one, but I'm scared sick. I'm worried I might hurt her and something might happen to her like Mom. What should I do?" I felt like a little boy asking how to confront a bully.

Granddad took his time, pondering.

"Does she know about us and what she is getting into?" he asked very seriously. I nodded.

"Does she want children?" I shook my head.

"Well Champ, what can I say? Life has dealt us a difficult hand, and no one would begrudge you a little happiness in it. If she knows what she's getting into, then you have done everything you can. As far as hurting her, I wouldn't worry about that. You won't."

Seeing I was about to interrupt him, he held up his hand. "I know the situation with your father was bad, but he was a good man, and it wasn't his fault that she died." The sadness in his voice didn't stop me from growing angry. I despised how he defended my father, and in my teenage years it was something we fought about at great lengths.

"What do you mean 'not his fault'?" I flared. "He killed her! How could he do something like that and live with himself?" Accustomed to my outbursts, Granddad's demeanor never changed. "Champ, you only know the situation from one side, how you remember it. Don't pass judgment on things you don't understand; and haven't you learned by now that memories don't tell a full story?"

Even though he was lecturing me, I didn't take offense. The young man who would have fought him on the issue had grown enough to experience my first full lapses, and now understood the lack of control while trapped in them. Understanding and forgiving were two separate avenues, and I wasn't ready to let my father off the hook. Not wanting to drag out the same old fight, I changed topics and told him all about Cara and her furry family as I tucked him into bed. He seemed excited to actually meet them in the morning and as I watched him drift off to sleep, I couldn't wait for him to have that chance.

Returning downstairs, I noticed the dimmed lights. Marisa stopped me in the hallway and explained in whispers that Cara had fallen asleep on the couch. I thanked her for all her hard work, and told her goodnight. Rounding my way into the living room, I found a most beautiful vision. Completely asleep, Cara stretched across the dark leather couch. She had removed her shoes and socks, and I felt drawn to her feet. I hadn't seen them so closely before. They had the same soft perfect skin as the rest of her, only topped with burgundy-colored polish.

I debated leaving her on the couch, figuring I could just grab blankets from the closet and make a small bed for myself on the floor next to her. But she looked uncomfortable, and having slept on that couch before, I knew she'd wake up with a backache. I couldn't let her be uncomfortable, so I picked her up.

She woke up a little and mumbled as she flopped her arms around my neck. Making my way up the stairs and into the bedroom, I placed her as lightly as I could on the bed. Once she was comfy, I readied myself. Removing my shirt and slacks, I headed to the bathroom to brush my teeth. Mid spit, I heard my name called. Worried she had rolled off the bed or was waking up from a nightmare, I bound into the room, toothbrush in hand.

She looked around hazily trying to understand the unfamiliar room, then as it all came back to her, she turned her attention to me. Eyeing me slowly from head to toe she purred, "Wow." Feeling a bit exposed, I went back to the bathroom and rinsed my mouth. Retuning, I found Cara now under the covers. At the foot of the bed in a neat pile were all of her clothes, and my eyes couldn't help but latch onto her lacy, black bra.

She had sat up and pulled the white sheet up over her chest. I walked over to turn off the room lights when she stopped me. "Leave them on please."

"You don't need to worry. I'll lock the door. No one will be coming in."

"That's not why I want them on," she said. "I want to be able to see you whenever I open my eyes."

"As you wish my lady."

I grabbed my book from under the bed and took it to the desk. I transcribed my notes from the night before, and detailed the day.

"Can I read it some day?" Cara asked.

"Of course. I would like that very much."

Ten minutes later, I closed my book and slipped into bed next to her. We folded our bodies together. She felt so delicate compared to the long wingspan of my arms.

"I am falling asleep," she whispered in my ear.

"I'll be here when you wake up." My body desperately wanted to make love to her, but my mind knew there would be a better time. The day's intensity played out in graying flashes as I fell asleep with her in my arms.

We never smelled the smoke until it was too late.

CHAPTER 16

People screamed in my nightmare. I wanted them to stop and let me sleep in peace, but they screamed louder. Opening my eyes, I realized the screams came from outside my head. Sitting up, I was knocked right back down to the bed by burning smoke filling my lungs. I coughed hard and grabbed Cara, pulling her down to the floor with me, yelling, "Fire! Fire!" She scurried toward the door on hands and knees grabbing her clothes as she went. I followed her, yanking a pair of jeans off a chair by the door.

The hall was dark and disorienting, and Cara began crawling in the wrong direction. I caught her ankle and tugged it. "Follow me!" In seconds we were in Granddad's bedroom. His lights were on but he was nowhere to be found. Worried he might be in the bathroom, I felt tempted to turn around and go back the way we came, but Cara's harsh coughing reminded me we needed to get out fast.

Heat billowed up the stairs in blinding waves, and the landing glowed with tall licks of fire. I knew the ground floor was our only way out, so I grabbed Cara's hand, ignored my instincts, and rushed us towards the blaze. Every breath of smoke coughed back and rejected by our bodies, I tried to use my jeans to cover my mouth and my nose, but it didn't help. When we reached the bottom of the staircase, the darkness we had crawled though was destroyed by firelight. I tried to guide us to the front door, but a bonfire that had once been the dining room blocked us. The air boiled so hot all the hair on my body began to singe. I turned us around and led the way to the back patio.

The sliding glass door was already open and we ran for it. We collapsed to the cold ground sucking for air when we reached safety. Gasping and hacking, I reached out and grabbed onto Cara to make sure she was all right. Mostly naked and smeared with ash, her whole body shook in the fusion of frosty mountain air and fear. Hearing again the screaming that had awakened me, I hurriedly pulled on my jeans and helped Cara dress.

Running towards the screams echoing from the side of the house just below my bedroom window, Granddad and Marisa were both still frantically yelling our names as we flailed into sight.

"I sorry! I sorry señor Shay! I not mean to burn de house!" Marisa sobbed.

"What happened?" I asked.

"Candles, I leave candelas quemando! One fall over. I try to put eet out but too late! Ohh, díos mío!"

Rosa, I whispered to myself, imagining her carelessly exploring the table, knocking over everything in her path. Cara's tears made their way down her smut-covered face, leaving clear tracks. She knew Rosa was dead.

I put my arm over Marisa's shoulder. "It's not your fault Marisa, I know that. You saved our lives. Your screaming woke us up. We're alive because of you. The house is just a thing. I'm just glad we're all OK." She wasn't convinced by my speech, but she did quiet her crying.

"We need to call the fire department," Cara declared in a moment of clarity the rest of us lacked. Finding none of us had a phone, I led Cara to the shed in the backyard. "There's a set of spare car keys hidden in the toolbox. You grab those and I'm gonna find some blankets for us." Finding two fleece throws, I wrapped one around Cara's shoulders as we rushed back to Granddad and Marisa.

They were much further back now. Granddad stood like a statue, watching silently with his fists clenched. The blaze had grown massive, heaving and roaring as windows exploded all around. I handed Marisa the other blanket and winced as I caught a glimpse of volcanic red and orange filling the window to my room before it burst.

"I'm gonna take Cara to the car so she can get help. Marisa, stay here with Granddad. And keep your distance."

"Sí, sí," she sobbed through a continual prayer mumble. I grabbed Cara's hand and between coughs and gags explained how to get to the nearest neighbor while we walked as quickly as our lungs could manage.

"Do you remember the code for the security gate?"

Her hands shook violently as she put the key in the ignition. I leaned into the window and kissed her on the side of her head. Her hair smelled burnt. Everything smelled burnt.

"Cara, are you OK? Can you do this?"

She responded with a shake of her head, "The code is 1958."

I watched her taillights disappear down the driveway. With little else to do but find my breath, I turned to watch my house burn.

Beginning to contemplate everything that would be lost, I leapt when I heard Marisa scream my name. I sprinted as fast as I could, but I was too late. When I reached the back of the house, she was standing alone.

"He run eenside!" she screamed. "He run eenside! He run eenside! Díos mío!!" I sprinted to the back door. Marisa followed and grabbed my bare shoulder and begged, "Nooo señor Shay!" Shaking my way loose, I ran through the door.

My eyes overflowed with tears immediately and acrid smoke refilled my lungs. I dropped to my knees and started yelling for Granddad. Hearing nothing but fire, I belly crawled to the stairs. Most of the house had been consumed since my previous escape. The walls, floor, and ceiling were burning. Only a small passage to the stairs remained passable. I called and called for him, but the fire's clamor garbled the sound. The sights and heat and panic triggered a memory. I couldn't ignore it, but I had enough control to know it wasn't really happening as it raced through my vision, melding with the inferno...

Flames engulfed the building. Black angry smoke burned my eyes as the horror of my screaming wife filled my ears. Our son was still inside and trapped. Muscling past the four men who tried to stop me, I ran straight into the conflagration. I had to save David. Crawling on my knees, I worked my way around to the stairwell. I screamed his name over and over while I climbed. When I couldn't breathe the smoke any longer, it became impossible to call out my five-year-olds' name. I reached the third floor and felt my heart break and fall from my chest. Large hunks of flaming debris crumbling off the high wall blocked the only path. My little boy was beyond saving. I wanted to lay down right there and go to Heaven with him... Then I thought of his mother. My wife. I had to live...

The memory helped me realize Granddad was searching for little David in the house, desperately seeking a phantasm he would never find. Splintery scratches and cuts knifed into my chest and stomach as I slid my way up the stairs. Blinded by the smoke, I kept gasping for Granddad, but only one of every three crackled out. For a moment I wasn't entirely sure where I was headed, but I knew I needed to keep moving forward.

The hallway felt like a foreign planet. I bumped into things I couldn't identify, and what had always seemed like a small walkway felt more like a football field. I yelled into each room as I came to them, keeping my left hand against the wall so I wouldn't miss one. When finally the wall curved into an empty space, I knew I had reached my room. As I crossed the threshold, I heard something fall and crash from above. The very real fear of being crushed by flaming pieces of ceiling slowed me briefly, but as I reached toward the side of the bed, I touched something soft.

Using my hands as eyes, I looked around. Granddad wasn't moving. I tried yelling in his ear but he didn't flinch. I tried to pull him across the floor, but progress was too slow and I could feel myself suffocating. Using strength I never knew possible, I hoisted Granddad over my shoulder and got on my feet.

No more careful steps, no more cautious moves, I ran in panic. The crumbling red glow of the house threatened from every direction. I held my breath but I could still smell my hair smoking as embers landed on my head.

I found the entire outside of the staircase burning and had to crush our bodies against the wall to make it past the flames. Flying sparks charred the exposed flesh of my bare back and arms, and the bottoms of my feet slickened with bubbling blisters. Halfway down, what sounded like a massive piece of ceiling crashed behind us, and I almost dropped Granddad while dodging it.

Finally reaching the bottom of the stairs, I found the small path to the patio gone. We were trapped. Without thinking, I leapt through the fire for the back door.

Marisa was still there when I stumbled out, and helped me lower Granddad to the grass. A huge gash in his forehead spilled blood across his face and soaked his grey hair. I leaned in to listen for breathing; there was none. Feeling for his pulse, I barely noticed Marisa using her blanket to smother the fire burning the cuff of my jeans.

When I was no longer aflame, Marisa used her blanket to put pressure on Granddad's wound. I started CPR. I had never done it on a real person before, and would have been nervous had I not been so desperate. As I tilted his head back, he drew in a large unexpected breath, and exhaled in a wheeze, "The blood of my life, the son of my line, you must survive in honor and learn from what has passed."

"Nooo!" I yelled. These were the famous last words of the Shay line. As he stopped unable to take another breath, I gave him every breath I had.

Still pounding on his chest and breathing into him when lights and sirens surrounded us, I barely noticed them. It wasn't until two paramedics removed me by force that I registered others were there to help.

As they tried to work on me, I shoved them away. "Save *him* goddammit! Save *him*!" I wanted all efforts on Granddad. They attempted CPR and shocked him a few times, but nothing moved his still body. Cara and Marisa clung to me as we watched from a helpless distance.

When they lifted him onto a stretcher and closed his wide-open eyes, I lost hope. By the time they loaded him into the ambulance, blind rage had taken me. Pulling away from Cara and Marisa, I marched around to the front of the house. I wanted to pull the hair from my head and peel the skin from my bones. Instead, I collapsed to my knees and wailed.

When I felt a small hand on my shoulder I leaned away from it. I didn't want to feel comforted, pitied, or loved. I knew it was my fault he was dead. I hadn't taken care of him. I had failed. All I wanted was to be left alone so the pain could destroy my heart, could burn me down to numbness.

"I love you," Cara said.

I couldn't accept her love.

"How could you!?" I yelled. "Don't you see how messed up we are? How dangerous? I could kill you any day! Any day! And even if I don't hurt you directly, at the very least I will obviously kill myself and leave you alone to feel just as horrible as I do now."

"Everyone dies, there's no changing that," she comforted, but it fell flat.

"You're right, everyone dies. But how many kill themselves by running around a burning building searching for someone who died before they were born? I don't want to be crazy. Granddad was my hero and I had to watch him die a lunatic's death."

"Granddad died a hero!" she shouted, pushing something into my hands.

It was my book. I looked at her dumbstruck. "One of the paramedics gave me that. They found it tucked in the waistband of Granddad's pajamas. He must have remembered your book wasn't in the safes. He died *very sane*, Chamberlain. He was trying to make sure your past wasn't lost."

I stared at my book. She was right. Granddad *was* a hero. Without my book, the transition into insanity would have been nightmarish. Granddad died for me.

I felt immense pain believing I hadn't saved him from the dangers of our curse, but it was a whole new level of torture realizing he had died saving me from my own error. It was too much to handle. The guilt I felt before had multiplied a thousand fold. Falling into the cold grass, I closed my eyes. Cara curled up behind me and let me weep.

CHAPTER 17

Sunlight stung brighter than I remembered. I squinted my eyes as Cara led me by the hand and put me in the car. After an entire month of writhing in physical and emotional pain, I knew it was time to face the world again, but I needed Cara to lean on. The burns on my feet had healed enough to walk, barely, but the laceration of losing Granddad would never close. Cara willingly assigned herself my guardian angel while in recovery. She had done everything, insuring we would have something to return to when I arose from the bleak.

As we drove, I peered out the passenger window, and it occurred to me I hadn't been driven by anyone but Granddad since I was a child. The thought forced a sharp inward breath. Hearing me, Cara took my hand and kissed it.

"Thank you for everything," I said.

"You're very welcome, but don't thank me *too* much, OK?"

"Why not? You deserve it."

"I'm just doing my job as the epic girlfriend after all. Besides, you haven't seen everything yet. I might have screwed up terribly."

She worried about some of the decisions I'd forced on her while I was down. The biggest of these became picking out a house, and using my money to buy it. The house lost in the fire was not just my home, but Marisa's as well, and I couldn't handle the idea of her having nowhere to go. I was determined to care for Marisa, and a new place to live gave us all an uplifting start.

As we pulled up to a small but elegant house, I knew Cara had done exactly as I would have. Nestled in a quiet area of town, it featured a large yard framed by a perfectly weathered picket fence. Leaning out of the car with Marisa's help, it was evident the former owner had lovingly cared for the yard. Broad plants and vines lined the walkway and crawled up the house, surprisingly healthy and vibrant for this late in the year. As we marveled at the greenery, I remembered the Royal Gardens of France when my family first met Dr. Lamarck. They were happy memories Granddad and I spoke of every time we did yard work. And when we killed something by neglect, or a seed refused to grow, he'd always say the same thing. His echoing words rang circles in my brain as we approached the door to the house.

"Champ, we may not have the green thumb ourselves, but at least we can remember what it was like to have one." I relished the sound of his voice in my head, and it made me feel at ease. I momentarily forgot all my pain in a swift blur.

When Cara knocked on the door, I fell to tears. It hit me that no one left on the planet would call me Champ. The ache I held off during our drive exploded in my chest, and when Marisa opened the door I threw myself into her arms. She cried as well, but found the strength to comfort me more than I could her.

Marisa wiped off her round face with her white apron.

"Gracias señor Shay. Muchas gracias!" She kept saying it, hugging me and crying and shaking.

"You're family Marisa. But I'm gonna kick you out of the family if you thank me one more time." She lightly smacked me on the arm, and then took my arm in hers sweetly. Cara took my other arm and we walked inside together.

The comforting smell of pot roast thickened the air as we entered the front room. Gesturing for us to sit, Marisa left to retrieve sodas from the fridge while Cara and I snuggled on a large plaid couch. This gave me a chance to look around.

"It came almost completely furnished," explained Cara. "And I just gave Marisa some spending cash to buy whatever was missing." By the way she explained herself, she sought approval on her actions.

"You did everything right," I said. "You don't have to explain it to me. I trust you."

"But it was *your* money. I don't want you to get mad about how much I spent," Cara said biting her lip.

"We talked about this. The money is ours, not mine, and you spent it caring for the people I love. How could I ever fault you for that?"

After Marisa distributed the drinks and settled herself into a brown recliner, I asked how she was getting along. She started out happily, telling me how much she loved the house and her neighbors, but then the conversation flipped. She burst into tears and started begging for my forgiveness. I told her over and over again that none of it was her fault, but she refused to believe me.

Realizing I couldn't convince her, I tried to salvage the visit by changing the subject. "Marisa, I've been wanting to ask - how's Gerald doing?"

This distracted her just enough to stop the tears. She reported that with Cara's help he had found a job as a groundskeeper at a local golf course. She went into all the boring details about his duties and his pay, and said she might learn how to golf just to see him more often. By the time she told us about how upset Gerald was that the golf club made him shave his beard, we were all laughing and relaxing like a family should.

Hours flew by as we reminisced about Granddad's spectacular history of antics and the comforts of the old house, and Marisa insisted we stay for dinner. I followed her into the kitchen to help. Watching her stir and shuffle about in familiar patterns, it occurred to me how much older she looked in a different setting.

"Are you really doing all right Marisa?"

I half expected her to lie in an attempt to spare my feelings, but I received truth instead.

"No señor Shay. I never fine again. I love meester Shay and I meess him."

Tears fell from her face into steam pops on the oven door as she pulled out a tray of homemade rolls. She kept working, not waiting for my reply. I knew they had grown close over the years, but seeing how badly she hurt made me understand the depth of her loss. She had been his constant companion day in and day out. They'd been living together through his worst and best moments like an old married couple. I had lost a mentor and father figure, but Marisa had lost a... husband?

"Will you do me a favor?" I asked.

"Claro que sí, señor."

"Will you call me Champ from now on?"

She froze, and her face frowned sadly into an understanding smile as the depth of what I had asked crept in.

"Sí... Champ." And she went right back to moving hot rolls onto a plate.

Cara called into the kitchen to ask if she could do anything to help. Marisa asked her to clear the dining room table. I decided to join Cara, and found her standing by the table reading a newspaper. I walked up behind and wrapped my arms around her waist. Closing my eyes, I breathed her in deeply and rested my head on top of hers. She folded up the newspaper in a very deliberate way as if she hadn't liked what she'd read.

"What is it?" I asked reaching for the paper, but she moved it out of my reach.

"I'm so sorry Chamberlain. I had no idea. I was so busy with everything else I didn't even think about this."

"Please give me the paper."

"No. It's a bunch of trash," she begged. "Please don't read it."

"Cara, I need to see it. Please give it to me."

Looking as if she might tear it up and swallow it, she deliberated for a moment while slowly crumpling the paper. Then she changed her mind and handed it over.

A large picture of the burnt out remains of my house dominated the center of the page. In bold font the headline read, *Fire Kills Famed Writer's Grandfather*. I had to sit down to finish reading.

In a very cold, calculated way, the article outlined the cause of the fire, reporting an immigrant staff was responsible for the fire when candles were left unattended. It also said a mentally ill man died when he ran into the burning house. It painted it so that mental illness had caused Granddad to run into the house, but that wasn't the truth.

"This is bullshit!" I yelled, balling up the paper and throwing it at the floor. "Granddad went back in to get my book! He knew what he was doing. And the whole thing was an accident! How dare they blame Marisa?!"

Hearing her name in my uproar, Marisa ran into the room. She took one look at the crumpled up paper and nodded knowingly. I was furious. "Marisa, don't believe any of this crap! They have *no* idea what they are talking about! We all know it was an accident. How were you supposed to know that the ferret would knock over the candles and kill Granddad?"

Cara made a squeaking noise and ran from the room holding her hands over mouth. Marisa, understanding my stupidity, pushed me out the door after her.

Jogging out into the front yard, I panicked not to see her. Knowing she couldn't have gotten far, I hustled around to the back and saw her sitting in a porch swing between two trees at the far end of the yard. Walking to her, my stomach swirled as I worried about how I could possibly take back the idiocy I had said.

I sat next to her. Cara pulled her knees up and buried her face in them. Her straight black hair acted as a shield, but I could hear her crying.

I tried to comfort her by placing my hands on her shoulders, but that only seemed to make things worse. Her whole body shook with muffled cries. Seeing her so beaten down raised the memory of a husband comforting his wife after the death of their child. The wrenching scene gnawed my mind, and seeing and feeling it pulled away my focus. I steeled myself against it, and a moment later my brain became my own again.

I chose my words carefully. I knew telling her that I sincerely didn't blame anyone for Granddad's death wouldn't fix what I had said.

"Do you know what I loved most about Rosa?" I asked.

She didn't answer.

"It wasn't her creepy red eyes, to be honest those things scared the hell out of me. They were like little cinnamon candies that judged my soul."

She allowed a little snort.

"No, what I loved most was that when I wasn't around, she was there for you, giving you the love and comfort you needed. I will always be grateful to her for that. That weird little ferret was your family - *our family* - and I swear I do not blame her. What happened with Granddad was going to happen one way or another. He had already put himself in so many bad positions it's a damn miracle it didn't happen sooner. And in all honesty, I'm glad his last moments were spent doing something he wanted to do, not something an old memory was forcing on him.

"My only regret is that I didn't tell Granddad that my book was useless."

Cara looked up at me.

My words made no sense. She knew how the books were used, and after watching Granddad die, she understood the extent we would go to in order to protect them.

"My book exists to remind me of the things in my past that were important - things I didn't want to lose. But now that I have you, I have everything I need. Who I was before and the things I went through mean nothing compared to what I have now. And I don't need the book for future generations to use because the curse dies with me. Do you see?"

"Yes, but if you want to let go of the past, does that mean you're giving up on finding your father too?"

"No, just the opposite. I've decided to double my efforts. Before, I needed to find closure for Mom, and to confront him with my anger. Now I have an even bigger reason - *you*. Until I know what caused him to kill Mom, I will always feel the need to be on guard around you. I can't trust myself." She tried to cut in but I stopped her.

"I know you love me, but evil *lives* in my head. I *need* to find him. Will you *please* help me do that Cara?"

She agreed and buried her face in my chest. We rocked slowly back and forth on the swing holding one another for a long time until Marisa called us in.

Our dinner paled a much quieter affair than the rest of the visit. The food tasted delicious as usual, but none of us had much of an appetite. When it was time to say goodbye, a new round of tears flowed from the women, and I did everything I could not to join them. We promised to visit again soon.

I decided to test my ability to drive, and Marisa waved excitedly from the doorway as we pulled out of the driveway.

"Are you ready to head back to the hotel?" Cara asked, wiping the last puddles of tears from her eyes.

"No, not yet. I want to go see our house."

CHAPTER 18

Cara let loose an incessant flow of mind wanderings without much input from my side of the car as we drove. I wasn't sure if she did it for my benefit or hers. Visiting the charred husk of the house and the spot where Granddad had died promised to be difficult, and she was attempting to distract what awaited us.

The driveway entrance gate had been removed. With all the people coming and going, I asked Cara to just have it torn out. It was useless with nothing left for it to protect. We held our breath as we pulled up to where the house should have been. Reaching my typical parking spot, I amazed at how unfamiliar it all looked. Without the house to block the vista, the mountains looked huge and ominous. The company Cara hired to clean up the wreckage had done a very thorough job, and even went so far as to fill in the basement. A smoothed over square of gravel remained the only sign a house had ever been there. The safes containing the books and all the items I had in the shed had already been moved into storage units. There was nothing left.

The air crisped quickly with the disappearing sun. As we walked to the house scar, I wrapped my coat over Cara's shoulders. I strolled around and around it several times, but couldn't find anything recognizable. I didn't know what I was hoping to see or find there, but whatever it might have been was gone. The only item to catch my eye was Granddad's boat. Without knowing a house used to be there, it appeared as though some greedy soul had cleared an entire acre of land to store their singular water vessel. It was covered in a thick yellow tarp, tied down to cement blocks.

Cara followed as I walked to it, and in familiarly practiced moves I untied and removed the cover. "Granddad loved this boat. He built it completely on his own. Every bit of wood was attached, sanded, and lacquered by his hands. He didn't use it often, but he loved coming outside just to look at it." Running my hands over the sides, I remembered dozens of conversations we'd shared in that very spot. When I was a mouthy teenager, he used to tease me and say, "If you don't cheer up, this boat will be my only pride and joy."

"We never talked about what you wanted done with it," Cara said. "I want to keep it."

I nodded and took her hand. We didn't stay long. There was no point. We had gone there to see what was left, and it didn't take much time to examine a bunch of nothing.

Back on the road, Cara asked me what I wanted to do when we returned. I didn't answer her at first. Granddad's death forefront in my mind, the visit felt like taking a strong shot of reality with no chaser. I knew every passing day brought us closer to the end, with no way around the fact we had no happy ending waiting for us. I would either hurt her, or she would run when I became insanely intolerable. She would be alone and miserable in the present while I was imprisoned in the past.

I pulled the car into the roadside and stopped. Cara looked panicked, checking behind us and out all the windows, looking for the cause of my maneuver. "What is it?" she asked. "Why did you stop?" Closing my eyes, I tried to picture a life without her. What should be done and what I wanted to do were raging a battle inside me. Working myself into frenzy, I pushed too far until I was in someone else's head in another time.

She looked even paler in her lacy white wedding gown. Carrying her into the candle lit parlor, she stole just enough vigor to whisper "Pretty" at my attempt to decorate with simple wildflowers from the field behind the house. The fever radiated though her dress and caused me to sweat as well. While I held her, every breath she attempted fell shallow and more labored than the one before. Making my way to the center of the room, I stepped over the pile of wedding invitations she and her sisters had carefully scribed by hand, sisters the Black Death had already claimed. I carefully placed her on the table I had made into a bed. Kneeling, I took both of her tiny hands in mine and said, "I'm sorry I couldn't get anyone else to come."

"I think God understands," she uttered in a voice so quiet I hoped I had heard her correctly.

Touching her face, I recited my vows, memorized from when she glowed healthy with rosy lips and spirited eyes. The words "Till death do us part" stuck in my throat. Finishing my devotional, I found her in a worse state. Her eyes had closed one last time, each inhale divided by agonizing pauses. With her final breath she gasped, "I do." Kissing the corpse that was my new bride, I thought of how badly I wanted to join her.

I had lapsed briefly, and when I came to I stood outside the car, several feet from the road. Cara stood beside me, shivering. Getting back into the car, this time on the passenger side, I could not speak. The memory had broken something in me. After several minutes, Cara asked, "Are you OK? Do you know what triggered the memory?"

"No, I am not. I knew we both agreed to take it one day at a time, but I don't think that situation will work for me anymore."

"What do you mean?" she demanded. "I can handle this, I promise. Please don't give up on me."

"I know I will lose you, one way or another Cara. I think you have a good idea of what loving me means, and I want to make the most of the time we have, so, I guess what I'm saying is that I want to marry you. If you will have me, that is."

She drove silently for many miles, staring into the vast forest beyond the shoulder. As time ticked by impossibly slow, I began to regret my proposal, and after several more minutes tried to think of a way to take it all back. I was on the verge of telling her to forget the whole thing when she asked, "Do you love me?"

"What?" I asked, surprised she would question such a thing. "Yes, of course. Don't you know that?"

"Well, you've never said it before, so I wasn't sure."

I was certain she was wrong and that I had told her how I felt many times, but thinking back, I realized she was right. I still hadn't said, "I love you."

"Cara, I am so sorry I never said it, but I'm saying it now. I love you. I *love you*, and even though I can't make many promises, I swear how I feel will never change."

"I love you too Chamberlain... And that's why I have to tell you something. I don't want any secrets between us, and there is something that might change your feelings for me. I leaned over and put my hands on the sides of her face, forcing her to look into my eyes."I am a man of my word. Nothing will change how I feel."

She smiled at me, a weak flinch that spoke volumes about her fear.

"Have you ever wondered why I thought the abandoned theater at school was so cool?"

"I was wondering, but at the time I was too busy trying not to lapse to ask you."

"Well, this story explains it, kind of, in my own way I guess. Remember how I told you about the day I tried to introduce myself to my biological Grandmother?"

"Yeah, I still despise her for that."

"I didn't tell you what happened afterwards. I was so upset by how she acted. I needed some alone time, but home was a tiny apartment with six of us living there. Back then I worked at a concession stand in a theater, and I knew it would be empty. I had a key, so it seemed like the perfect place to go and cry without an audience, but when I got there I felt worse. I felt alone. My whole life I had been invisible to everyone around me. No one ever went to my awards assemblies or my soccer games, and that was at the good homes. At the bad ones I went so unnoticed that I had to steal food because they forgot to feed me. But if I did it on the stage in a grand theater, someone would have to see me, have to notice me."

Terrified by what she said, I asked, "Cara, did what? If you did what?!"

"The stage was empty except for a piano and a thick rope coiled up under a dusty purple curtain. The curtain was soft, but very heavy, and it took all my strength to pull out the rope."

I couldn't believe what I heard. I squeezed my eyes closed trying to block out the forming mental image, but she kept going and it kept focusing clearer and clearer.

"I tied one end of the rope to the piano. Light terraces hung high above the stage, and it took me several tries to get the rope over it. When I got it, I grabbed a chair from the side of the stage, stepped on it and tied the rope around my neck."

She faltered a sad, embarrassed laugh. "I stepped off the chair, and a weak spot in the rope snapped. I fell on the floor and I didn't know or care if I was dead or alive. Once I figured out what had happened, I just lay there and cried, but I wasn't crying because I was sad. I was crying because I was happy. I was glad I didn't die. I had made a rush decision that almost ended everything.

"I took the rope off and sat on the chair for a long time, thinking about all the wonderful things in life I would have missed. Some of them were kinda small, like the smell of fresh buttered popcorn, but I thought of thousands of them. Sitting there, staring at the empty stage, I knew I had a new start. I could feel the fight and hope flow back into me. It was such a great feeling that from that point on I went to theaters just to remember that day and all of the amazing things I'd experienced since then.

"I wanted you to know that I have faced the worst. I promise I can cope with whatever waits for us."

Cara's description of her attempted suicide triggered the memory of a woman whose rope didn't snap. In my head I was a man cutting the tether attaching his dead wife to a barn rafter. While I felt a painful sympathy for what Cara had revealed, the relative in my head was jaded and annoyed. His wife had left him alone with three children. By the time the last thread of rope split and his wife's body thumped to the ground, he had already compiled a list of women he would pursue for his next wife. The man's coldness repulsed me.

After an extended silence, Cara began pushing me to speak. She wanted to hear anything comforting, but I flipped halfway between two worlds, and when I opened my mouth, my relative's appalling words came out.

"How could you be so selfish and weak?"

The vileness of my response churned my gut. As soon as I said it, Cara jumped out of the car and ran into the dark forest. I hurried out after her but couldn't tell which direction she had gone. "Cara, please come back! I'm sorry! Those weren't my words! It was memory! I don't think you were being selfish or weak, not at all."

I kept yelling, and several minutes later saw visible breath clouds in the icy air in front of a dark figure emerging from the trees. When she neared, we hugged, and I repeated all the things I yelled. I described the memory and apologized too many times.

"I'm sorry I ran away. I worried that was exactly the type of thing you would think, so when you said it I..." She started crying and shaking uncontrollably.

I helped her into the car and ran around to get in and crank the heater. Her teeth chattered loudly, and the mixture of tears and cold reddened her cheeks. I rubbed down her arms and hands to bring the warmth back into them. "Thank you for sharing your past with me," I said. "It doesn't change how I see you, it just makes me realize how much you have overcome."

"So, you knew what you were saying even though you were lapsing?" she asked.

"Not exactly. I could still hear you, but all the emotions from my relative were spilling over."

"He wasn't a good man, was he?"

"No, and I'm glad he had his son and died not too long after that incident. I wouldn't want any more of his memories in me."

Warmed and calmer, Cara suggested we start driving again before it got too late. I pulled onto the road and watched Cara out of the corner of my eye as she stretched her thin arms out in front of her and yawned.

"Was that the only time one of the wives killed herself?" The tone she used asked more curious than concerned.

"No, there were others. Typically they just ran away though, that's what Granddad's wife did."

"That's so sad. Was it because they couldn't watch what it was doing to their husbands?"

"Some, but for most it was because their sons had the curse. I think they all hoped to have girls or have sons that the curse skipped. It doesn't matter anymore though, you'll be the last to have to put up with it."

"What do you mean? Are none of the other Shays married?"

"As far as I know I am the last of our line. As time went on, more and more of my relatives learned not to reproduce, thank goodness." She put her hand on my neck and traced little circles with her fingernails. My skin tingled and I could feel her eyes examining every inch of me.

"Is the marriage proposal still on the table?" she asked.

"Yes" I answered, balancing staring at the road and studying her expression.

"Good, because I want to be your wife, if only for a little while." She kissed my cheek and I smiled. She yawned again and curled up in her own seat.

"So do we restart Mission Find Dad tomorrow?" she asked dreamily.

"No, tomorrow we start Mission Marry Cara."

In the dim lights on the dashboard I could see her smile gleam. She slept the rest of the way home.

CHAPTER 19

Standing outside Kaliska's office, I prepared myself for the conversation. When Cara contacted him after the fire, he was more than happy to allow me recovery time off. He even volunteered to teach my classes. It was a generous gesture, but I knew with certainty he'd done it under selfish pretenses. With me gone, he'd have a break from my judgmental presence and the guilt I knew he felt every time he saw me. I also hoped that if I weren't around to stir the pot, Amber would get off his back about me. That's why I knew it had to be serious when he called and requested a meeting.

It took well over a minute for my knocks to be answered. I started to think he wasn't there when the door opened. The second our eyes met, I knew something was up. His normally pulled back, long black hair hung loose, and the collar of his shirt bent up on one side. The expression he wore told far more than his attire; he was obviously entertaining a female. With the look of a child caught picking his nose, he didn't seem pleased to see me. Stepping out into the hallway, he closed the door quickly behind him.

I was in a good mood. Cara had that effect on me, and I decided to push through this with as little drama as possible.

"Hello Edmund," I said, extending my hand. "You did say we were meeting at one o'clock, right?" He looked at my hand for a moment like it was a poisonous snake that might bite him, and then hesitantly took it. I tried to block out the images of where that hand might have just been.

"Hey, Chamberlin. Good to see you buddy. How's things been? Sorry 'bout your loss. Have you found a new home yet? Oh, and congratulations on your wedding by the way. How's marriage treating you?" His words ejected too fast and he asked too many questions in a row for me to answer. He was stalling, keeping me out of the office until whatever girl he had in there, who I really hoped was not Amber, could put on clothes.

"I'm doing better I guess. Thanks for taking my classes." Before I could say more, a slight knock came from inside his office.

Kaliska opened the door, and I felt wholly surprised by who I saw. It was his wife! Straightening her very short yellow sundress, she looked not only beautiful but also happy. She didn't come to the school often, and when she did she kept to herself. I first met her at a faculty Christmas party where she hovered behind Edmund wearing baggy, drab clothing and looking miserable. The contrast between my memory of her and how she looked, all smiles and glowing, stunned me.

"Hello Georgia! It is very nice to see you again," I said as she walked through the threshold into the hallway.

"It's nice to see you too. I'm sorry I can't stay and visit, but I have a lot of errands to run. I was just dropping off some lunch for my honey." As she very affectionately said *honey* she leaned up and kissed him on the cheek. We exchanged goodbyes and I stared dumbfounded as she almost skipped down the hallway. My surprise at the change in her must have been playing on my face because Kaliska slapped me on the back and grinned, "Come on in and I'll tell you all about it." I followed and shut the door behind me.

His office couldn't have been more different than mine. Juxtaposed to my old-fashioned oil paintings and oak desk, his glistened at the height of modern style. A huge oval desk of clear glass hovered over white carpet. In the corners sat bleak black sculptures of random shapes, and his computer was attached to a large plasma screen hanging on the wall. No doubt many visitors were very impressed by the space, but to me it looked and felt cold and soulless.

"So, you probably weren't expecting my wife in here with me, were you?" I didn't answer; it was a rhetorical question. "Strangely, I have you to blame for that Chamberlain."

I wasn't sure if he meant the blame as a good thing or bad. "Amber was an absolute nut job, and because of you, she preyed on me." I lifted my eyebrows, tempted to reply, but he stopped me. "OK, OK so maybe we preyed on each other. The point being she came to me to get revenge on you, and whatever it was that you did to her, dear lord, don't ever do it to a girl like that again." I tried to cut in and explain I hadn't done anything, but he waved me off and kept talking.

"Anyhow, after we saw you that day in the greenhouse, she made good on her promise." I couldn't remember what he was talking about. "When I got home that night, I found her talking to my wife on the phone.

"I was completely freaked out and mad, and in a lot of ways blaming you for it. I had to stand there and listen to Georgia's side of the conversation unable to defend myself. I wanted to rip the phone from her hands or start screaming so she couldn't hear what Amber was saying, but Georgia acted calm for the whole call. When it was over, she hung up the phone, looked at me for a second, and went into the kitchen to make dinner.

"I had expected screaming, crying, bags being packed, anything but what she did. So I followed her into the kitchen and asked what Amber had said, fully prepared to denounce whatever she said as a lie. That's when she turned to me with no emotion whatsoever and said, "The same thing they all say."

I couldn't believe what I'd heard. She knew. For years she knew and never said a word. Not only that, but she blamed *herself* for *my* affairs. I felt so horrible for what I had done that I begged her to forgive me and promised never to do it again. And since then, things have been copacetic, even romantic. She's so happy now, and she comes to visit the school often, if you know what I mean. So, thanks. If you wouldn't have sicked that freak on me I would've never fixed things with Georgia."

Finishing his story, he slapped me on the back and pointed to a black leather chair for me to sit in. While happy for the way things turned out, I still couldn't help but wonder how long it would keep. I'd seen him in such a bad light for so long that it was hard not to think he'd be right back at his old ways again soon. I pitied Georgia even more than before, imagining her newfound happiness existing for only a short time before being stolen from her again.

"I'm happy for you, but what happened to Amber? I asked, genuinely concerned. "Is she still running around causing problems?"

"In fact, that's why I asked you to come in. Sometime after your wedding announcement came out in the paper, she went super psycho. I didn't even know you had a girlfriend, you dog. Anyone I've met?" The idea of him being anywhere near Cara made me feel ill. "Nope," I said, relieved it was true. "Probably a good thing right?" he asked, inappropriately winking at me. I ignored him and asked more about Amber's increased craziness.

"The other day Libby went into your office to drop off mail and update some files. When she went in, Amber was wrecking the place. We have no idea how long she had been at it, but it looked like she might have been sleeping in your office. Super creepy. Anyways, she did a lot of damage. That girl was so batty that even after she was caught, she kept trying to demolish your stuff. The security guards had to handcuff her and physically remove her from your office. After expelling her, I called her mom and told her that if she didn't personally come find professional help for her daughter, the university would press charges. Her mom agreed and we haven't heard a peep since.

"So, good news is she's gone, and the bad news is that your office is trashed. So, when do I get to meet your new bride?" Again I ignored his question and asked if they had done anything to clean up the mess Amber made. The thought of someone having that kind of time to look through the files I had on my father made me nervous.

"We left it. Being the private person you are, Libby and I decided that was best." What he really meant was that Libby told him to leave my stuff alone or she'd kick him in the face. I owed her a massive thank you.

"Well I better go take a look at the damage. Thanks again for the time off, and I hope things work out well for you and your wife."

"We had to change the lock. Amber took a screwdriver to the last one." Kaliska threw me the key and made a nauseating joke about our honeymoon. I ignored him one last time and took my leave after a quick handshake.

Almost running, I hurried to my office. The door was the same, but a large padlock covered the doorknob. I took a deep breath as I put the key in and turned, letting the lock drop into my hand as it opened. I turned the mangled handle and opened the door into a room I barely recognized. Although I had been warned, I was astonished.

I had to wade through a half-foot of loose papers to travel the swath of destruction. Each turn of my head offered new signs of ruin. With a red marker, Amber had covered the walls in a collage of scribbled obscenities, and in a more creative moment, she had penned a poem in which she called me a "rigid frigid freak." To fill the spaces where words escaped her, she drew stickmen dying in disturbing ways, most of them with little nametags that said Chamberlain. The ones with Cara nametags scared me the most. Fluff from my eviscerated comfy chair was everywhere. My once elegant wood desk had deep, swirly scratches all over the top, and its drawers had been removed and smashed to pieces. The small amount of emergency clothes I kept there had been made into a makeshift bed, complete with a pillow I didn't recognize.

Looking further, I realized Amber had left many items. I found several pairs of her underwear, balls of hair, pictures she had taken of me, and a fly-infested pile of empty fast food containers.

My file cabinet containing all of my father's paperwork, all of my class notes, and several research documents had been pushed on its side and had spilt onto the floor. As horrible as it all looked, only one wrecked item caused me to sit in the middle of the mess and bury my face in my hands. My cherished painting of Lamarck had been sliced into ragged strips and hung lifelessly from the frame.

I let myself sit there for a while coming to terms with the mess I had to clean up when I heard the door open behind me. Turning, I found Briggy. He used great effort to push the door open far enough to accommodate his wide girth. The mountain of papers he toppled just fell right back at him, promising the same effort when he left. What could only be described as a miniature oak tree stuck out of his lab coat pocket.

"Oh my! What a mess that girl made," he said, trying clumsily not to destroy the papers he trampled. I heard what happened, but I never dreamed it was this bad. She really needs to drink more green tea."

"Don't worry about where you step. It's all mostly trash now anyways." He relaxed a little, but he felt too nervous to tread any further into the room and held his ground by the door.

"I just wanted to come by Chamberlain, and tell you again how exceptional your wedding was, and how happy I was to be there." The happiness of remembering that day lessened the blow of the chaos around me.

Having very few people to invite made the big day both easy to plan and intimately perfect. Both Cara and I decided the valley behind where my house used to sit was the ideal spot to tie the knot. Not only was it picturesque, but in some sentimental way it meant that Granddad could be there too. Entirely the wrong season for an outdoor wedding, no one complained much about the cold. A local minister performed the ceremony, and Briggy stood as my best man. Cara had Marisa as her matron of honor. The entire ceremony passed simple and casual, except for one detail. Inviting Briggy to be involved in the wedding also meant he insisted on being in charge of the flowers, a job he took very seriously.

I watched with awe as several of his grad students set up and arranged three hundred of the most incredible flowers we'd ever seen. Under Briggy's watchful eye, each flower was placed to look like part of the valley. Only upon closer inspection did they seem out of place, and if a person didn't know better, they would've sworn the flowers had been growing there for years. They were shaped like roses, except the petals were longer, and they were the size of footballs. Confusingly, none of the flowers were in bloom. I couldn't complain, given that Briggy had only a week to prepare, and they still looked beautiful closed. I never even mentioned it to him.

By the time the ceremony began, I had all but forgotten about the flowers, my eyes glued to my bride. After an unforgettably gentle kiss to seal the deal, Cara looked around and said, "Wow!" At first I thought she commented on the kiss we shared, but following her stare I saw it was meant for the flowers. Each one, including those in Cara's hand, had exploded open. The giant buds transformed into watermelon-sized blooms. Hundreds of cerulean flowers opening before our eyes, it looked like a wave ran through the valley, changing it entirely. Unlike anything I had ever seen, a shimmering lake appeared below us. Cara must have been feeling the same thing I was because she pulled me close and whispered, "They're magic, just like you." Briggy was a genius.

As we stood there in the disaster of my office, I thanked him again for being my best man, gushing again how incredible the flowers made the experience. He laughed it off like it was nothing, and offered to help me clean up. "We could get a group of grad students in here and have this all shipshape in no time."

"I appreciate the offer, but I really need to go through this stuff piece by piece." Understanding, Briggy departed, "Very well then, say hello to Cara for me. And let me know if you need anything at all. Very carefully, he let himself out, and the room instantly felt lonelier without his presence.

Lost as to where to start my task, I decided to call Cara and let her know what happened and why I would be delayed. Cara answered after only one ring. "This is Mrs. Shay speaking, and she is not at all surprised you miss her already." I laughed, but quickly turned more serious. It was a long, one-sided conversation. I hadn't explained any of the embarrassing Amber situations to her, and it needed to be done.

She listened quietly as I told her about the day in my office when Amber threw herself at me, the day she tried to attack me in the greenhouse, and Kaliska's involvement. I expected her to be a little upset, or at the very least jealous of the girl stalking me. But true to form, Cara carried a cool head. She said nothing bad about Amber, and instead expressed her sympathies for my office and the stress I was facing. She even offered to come and help clean up, but I told her not to. She was busily packing what remained in her apartment, and I didn't want to burden her with anything else. I told her how much I loved her, and that I would call her when I finished.

Revamped by her voice, I decided to start by putting the file cabinet right side up. After clearing a space on the floor for it to sit, I had heaved it half way up when someone pushed the door open. *Please don't be Amber please don't be Amber,* I said to myself as I turned around. To my great relief I saw Libby instead.

In a pinstriped pantsuit tapping her toe with arms crossed, Libby looked pissed.

"You married the coffee girl!" I didn't know what she meant.

"Libby, what's eating you? Is this why you didn't come to the wedding? I really wanted you to be there."

"First of all, she is *not* your caliber. Secondly, you have no time to spend being domestic. Did you get her pregnant or something?" I usually expected Libby to be mad about something, but I didn't expect she'd be so personal.

Her reviling of my wife threw me on the defensive. I boiled with scalding rage preparing to attack back. As acidic words formed in my throat, I couldn't keep ahold of them - an intruding memory erased them from my mind. My real-life emotions were matching up too closely to those in the memory, and I could feel it dragging me from reality. Helpless against it, my revulsion had slipped too far, and I was going to lapse in front of Libby. It was a memory of my father... helpless to protect my mother...

"You disgust me, Nichole! I knew you were dumb, but I thought you were brighter than this. That kid is a nothing and everyone knows his family is crazy. He's only using you to get to my money. Did you actually think someone could be interested in an ugly, nasty thing like you?"

Standing by the front door, I could clearly hear the insults Nichole's mother slammed into her. I wanted nothing more but to kick the door down and rush to Nichole's side, but she had made me promise to wait outside, no matter what.

"Mother, I know you paid one of your lackeys to try and kill him. How could you do that? I love William, so you might as well have paid to have them kill me too." As Nichole mentioned my near-death experience, I reached up and felt the stitches below my ear where a man I had never seen before tried to cut my throat.

"How do you know I didn't? You can't prove a thing. And besides, if he had done what I paid him for you would have forgotten that boy by now. Pity that no one lives up to expectations anymore. This is it Nichole, no more games. If you are determined to stay with him, you are no longer welcome in this house, and I promise you a life of misery."

"Like it hasn't already been miserable the whole time I've lived here with you! Goodbye Mother. I am leaving and you can't stop me. I hope you rot in Hell."

I heard a tussle and the sound of something being thrown against the wall. Then silence, followed by the sound of a slamming door. I was dying to know what happened and pushed my ear against the door. Just about to kick it in and find out for myself, Nichole finally came outside. She had a black eye, her shirt was torn at the collar, and her smile smeared with blood. "I am free!" she cried as she threw her arms around me.

"Are you even listening to me Chamberlain? I know you can hear me. Don't stare into space and pretend like I'm not here. I can't believe you would tie yourself to such low grade trash."

Libby continued to spit fury at me. My head was splitting, and I had to shake the sight of my mother's broken face from my head. I quickly checked my tattoo, just to be sure I was who I thought I was, and then fired back at Libby.

"You... You will not speak of my wife that way. She is an incredible person and the love of my life. And if you insist on having these feelings about her I advise you to find a new job." Libby stared at me like I had slapped her. When she finally did speak, I was floored.

"Why her Chamberlain? Wasn't I good enough for you?" She sounded like a child, a tone of vulnerability I didn't know she was capable of.

Unknowingly, I had hurt Libby, and thinking back on everything she had done for me I felt horrible. Every extra task, every moment spent together had meant something different to her than it had to me. I always assumed she was a diligent person by nature, and it had never dawned on me that she acted on anything other than work ethic. I needed to be firm and clear about where we stood, but at the same time I didn't want to hurt her unnecessarily. I chose my words very carefully.

"Libby, I had no idea how you felt. I am *so sorry* I hurt you. It was never my intention. You are a tremendous person and you will someday make a man very happy, but not me. I never wanted a relationship, or a wife, until I met Cara. She is the one. I know she isn't perfect, but I love her. I would very much like for us to continue to work together, but only if you can do it without emotions getting in the way. There are boundaries you cannot cross, and insulting her is one of them."

I took her hands in mine as I spoke; it was the first time I had ever touched her. At first she fixated on our entwined hands, then the wall behind me. She looked everywhere but at me. After a minute she closed her eyes, took a deep breath, and pulled away her hands.

"I still don't like her. But I get it though. It's not like you knew I was open to a relationship. Besides," she added ruefully, "now that I see what you prefer in a person it's obvious we would have never worked out."

She had spun it as my loss and I was OK with that. It didn't matter how she justified it, as long as she grasped the point.

"Thank you Libby. You don't have to like Cara, but I will not tolerate you saying anything bad about her. She's my wife..." She nodded knowingly.

"And by the way, thanks for keeping Kaliska out of my office." Libby always responded well to compliments, and once again she did.

"Yeah, he was just chomping at the bit to get his greasy fingers on some dirt on you. I threatened that if he stepped one foot in the door you would bring a privacy suit against him that would cost him his livelihood. I think the idea made him pee a little, and he backed off without a word." Her weasel smile gloated at the thought of how she made him squirm. I couldn't help smiling too.

"Libby, why on Earth did you decide to go into history? You would have made an excellent lawyer."

"Too many lawyers in the family already, and I love solving mysteries. My parents weren't too happy about it. They think I'm wasting my time." Her reluctant face revealed she still wondered that as well.

"Are you telling me you want to hunt treasure?" I asked, laughing more than I intended. "Like on the reality shows?"

"Don't be silly, I don't hunt. I *find*. Speaking of which, I have a present." She reached into the chest pocket of her blazer and handed me an envelope that had been opened. Confused, I pulled out the contents and read in disbelief.

Dr. Shay,
It has come to my attention that you are seeking information on your father's whereabouts. Please come to the Walsenburg Prison on November 21st at 6 a.m. and I will give you the details of his location.

Regards

I read it over and over. I couldn't speak, scared of that which I had sought for so long.

CHAPTER 20

Libby couldn't look more pleased as she watched me stand there, dumbstruck. "A thank you would be very appropriate right now Dr. Shay."

Overwhelmed with joy and without thinking, I grabbed her into a massive bear hug. She didn't hug back, but stood limply with her arms at her side not knowing how to respond to my physical display. I let her go and thanked her repeatedly.

"Before you get too excited, well even more excited I guess - I want you to think this through. The letter didn't say who it was from and it also mentioned your father." *Of course it mentioned my father, that was the whole point* I thought, and then her meaning became apparent.

Only two people left on the planet were supposed to know that William James was my father - Cara and I. Looking back down at the letter, there indeed was the word *father* spelled out in plain sight. Who could have made the connection? Not even Libby was supposed to know, though I had assumed she had guessed.

"Do you think Amber figured something out?" I asked, gesturing around the room, already feeling like the butt end of a sick joke, my hopes fading.

"Impossible. The letter arrived before she broke in. Plus, nothing she would have found in here could have clued her in about your connection. The only plausible explanations are that this person had spoken directly to him, or *is* him. I think this is proof that this is the real deal. You need to be careful though. No signature could mean something illegal or dangerous, like maybe they mean to blackmail you." What she said made sense. It was the real deal, but the information might come at a heavy price.

"What did your father do?" Libby asked. It felt wrong even contemplating answering her question, but she had proven herself in so many ways. She deserved at least a little of the truth.

"He killed my mother when I was a child," I said flatly.

"...And you want to find out why," she said finishing my sentence. A simple nod told her everything she needed to know.

"Well we have a month before the big meeting, so in the meantime let's get this mess taken care of, shall we?" I agreed, feeling anxious about how long a month would be, and tucked the letter into my back pocket.

I began scooping a handful of papers into a pile on the floor, and Libby laughed. It came out low and awkward, but clearly a laugh. "What?" I asked.

"I already hired people to clean up this mess. Dr. Slimeball told me you were coming in today, and I was just waiting for you to show up and supervise."

"Most excellent" I said, dropping the unwieldy armful of papers.

"All of your class files are backed up on a portable drive and I have an art restorer coming to look at the painting this afternoon. Your furniture is screwed, but you really needed to update it anyways." I was relieved. We seemed to be going right back to our normal routine. Libby may have been hurting inside, but at least she wouldn't let it affect her work.

The rest of the morning flew by. Libby hadn't exaggerated when she said she had already taken care of the clean up. After a brief phone call, men in white jumpsuits arrived and expertly organized and emptied my office. We watched in awe and relief as the marker came off the walls with a simple cleaning solution. The art restorer came shortly before lunch, and removing what was left of the Lamarck painting, she promised to bring it back to near original condition. I believed the restoration would require a feat of dark magic based on the damage, but I was very willing to let her try. Watching her wrap what was left of it in a sheet like a corpse, I mentally waved goodbye to my friend Lamarck, and silently promised him he was in good hands.

With the office completely empty, Libby started making calls to fill it back up. It worried me that she had taken the liberty of ordering new things for the office without my input. It wasn't that I was unusually picky, but it was stuff I would have to see and use day in and day out. She dismissed me with a talk-to-the-hand motion when I tried to intervene.

"Chamberlain, I know what you like. OK? Now quit your fussing and go get some lunch. If you hate it, I'll send it all back. Promise."

Like Pavlov's dogs, at her mention of food my stomach growled on command. Eager to share the letter about my father with Cara, a lunch break made the perfect excuse. "You're right. Thank you Libby. I'll be back in an hour or so." She didn't even acknowledge my departure as she dialed straight into the next round of phone calls.

My strides stepped swift and long as I made my way to the car. Although only a few hours had passed since I'd seen her, I missed Cara intensely. I felt elated and giddy that in a short while she would be back in my arms again. We had been married only one week, and the passionate glories of our honeymoon swam warmly in me.

I decided to stop and pick up food for us, and thought the café near her old apartment would be the perfect place. Parking in front of the brick building under the large sign, I thought back on our first time there and wondered if Bible Bob might be inside once again.

Walking in, I paused in surprise by how busy the place bustled. Almost every stool at the counter had an occupant, and many of the tables had been pushed together to accommodate large parties. At least three waitresses worked the floor, and two more hustled behind the counter. I looked for Bible Bob among the gaggle of faces but didn't see him.

"If you're looking for a table it's going to be a few minutes," said a short, plump, middle-aged woman from behind the counter.

"No, I was just wondering if I could get something to go?" She handed me a menu and shuffled off with a nearly overflowing glass coffee pot in her hand. When she returned a few minutes later, the coffee pot was empty. Setting it on the counter, she pulled out a pad of paper. She took my order and suggested I take a seat at the crowded counter until my burgers were done.

Taking her advice, I squeezed my way between two elderly men, one rail thin and the other quite large. They were talking about the newest storm that was sure to hit us in the next couple of days, but neither could remember which day. Wishing to be helpful, I grabbed my phone and pulled up the latest weather forecast. "It looks like it will hit us in two days," I said brightly to the larger man.

"Got that off your phone didja?" he asked in a slow, annoyed drawl.

"Uhh yeah. Would you like to see for yourself?" I tried to hand him the phone but he waved it away. "Nope. I don't go in for all that fancy phone stuff," he said, giving his friend on my other side a knowing look.

My apparently untrustworthy phone sparked a new conversation between them. Forgetting the weather, they joked back and forth about the changes they had witnessed in technology. Having very little input on the subject personally, except for borrowed memories, I sat back and listened, though not intently as they linked together a range of topics from the television to the microwave. The rollercoaster of emotions from the day had worn me out. I was drifting out when someone tapped me on my right shoulder. I turned, expecting to see the waitress with my food. Instead I saw the thinner man staring at me with a puzzled expression.

"You all right son?" he asked in the same slow accent as his friend.

"Yeah, I'm all right, just dozed off there for a bit. It's been a long day," I said a little disoriented, wiping my eyes and looking around.

"Tell me again 'bout those voice pipes you used in the war," he requested. "I can't say I've ever heard of'em." At first I assumed he was talking to his friend, being that I hadn't been part of their conversation. When his friend didn't answer, and instead looked straight at me, I knew. For the second time in one day I had lapsed.

Apologizing for butting in on their conversation, I stood up and asked the waitress how much longer I would have to wait for my food. She looked irritated at my impatience, but answered assuredly, "Only a few more minutes sugar."

"Thank you ma'am. I... I need to step outside for some air." Smiling with concern, she hurried off to deliver the three plates of sandwiches she was balancing.

Pushing through the door, I walked into the alley on the side of the building and almost threw up. With my hands on the cool wall and my head bent over, I tried to force myself to retain the contents of my stomach.

I hadn't had a single lapse in three weeks, but on my first day back in real life I had already racked up two. It had been so easy to ignore my impending doom with Cara around, but I was running out of time far more quickly than I hoped.

I stood up straight and stared at the sky.

"It sucks being crazy doesn't it?" said a man's voice from behind me.

Turning around, I saw a dirtier, hairier version of myself. It was Bible Bob. He was dressed in the same clothes as the first day we met, and he smelled just as bad.

"Oh! Hello Simon. I didn't see you back there. What did you say?" I asked, trying to hide the nervousness of being in an alley with someone so desperate looking.

"I said that it sucks being crazy, doesn't it?" He hacked up a chunky phlegm ball and spat it onto the wall behind me.

"Yeah it sure does," I agreed. I tried to persuade him to come to the diner and let me buy him lunch, but he refused. Instead, he launched into a story about being kidnapped, which I knew was his version of my attempt at helping him. Throughout his tale he sweetly referred to Cara as The Angel. I was hoping for the end when for no apparent reason he changed his tone and started shouting Bible verses at me.

Refusing to flashback into the old St. Patrick memory again, I gave up and turned back toward the restaurant. The waitress was holding open the door calling to me, waving a white paper bag. "Sir, your order is ready!"

I thanked her and apologized, and as we stepped into the diner I asked if I could add another burger to the order for whenever Bible Bob came in next.

I could feel the eyes of the two older gentlemen on me. The waitress' accommodating face bent into a frown. "Oh sugar, I'm so sorry to tell ya, but..." She swallowed hard and fanned her welling eyes with her fingers. "Bible Bob was hit by a semi truck a few weeks back. He ran outta here one day yellin' something about fire and, and, he never saw it coming. And he didn't suffer any neither."

She walked behind the counter and started to ring me up, but I couldn't stand there one second longer. I pulled a fifty out of my pocket and shoved it in her hand. "Keep the change," I said, and ran out the door.

Getting into my car, I listened for Bible Bob's ranting, but only heard silence. He was gone.

Pulling up to Cara's old apartment, the white moving truck we had rented was parked in front, taking up two of the three spaces. Claiming the last, I pulled the keys from the ignition. I took many long, deep breaths to pull myself together before I went inside. Unfortunately, all I accomplished was dizziness, so I grabbed the food, and made for the door.

CHAPTER 21

I didn't knock as I snuck into the apartment. Watching from just inside the door, Cara obviously had no idea I was there. She spun in the living room, dancing a waltz with a broom. I guffawed at her goofy elegance, but the music was too loud for her to hear me. Looking straight out of the fifties, a pink and white floral scarf held back her hair, and over her snug jeans wrapped an old-fashioned apron with bits of frill. Memories tugged at me, but I managed to push them aside to enjoy the view.

Unable to resist, I snuck up behind her and whispered in her ear, "Can I cut in?" In one swift pirouette Cara spun around and belted me in the mouth. The stupefying force of her blow sent me straight to the ground.

"Oh crap Chamberlain!!! Oh no! I'm so sorry!!" She joined me on the floor, and helped me to my feet, touching her fingers lightly to my already swelling bottom lip.

"I should have warned you!" Cara exclaimed as she ran to turn down the music.

"Apparently I should have warned *you*!" I joked back.

I laughed, but Cara looked solemnly serious as she examined my lip.

"Sit back down while I grab some ice," she said, pointing her finger at me like a dominatrix nurse.

"Yes, ma'am, just please don't hit me again," I teased, shielding my face with my crossed arms. Her flustered groan from the kitchen said she did not see the humor in it.

Returning with ice wrapped in a paper towel, she held it to my lip lovingly.

"You know how people have the flight or fight instinct when they are frightened?" asked Cara.

"Let me guess, you take flight," I assumed, putting an arm around her to give her a squeeze. "Ha ha funny guy. I'm sorry I didn't warn you about my weirdness. I forgot." She was looking at the ground. Taking her face in my hands, I looked into her luminescent blue eyes. "It's fine Cara. Weirdness is fine. And your particular brand of weirdness is exactly what I love about you." This brought the joy back into her face and she kissed me lightly, avoiding my double-sized lip.

"What are you doing here anyways? I thought you would be at the school all day." I took the ice from her and retrieved the food from the door where I had left it.

"I decided I needed to feed my wife," I announced proudly, holding out the bag.

"Sweet!" she squealed, nabbing it from my hands and plopping down on the floor. Three bites into her burger by the time I joined her, she had obviously been working all morning without stopping to eat. The burgers were wonderfully greasy and heavy on condiments. The fries were salty and perfectly hot for the taste buds, but burned my engorged lip. Both famished, we barely spoke as we enjoyed our meal.

After not a single stray fry hid in the folds of the bag, we looked around at her progress. All of the smaller items and her clothes were packed. The walls seemed suddenly massive with all the bits of paper gone. Only the larger furniture remained, which I promised to help her move when I finished at work.

"Are you sad to be leaving?" I asked, thinking about all the massive life changes she'd undergone in the last few months.

"I don't know... This was the mansion of my dreams..." She pined away and snorted a smile. "No seriously, I'm not sad at all. I'm ready to start our future properly, and I can't do that hanging onto this."

At her mention of the future, all of the events of the day that she and food had deftly distracted me from swept back in and clouded my mood. Seeing my change, Cara grabbed my hands and asked, "What's wrong?" Embarrassed and deeply disappointed in myself, I brushed her off. "Nothing."

"Lying to me isn't going to solve anything," she intoned gently, calling my bluff. She was right. I had no shame or reason to keep secrets from her anymore. The truth of my future, for good and bad, was hers to share.

After a deep breath to organize my thoughts, I told her about my two lapses earlier that day. She listened patiently to what happened, but disagreed with me about what it meant.

When I told her about Bible Bob, she seemed unusually sad.

"Chamberlain I have to apologize. I knew about Simon's death the day after it happened."

I felt irked she had held it a secret. "Why didn't you tell me?"

"I didn't mean any harm by it love. You were recovering and doing so well with no lapses, and I went to the hotel to settle the bill on his room, but the desk girl said he never checked in. So I went by the diner and Vera told me. I'm sorry I kept it from you. I was gonna see how your first full day at work went today and maybe tell you tonight. I promise."

Everything she said made sense, and I felt more worried about having talked to Simon. Warm blood showered in my chest as I realized how much she always looked out for me.

"You were under a lot of stress today," she said, straddling me. "Having to deal with your office being destroyed, Dr. Sleazy Snake, *and* that whiner Libby would put anyone on bad footing, mentally speaking. You went a long time without any issues, so I think this is a learning opportunity. Less Libby Whiners, fewer snakes, and more Cara."

I hoped deeply she was right that the setbacks were simply products of stress, and not evidence of my rapidly progressing illness. Past experience forced me to believe she was wrong, but I couldn't pollute any positive thoughts she wanted.

"More Cara, huh? Well, if that's what Nurse Shay prescribes, I think I should probably listen." I growled and pulled her hips hard into mine and kissed her deeply. My lip stung, but my wandering hands pulled the pain away as they climbed inside her t-shirt. Our grinding made a crackling paper sound from my pocket, reminding me I hadn't shown her the letter.

Sliding my hands down her back, I gently pushed her hips away. She moaned in disappointment, "Oh, come on professor. We have time." I kissed her on the tip of the nose while I reached into my pocket.

"What's this?" she asked without unfolding it.

"Just read it love." I laid back and crossed my arms into a pillow behind my head. Closing my eyes, I waited for the sound I knew sure to erupt.

Her adorable squeal filled the room, followed by rounds of "Oh my goodness!" and "How could this be?" After the hoopla and a lot of hugs and kisses, she went quiet, obviously contemplating the implications.

"They must know him or maybe just you," she guessed, finding the same connections Libby and I had divined. "Yeah," I said a little more blasé than how I really felt. "Either way it should be interesting."

The thought of seeing my father again suddenly reckoned too overwhelming to contemplate. Receiving the letter reignited my hopes of finding exactly which memory caused him to kill my mother, but confronting him with it required a difficult ride on a rollercoaster of emotional dread.

Getting up, I held out my hand and helped Cara to her feet. "I should get going. Libby ordered new furniture and I really need to help before she organizes the entire office for me." Upon mention of Libby, Cara said with a rueful squint, "Maybe I should go along and help too. I'm done with what I can do here anyways. That's why I was waltzing with you, I mean, the broom." I knew it would be more than awkward having them both in the same room, but I couldn't resist extra time with her, so I agreed.

Driving back to the university, I told Cara about my earlier conversations with Libby about her feelings, leaving out all the rude things Libby had said about her.

"I can't blame her. You *are* a sexy piece of man meat. Do you think she will try and cause problems for us?" Cara asked levelly.

"I don't think so. I made my feelings for you very clear, and she's not really the type to grovel for something."

"She may not grovel, but she will fight dirty," Cara said.

"And how do you know that? I didn't want to tell you, but she called you Coffee Girl today. What's the deal with you two?"

"Let's just say *Psycho* and I have a past."

"Annnnnd..."

"Short story. She is a picky control freak and I can't stand her."

I raised my left eyebrow to let her know I was seeing through her.

"I'm guessing you want a little more detail than that."

"Yeah, that would be nice."

She sighed. "Well, I was working in a coffee shop, and Libby was one of our regular customers. She always ordered the same thing, a tepid low fat latte, and since none of us knew her personally, that's what we called her. Tepid Low Fat. She was a total pain in the ass every day, and I wasn't the only one who thought so."

I realized what she was about to regale and I couldn't wait to hear it.

"She would come in and lord over us that she worked for *the distinguished Dr. Chamberlain Shay*. Hardly ever was there a day she didn't complain about how we made her stupid drink, and way too many times she forced us to remake her order *two or three times*."

She pulled in a big breath and exhaled with a growl.

"I liked my job, and I knew that dealing with her was part of it. I was polite and kept my mouth shut even though I thought we had every right to refuse her service. When I had to wait on her, I fantasized about how I could get away with dumping the drink all over her."

I shook my head and tried not to laugh. I had seen the proof the day Libby came to my office latte soaked.

"Wait, let me explain. I was busy one day, and I was rushing to get all the orders done, and when I went to take Libby hers, I tripped over a chair leg and spilled it all over her. A total accident, I swear." She held up her right hand as if to take an oath. "I told her I was sorry, but she was convinced it was on purpose, and she complained to my boss. I'd been late a couple times that week, and I got fired and lost half of my last check to pay for her stupid shirt. Don't laugh you jerk."

"I'm sorry, but you should have seen how she looked in my office that day."

Cara pouted. She wanted me to agree that Libby was the worst person on the planet, but I couldn't. "Love, I know she lacks all your explosive sweetness and happiness, and I know how difficult she is, but Libby has worked *very hard* for me. Because of her I might find out what happened with my parents. Please just try to get along, and I promise I won't let her insult you or talk down to you. But no one can force her to be nice."

Walking down the hall to my office, we could see from a distance a note taped to the door. I didn't bother looking at it, assuming it was from

Libby to explain she went to lunch. Stepping through the door, I was awed by the transformation. Incredibly, the room had been magically shaped once again into *my* office. The layout felt the same as before, but improved with more expensive items. Running her fingers along the top of the glossy cherry wood desk, Cara couldn't help but comment cleverly, "I'll give her one thing, that weasel sure has good taste." She winked at me, looking me up and down with bedroom eyes.

Looking around at the furnishings, I couldn't have agreed more. In addition to the desk, Libby had brought in bookshelves and matching leather chairs. The computer was sleekly updated, and behind it a beast of an office chair that looked tenfold as comfortable as my previous. Where the Lamarck painting would hopefully hang again, Libby had placed a passable nature print to hold its place.

The room felt right, complete with a towering comfy chair by the window. It was still yellow, but a softer, paler hue. Taped to it was another note I read aloud, "I hated putting such a monstrosity in here, but I knew if I didn't you would eventually." I motioned to Cara to sit in the chair, and felt elated she found it comfortable. Fantasies of her sitting there every day between classes filled my head.

"What do you think? I asked.

"It's perfect. Tepid Psycho did a really nice job." I rolled my eyes at her less than pleasant nickname.

"Play nice Cara. You agreed." She smiled and twisted innocently in the chair like a sexy, bashful nymph.

After completing my inspection, I unfolded the expectedly plain and to the point note Libby left on the door.

Chamberlain,

I am done with the office and will see you tomorrow. Please do not destroy my progress by piling random books and papers all over the floor.

- Libby

The last part was just a joke because she knew that would be exactly what would happen, eventually. Cara laughed, knowing all too well my ability to create copious literary clutter.

"We could always live here," Cara said trying to sound serious.

"Alright," I said plopping into the big office chair behind the decadently regal desk.

"Seriously though," said Cara staring out the window onto a view I knew by heart. "We need to start looking for a place."

She was right. We were renting an apartment near the school for the time being, but it didn't feel like home, not in the least. It was larger than Cara's old place, but still too small for two people with so many books.

"We need to find a place to make *ours*," she said. She had read my mind, and we both knew renting an apartment wouldn't let that happen.

"Maybe we should have Libby help out?" I suggested reflexively.

"Great idea," snapped Cara. "And then maybe she could wash your underwear, feed you by hand, and even have sex for us too."

"OK, OK, I get it. Never mind. It was just an idea."

I sat there for a long time watching my wife stare out the window, and I couldn't help feeling like everything would work out - a powerful side effect of spending time with her. When we were apart, reality stabbed through and I knew my illness worsened every moment. It was hard to start looking for a new house when I had no idea what my life would resemble in a month. Would I still be able to work? Would I be able to handle meeting up with my father? Could this marital bliss really continue after what happened this morning? All these unanswered questions made settling into thoughts about something as important as a house appear pointless, but as Cara got up from the comfy chair and crawled into my lap, my perspective instantly changed. I wanted to give her everything she desired, and if it were a house we needed, I would force myself to focus.

CHAPTER 22

I thought Cara might eject straight out of her seat and through the roof of the car. Coffeed up heavily, she bounced in her seat like a five year old on a sugar high.

"If you don't calm down, people will think I kidnapped you." I pointed subtly to a fat gentleman staring at her in the car next to us at the stoplight. "Maybe you have, and now you're taking me to my dream house where you'll force me to stay forever and ever and ever."

After looking at twenty plus houses over the last two weeks, Cara promised this was indeed the one we sought. Unfortunately, this was not the first time she'd laid that claim. She had sworn three others were The One, but after spending a little time at each, they proved not to be. It wasn't me who turned them down. I would've been content living in a dumpster as long as Cara was there, but she wanted The Perfect House. We talked about building one from scratch on the property of my old home, but we quickly dismissed the notion in favor of starting with a clean slate, somewhere closer to the school.

Busily back at work, and with the mysterious meeting about my father fast approaching, the weekend house hunting distraction gifted a nice respite.

"That's the street!" Cara squeaked as she pointed down a small dusty road. I turned onto the gravel and asked her the details. I knew before I asked the question that I wouldn't find out how many bedrooms or square feet. To Cara, those tidbits were not important. She was much more interested, if not obsessed, with their history and what memories the houses provoked for me. At first she wanted to find one that allowed me to be totally free of any triggers, but once I convinced her that a house of this variety couldn't exist, she honed in on finding one that inspired good memories.

I only half listened as Cara explained the house was built in the fifties, and then babbled on about the owners. I wanted to listen, but I was discombobulated and distracted. I tried to nod in approval, absently saying, "That's nice" in all the right spots to what she was saying, but I must not have been doing a very good job. She busted up laughing and said through a coy smile, "Really Chamberlain, you think it's *nice* that if this isn't the right house we might have to use Libby as our personal whipping boy to find one."

I hated losing face, even if I knew I had done wrong.

"Yep, I sure do."

Irritated I didn't cop to not listening to her, Cara sulked at the window. I took her hand and kissed it. "I'm sorry love. I just have a lot on my mind with the meeting tomorrow." She continued to look away and answered in frustration.

"I know. But I still wish you would let me go with you, or at the very least take a bodyguard like Libby suggested." The three of us had been repeating this argument ad nauseam since I received the letter. Cara wanted to be there for emotional support, but I had no idea what I would be facing and didn't want her involved if things got weird. I almost did take Libby's suggestion, but rejected it after thinking it through because I thought the presence of someone else might scare off our source.

I was being arrogant and I knew it. I wanted to face the moment alone. I thought of it like a birthright. Besides, they were being paranoid. We were meeting in a prison parking lot after all. What could happen? I had made up my mind about it, and had begged them too often to drop it. Cara bringing it up yet again wore on my nerves like a wire brush. I didn't want to argue, and instead changed the subject.

"Hey, do you want to know something cool?" Out of the corner of my eye I could see her nod sarcastically.

"Do you know where the phrase 'whipping boy' originated?"

"No, but I guess I will shortly." Her words bit sharp, but playful. I was already forgiven, mostly.

"It started with families of noble blood and bratty children. Important people had servants take care of their kids on a daily basis, and like all kids they had to be punished. The problem was that a servant was never allowed to punish their 'betters', so they invented a whipping boy. From an early age, a common child would be raised side by side with a royal kid, and most of the time they would grow close like brothers. Then, when the royal kid screwed up and needed punishing, their caretaker would beat the common child in an attempt to make the royal child feel bad, hence "whipping boy." Many wealthy families practiced it, and it worked most of the time, but always there were the emotionally deformed who'd do bad things just to torture their whipping boys."

No longer looking out the window, I could feel Cara peering at me with intrigue. "Why would anyone let their kid be used like that?" It was a fair question, and I explained how poverty developed a powerful social divide wherein having your child raised as a virtual brother to a someday king was a gamble many families couldn't refuse.

"Did your family have a whipping boy back in that era?" Her notion my family ever held that kind of wealth made me smile. "Nope, we were always commoners. We never even got picked as whipping boys. I just have memories of the practice being discussed."

Pointing out a driveway for me to turn onto, Cara said astutely, "Your family has never been common."

She began repeating the details she thought I'd missed about the house.

As she talked, I enjoyed the landscape. The dirt driveway was lined with dark green cedars, branches drooping precariously with heavy snow. As I pulled in, Cara squawked joyously and jumped out right before the car completely stopped. I parked and followed her, seeing where she'd found the inspiration for the house. It was a two-story stucco, complete with a large wooden front porch and classic swing. The view from the front matched the description I had given Cara of the house I grew up in with Granddad. Standing there in admiration, feeling an instant sense of arrival, I teased her.

"You cheated."

"I did not! You told me you loved your childhood with Granddad, so I thought that if I found a house like it, you would have good memories triggered most the time." I put my arm around her as we walked up the creaky steps. She had nailed it again. I flooded with my own happy memories of playing on the porch while Granddad sat in the swing.

Cara unlocked the door and we stepped inside. The general layout was very open and typical, with a large front room, and a master bedroom on the second floor. Fumes of new carpet and fresh paint lingered annoyingly. Most of the house looked quite different from the one I was raised in, except the kitchen. The cabinets were wood, but painted over with thick, sticky white paint. The tiles bore the same tacky green color. Walking into the kitchen, I explained the commonalities and watched Cara's face light up.

"Are the memories you're experiencing all good?"

"Most," I admitted reservedly.

"What are you seeing?"

"I'm getting a few head rushes from memories of Granddad's struggles with his wife before my father was born. But they're safe memories, not violence provoking or anything. I can deal with them happily because they're paired with so much good."

I grabbed her hand. "Well my love, I like it. I love it. The memories are the best yet. What do you think?" We squeezed our hands tightly together, taking in the backdoor's snowy view.

"We're home."

CHAPTER 23

I arrived at the parking lot an hour early as a pink sun broke light. The lot was much fuller than I expected, and a dusting of snow covered the cars of the overnight guards. I drove two trips around to find a spot both empty and with a decent view of the entrance. When I finally found one, I backed in tightly between a light blue minivan and a big, tan suburban. It seemed a bit silly to go through that much effort to see them coming when I had no idea who to expect, but I felt desperate not to miss them.

I had little to do but sit and wait. Like sitting in traffic on the way to a funeral, I felt both determination and dread. Having not slept the night before, my eyes ached with exhaustion, but the profuse adrenaline volcanizing my blood kept me awake while butterflies tried to kill each other in my guts. To keep myself busy, I traded off between staring at the entrance and checking the time on my phone.

Two cars came down the road to the prison. Neither of them turned in, but both caused the knots in my stomach to implode. As the meeting time grow closer, I started to sweat from everywhere. A few minutes before six, I turned the key on and rolled down the windows. The very cold morning air rushed in, refreshing my eyes.

Eagerly expecting that at any moment a car should be pulling up, I was startled when a loud metallic sound clanged from behind me. Craning my neck around, I could see three people standing behind my car. I couldn't make out their faces in the dawn, but I could tell by their stature that a woman stood in the center with a man on either side. Neither was my father. I wasn't sure if they could see me, so I watched them for a few minutes.

The woman was impatiently waving her arms, and she stretched out her hand and hit the trunk of my car. The same metallic clang as before reverberated from her very large ring.

Perturbed that she was doing damage, I stepped out holding my keys in one hand and my phone in the other. Seeing my abrupt exit, the elderly woman wearing a large fur coat slinked behind the two large men as they stepped protectively in front of her. As they moved, the old woman spoke in a firmly evil voice, "Well you're tall like your father, but pathetically skinny. You can thank your mother for that. She always was a scrawny, sickly thing."

My spine chilled and tensed with her words. It wasn't what she said, but the fact that she said it in a voice I had never heard, but recognized immediately. She was my mom's mother. Granny.

As quickly as I could, I pulled up the only two memories my father had of her, neither of them good. I then tried to remember any conversations my parents had about her, but there were none.

"Speak up! You can talk, can't you moron?" she asked indignantly, but I was too flabbergasted to speak. All I knew about her was that she hated my father and beat my mother. Pleasantries like "It's nice to meet you" or "How have you been the last twenty-five years?" all seemed superfluously wrong. I had no love for this woman, and it was clear by her mannerisms that she hadn't changed since my father met her. I tried to think logically about the situation, but none of it made sense. All I could think was, *why her?* I decided to ask.

"How do you know where my father is?" My voice sounded frail after her strong and abrupt tone.

"Right to the point then? Fine." She snapped her fingers and the two men charged me.

I instinctually tried to get back in my car, but one quick pull at the handle and it was too late. The huge men advancing on me rapidly, I abandoned the idea and tried to run. I had barely reached the middle of the hood when I felt a strong hand grab my shoulder. I pulled away but lost my footing and fell. Plunging forward, I used my hands to protect my face, but the rest vulnerable. With a crackling pop like snapping celery, my knees hit the unforgiving ice-covered asphalt. The pain shot up my thighs and I opened my mouth to cry out, but one of the men threw himself on top of me and crushed the air out of my body. The other man shoved a rag into my mouth. I kicked and thrashed and fought as hard as I could against them, but it was futile. I was no match for men that large and experienced. They pinned me instantly, and I felt a sharp sting in my arm. Wrenching my head to the side, I watched helplessly as the old woman injected something into my arm, grinning like a demon.

Drowsiness overcame me as I heard her say one last thing.

"What a wimp. I told you this would be easy."

CHAPTER 24

I awoke with a stabbing pain and high-pitched ringing in my head. I reached across the bed to pull Cara in next to me, but instead of finding her, my hand hit a wall that shouldn't have been. The unfamiliar feeling jolted me back to the horror of what had happened. I jumped up from the bed, unfortunately having forgotten the damage done to my knees. Moving to a standing position burned like someone pushing scorching, white-hot knitting needles through my kneecaps. I was alone. With no apparent threat, I buckled to the floor.

From my low vantage point, I took a minute to survey my surroundings. My mind defaulted to the worst conclusions and I expected a torture chamber with chains and blood-soaked floors. What I found instead was boring by comparison. I was in a simple, sparsely furnished bedroom.

The bed I had been laying on was small, but graced with a rosy canopy and an expensive matching feather comforter. In one corner sat a wooden chair with a pink velvet seat facing the center of the room. Along the wall opposite the bed stood a small nightstand with a brass lamp. The meager light languished under a faded cream shade filtering the light into urine yellow. Without windows, most of the room was in shadows or darkness. The walls and hardwood floor were bare. The off to the side bathroom had only an unkempt toilet and dirty white porcelain sink.

I reached into my pocket for my phone and found it gone, along with my car keys and wallet. Egged on by the pain, I pulled up my pant legs to examine the damage underneath. Large purple bruises covered both legs around my distended knees, but nothing felt broken. My clothing was still wet and torn from the struggle, and scratches decorated my arms like I'd been arguing with feisty cats. Completing my physical evaluation, I moved excruciatingly to a standing position and practiced putting weight on both legs. It hurt blindingly, but the pain blurred meaningless against my anxiety for escape.

Reaching for the handle, I hoped the kidnapping was just a poorly constructed reunion designed by my insane grandmother. My hopes nulled as the knob held stiff. Trying again, I put my weight into the door several times. It wouldn't budge. I banged on the door with my fists, screaming for someone to let me out. Infuriated, I tried ramming the door with my shoulder, only causing more pain from my knees, and crippling shoulder pain. With each failed attempt I felt myself falling further into full-blown panic.

Heaving for breath, I looked closer, and the door was actually made of steel, bolted from the other side. I felt so stupid that I immediately tried to use the objects in the room to break open the door, but the seemingly innocent furniture proved to be just as sinister as the door. Everything had been bolted down. Even the lamp was secured to the table with rivets.

I was out of breath, and my throat burned with thirst by the time I had given up on escape. I decided to rebuild my energy, and limping my way into the sad little bathroom, I turned on the sink. Being held prisoner made me paranoid, and I tried to smell the water before I took a sip, even though I didn't know what I was sniffing for. It seemed normal. I cupped my hands and brought a small amount to my lips. It was cold and tasted clean, so I put both hands on either side of the sink, leaned my head down and drank it straight from the faucet. Long, desperate swallows cooled my throat and helped me feel slightly better, but only momentarily.

Trudging back into my cell, I sat in the lone chair, hung my head and tried to unravel the unknown. I knew my grandmother hated my father, and that she despised my mother for marrying him, but why any of that would cause her to kidnap me years later was baffling. And why go to the trouble only to be left in a room to rot? At some point, someone would have to come in, or I would be taken out. If my grandmother wanted me dead, she could've done it in the parking lot. Instead she brought me to this prepared prison, which made sense only if she wanted something from me. If it were some kind of family relationship she was seeking, she definitely would not receive it.

While I tortured myself trying to puzzle out what was coming next, I worried sadly about Cara. She had no idea where I was or if I was OK. Her concern would have been immeasurable, and my inability to console her was killing me, causing pangs of pain so strong I thought I'd explode. Needing to slow my garbled mind and be productive, I carefully considered my situation, and planned what I would do when someone entered my space. Using force to claw my way out tempted as the most satisfying physical retribution, but based on the brutes Granny sicked on me earlier, I knew it would be fruitless. The only power I held against her was my mind.

I waited for hours. When my legs numbed from sitting, I paced the floor. When my knees tired of pacing, which was far too quickly, I sat back down. My routine finally broke by the sound of footsteps from outside. I strained to hear the direction they were coming from, and when it became clear that they were heading for my room, I sprinted to the lamp and pulled on the shade. I wrenched it off and threw it on the floor next to the nightstand. With nothing impeding it, the room light doubled. I only had seconds to observe the changes before the door was unlocked and pushed open, my eyes flashing light bulbs with each blink.

Making my stand at the foot of the bed, I held my breath as the same men who had kidnapped me walked slowly and deliberately into the room. They followed each other closely, and kept their hands out in front like they were expecting me to attack at any moment. No longer sporting their heavy coats, they were dressed like little boys in too tight church clothes, still as menacing as dragons.

The younger one looked thirtyish, and walked with slumped over shoulders. Everything about him revealed he was a follower who wouldn't act without a command. The other man terrified me the second he came into view. Well into his fifties, I instantly recognized him - not just from his brutal parking lot attack.

The grey in his hair and the wrinkles around his eyes couldn't disguise Jeremiah's pocked skin and dead stare, same as he wore thirty years ago when he tried to slit my father's throat. I pitied him for still being employed to carry out my grandmother's dirty work, but not enough to forgive him. I remembered well the cold, sharp feeling of his blade slicing the skin below my father's ear. It may have been the exhaustion or the stress, but the tug of the memory was stronger than ever, trying to force me into lapse. As they loomed huge in front of me, the room around them blurred.

The day's warmth had retreated, giving way to a crisp winter's night. It was the worst and most dangerous time to lapse, and I started pinching the back of my hand to focus on the present. It didn't help. I pulled up my sleeve and stared at my tattoo, but still I slipped. I desperately needed something to happen to pull me out, so I started talking. "My name is Chamberlain Shay. What you're doing is wrong." Saying my name out loud helped bring me back in control, a little. I said it again, louder. And again.

The younger milquetoast man shifted his eyes to the floor and winced, while Jeremiah seemed to not even hear me. Granny's gnarly voice scraped in from the door behind them.

"Grow up child. These men have no morals, otherwise they wouldn't be here." Crippled by bitterness and age, she balanced her boney frame on a plain silver cane. Her drooping face matched my father's memories, only ravaged deeply by remorseless time. Where once blushed high cheekbones protruded a shrunken skeleton through loose skin.

Salting my words heavily I said, "Hello Granny."

She said nothing and eyed the room, noticing it was not nearly as dark and shadowy as she had intended. When she glanced over at the removed lampshade, I watched her face intently and saw exactly what I had hoped, both irritation and rage. I had won a small battle. With the very few memories we had stored of her, one thing was abundantly clear - she was a bona fide control freak. I had stolen some of that control, and whether or not she realized it, I had made my statement. I would never give her complete power over me.

Turning away from the lamp, she shuffled her way over to the chair. The young guard stood in her way, and as she approached him she harshly whacked him on the back of the leg with her cane. He didn't cry out despite the obvious pain, but moved aside subserviently, bowing his head and clasping his nervous hands at his waist. Watching his face, I could see what Granny didn't care to see as he squeezed his eyes shut in shameful anger.

Once settled into the chair, Grandma decided to speak again. "I guess introductions would be redundant to a mutation like you, wouldn't they? You've no doubt seen me in your father's memories. Oh, don't look so surprised Chamberlain. We all know about your sickness here, and none of us would be in this mess if your father hadn't infected my daughter with his genetically flawed spawn." Her words didn't hurt me. On my bad days I would have agreed with her.

"Why am I here?" I demanded, instantly answered by the wicked snap of her fingers. Before I could react, Jeremiah bolted forward and slapped me hard across the face. The impact knocked me back against the bed, and before I could right myself he had returned to his guard stance five feet away.

"You will not speak unless I ask you a question!" she yelled. My face stung and I tried in vain not to tear up. "Sit," she commanded, pointing to the floor in front of the bed. I hesitated at first, but when I saw her raise her fingers into a snapping position I obeyed. A trillion needles flared in my knees.

"You are here because you are stupid. Of course your father is dead, where the hell else would he be? If you don't believe me you can go in the backyard and dig up his rotting body yourself. Really the best place for him I think. I should get a medal or something..." She continued disgustingly, patting herself on the back for being an accomplished murderess. I stopped listening. I didn't want to believe her, and fumbling to find a reason, I asked, "Why?"

I knew the question meant more pain, but I was beyond caring. I wanted answers.

I braced myself as Jeremiah kicked me in the hip. I bit down hard and resisted screaming, and never let my eyes stray from the face of the younger guard. He seemed like the only perpetrator in the room with a sliver of soul, and I wanted to exploit any piece that hadn't been beaten out of him. He cringed when the dead thud of a big boot hitting bone beneath flesh stilled the room.

Granny sneered. "Slow learner, aren't we? As I was saying, the world is a better place having him gone. I know Jeremiah feels quite happy to have taken care of him." As she gestured to him, his expression changed for the first time as the corners of his lips pulled into a greasy smile. The deadness in his eyes never changed. Having failed at slitting his throat the first time,

Jeremiah seemed deeply happy to finally succeed at it decades later. I felt ill as the image played in my head.

"No one takes what is mine without paying for it," said Granny while cracking her arthritic knuckles as if she was Queen of the World. Her thirst for control was so strong that it had warped her view of people. They were no longer individuals, but objects that were hers, and my mother must have been her prized possession.

"You may speak now, but control your tongue."

I took my time and fought internally with what I wanted to say, and what I should say to get more answers. Growing quickly impatient, she began tapping her cane on the ground.

"Out with it!" she commanded.

"I never took anything from you." I tried to hide the anger in my voice, and instead projected sorrow. I wasn't looking for pity from her; I knew that emotion didn't exist in her pallet. I stared at the young guard.

"You tried to take away my freedom Chamberlain. Your ridiculous hunt for your father left me in a difficult situation, so I solved it. Too many people came poking around once your damn assistant found out about the prison. I may not have much time left to live, but I *will* outlive you." With help from her henchmen, Granny rose from the chair like an addled empress. She walked slowly toward the door.

"Why keep me here? Why not just kill me?"

"Because I own you now Chamberlain. Oh, and if you decide to kill yourself, please do it cleanly. Not for my sake mind you, but if you make a mess, Charlie will have a lot of extra work to do." They slammed the door shut, and my heart sunk to thoughts of Cara.

CHAPTER 25

Many hours trickled by before I moved from my spot on the floor. I lay physically still, but my mind ran Olympic-sized laps over our intangible conversation track. I wouldn't have changed my position for many more hours had Charlie not come in with food. His eyes never left the floor as he placed a white tray on the small table. Before he turned to leave I said, "Thank you," as imploringly as I could, and he offered a recognizing grunt. The odor of the stew filled the room and nauseated me. I had no appetite. Starving myself in protest initially seemed like a good idea, and while I contemplated flushing it down the toilet, a memory filled my head refusing to be ignored despite the mountain of more pressing issues.

Roasted rat was on the table, and a family sat around it looking miserable. The memory emanated from a child who'd decided he would take a stand and never eat rat. When he refused, his father yelled at him. Scared to further anger his father, the child took bite after bite until only little bones remained. The meat wasn't as rancid as the boy imagined, despite its horrible origins, and the gathering grew more pleasant as the rest of the family tasted the same revelation.

Granddad reminded me of this memory many, many times when I was a child being picky about what he had served. He would say,

"Champ, if rat can taste good, so can those peas. Strong men have to *eat*, so get to it." His coaxing always worked, and I always ate what I was given. Thinking of Granddad brought a cathartic release and momentary escape from my predicament. Heeding his advice, and knowing that I would need my strength, I crawled over to the tray and forked oversized cheek-filling portions into my mouth. The stew was hot and thick, burning as it slid down my throat. I washed it down voraciously with the glass of milk Charlie had left.

I stared at the remains of my dinner while my mind tried to decipher what it meant. Stew indicated evening perhaps, or at the very earliest lunch. Without windows, I had no sense of time, and hoped I could use my meals to track how many days I spent locked up. It was only a shred of knowledge, but I was clinging to anything. I still had no idea where I was, or how many hours I had been unconscious. My clothes were still damp from the parking lot tussle, so I couldn't have been out for too long.

Frustration overwhelmed me as I thought of Cara. I had to escape and get back to her. My strength reignited, I began to search the room once more. The door was impenetrable, but I hadn't checked the walls. I walked slowly around the entire perimeter, and knocked lightly every foot or so. Each knock thudded flat. No hollowness could be heard. I checked the walls of the bathroom as well. Nothing. Running out of walls, I became desperate and repeated my bathroom sweep, this time knocking every four inches. Straining to hear, I was at last rewarded with a distinctly higher sound. Tracing it, I realized there must have been a small, boarded up window there. Excited, I ran into the bedroom to look for anything I could use to make a hole in the wall.

Since everything but the bed linens and lampshade were bolted down, I thought about breaking a leg off the bed. Too noisy. I contemplated wrapping the sheets around my hand or foot to pound my way out, but same problem. If I didn't get through within the first few blows, the disturbance would bring in the guards and I would be moved or chained up. Turning to the only other objects in the room, I grabbed my dinner fork and ran back to the bathroom. It was a thick, old-fashioned utensil, and my first few scrapes effectively removed the paint and created a sizable gouge. The sound was slight, but still audible. Between every scrape I froze and listened for some reaction. Nothing but silence.

Working diligently for I wasn't sure how long, I managed to etch through the hard plaster layer, but only a small hole about half an inch deep. I hid the bits of plaster and powdery drywall crumbs in the toilet. Creating a weapon was never my intention, but after hundreds of scrapes against the rough plaster, the handle of the fork shaved into a dagger shape. The fork wasn't the only tool being modified by my work, as puffy blisters formed on my thumb and forefinger.

I eventually tore off part of the white bed sheet and wrapped it around the fork to lessen blister damage and alleviate some of the pain. The added protection allowed me to continue working, but the pain only dulled slightly and my blisters popped.

After gaining another half inch, the drywall fell away and revealed darkness behind. Using my fingers, I felt around inside the small hole and found the space vacant. With excitement, I pinched my fingers hard and braced myself to break away more of the wall, but quickly realized it was far too strong. The noise and mess would've been obvious. I decided to cautiously bide my time and return to the scraping method. I had just started rewrapping the knife when the clang of the lock being slid open echoed in the room. I quickly put the fork in the waistband of my pants and covered it with my shirt. I tossed the remnant of sheet in the sink. Barely making it back into the bedroom before Charlie walked in, I stood strategically between he and the bathroom.

Sadly staring at the ground as he took small, careful steps, he couldn't see the expression on my face as I reacted to what he carried in. Piled in his large arms were several changes of clothes. On top of the pile was what looked like a large red dog collar with a black box attached to it. As he put the clothes on the bed and opened the collar using a key, I realized I was the dog. Charlie didn't want to put it on me. He hesitated, and couldn't look me in the face. "Please come here," he asked in a soft voice that made me believe he was even younger.

The humiliation of wearing a dog collar was nothing compared to the fear of what the black box did. I'd seen something like it once before being used by a rancher to stop his dogs from chasing livestock. It was a shock collar. Human instinct fought my logic and every ounce of anguish ached to fight back. I stood still and refused to walk near him. Giving me only a few seconds to comply, Charlie walked towards me with the collar stretched wide in his two burly hands.

I thought about how easy it would be to extract the fork dagger from my waist and plunge it into his chest or slice open his throat. I could grab the jingling keys at his side and run for the door. It was a good plan. Even if Jeremiah waited on the other side of the door, I would have the element of surprise working for me. My heart pounded and sweat pooled in my palms as I thought through every motion. Charlie approached and I began to reach for my makeshift knife, but I made the mistake of looking him straight in the eyes.

What I saw stopped me cold. Charlie was drowning in desperation. He despised the task placed on him, but he had no other choice. He was acting on orders, and I knew I couldn't take his life, not when he wasn't directly threatening mine. I might have been more determined and willing to draw blood if I hadn't a plan already in the works.

Taking me by the shoulder, he held me still as he attached the heavy collar around my neck. I didn't struggle or say a word. He carefully made sure it fit securely, but also asked me twice if it was too tight, a gesture I appreciated. Releasing me as soon as he could, Charlie collected my dinner dishes.

I watched him carefully as he placed the empty glass on the tray. I waited nervously to see if he noticed the missing fork, but he didn't, and as the door closed behind him I exhaled a huge breath of relief. No one died, and I still had hope of breaking free.

Tugging at my new collar invigorated me once again. I rewrapped the fork and went back to work. Before too long, the hole was big enough to use the back end of the fork as a pry bar. This removed inches at a time, and I progressed quickly. As handfuls of white wall innards fell, I could fit my entire hand through. I reached inside and my fingertips met the glorious feeling of cold glass. Covering my hand with my mouth to stop the urge to shout for joy, I worked double time, paying little attention to any noise I was making. Once the opening was large enough, I used both hands to break away the drywall in chunks.

At last I was staring at my own reflection in a window just large enough for a man to crawl though. Pressing my nose against it and using my hands to shield the light from inside the room, I strained to see the outside world. A large wall of clouds dulled the stars of a pitch black, moonless night. A few faint lights could be seen in the distance, but I couldn't see the ground beneath the window.

My bedroom prison was not on the first floor. The distance to the ground was nigh impossible to gauge in the dark. I could have been fifty feet above or just ten, but it didn't matter. Until the sun came out at least a smidgen to answer the question, I risked unintentional suicide.

Covered in the fine gypsum dust filling the air, I washed my hands and face in the sink. My body limped sore and tired. Pulling the blanket off the bed, I drug it into the bathroom and curled into a ball under the window. I couldn't let myself fall asleep. I needed to be ready to leap from the window the second light touched it.

CHAPTER 26

The colors of the sky arrived slowly. The unchanging void I had been staring at for hours turned grey before light purple. By the time pinks morphed in, I was heartbroken. The window revealed I was either on the third floor, or in the attic of a tall brick home. A jump from this height would have killed me. I cursed and kicked the wall. All that work was pointless since I wasn't ready to die. Returning to the bed with the blanket, I lay down and closed my eyes. I knew I had to come up with another escape plan, but that required the use of my uselessly exhausted brain. I mustered just enough foresight to tuck the fork in between the wall and the mattress before sleep found me.

I dreamt of being choked to death. A man held his hands firmly around my neck, squeezing the life out of me. I struggled to pry off his large hands, but found it impossible...

I awoke with a start as Charlie came through the door. He was carrying another tray of food, but this time he wasn't staring at the floor. His face was blasted by shock as he looked towards the bathroom. The once dimly lit room was full of streaming morning sunshine.

He put the tray down on the nightstand and rushed towards my escape attempt. It was too late to hide what I had done, so I just stayed in bed and waited to see his reaction. He did not move or make a sound. I kept anticipating him to yell for Jeremiah, or run out of the room or tackle me, but nothing happened. He came back into the bedroom, stood at the end of the bed, and said, "Eat and change yer clothes, please." I nodded eagerly, and as he closed the big door, I ran to the window. I wanted badly to see the outside world in full light.

We were in the mountains. Snow frosted evergreens surrounded the house and beyond. From the high angle of the window, I could see a tall, black iron fence skirted most of the property, and beyond it a dirt road. Any other day I might have found the Zen landscape beautiful, but standing in a window too high to escape from while sporting a shock collar, all I could do was curse it. I wanted to be free, and all my work on the window hadn't gotten me any closer. My only hope now was that Jeremiah would be assigned to my care. I still had my weapon, and he was one man I wouldn't mind killing.

The clothes Charlie had dropped off the night before were still on the bed, crumpled into a ball from being slept on. As I touched the brown wool slacks, I wondered how old they were, and which dead man had worn them before. They itched as I slid them over my skin, and they were too short, leaving my ankles exposed. Much like the pants, the creamy button down shirt from the same time period reeked of starch and mothballs. It was tailored for a much shorter man, and barely ran past my elbows, leaving my tattoo out in the open. It suddenly felt odd to have it exposed. I was thinking about putting my dirty shirt back on despite its stench when the door opened behind me.

"I hear someone has been a naughty boy." Her voice grated like sandpaper on flesh. Turning around, I was amused by what I saw. In the bright light of the sun, all of her frailties were amplified. Still armed with her cane and guarded on either side by her henchmen, she took her customary seat in the one chair.

"I thought the room could use a little light. I hope you don't mind, I took the liberty." Granny may have had control of me physically, but mentally I retained an annoying bit.

"Please, don't act civilized. I know you clawed at the wall like a caged animal. Look at your hands, all blisters and blood. Since you're still here though, I can only assume you're spineless. Even that weak mother of yours had the nerve to make the leap. Cost her a broken back, but at least she wasn't the coward her son turned out to be."

After her vicious words, my entire perception of the bedroom changed. This had been the torture chamber of my Mother's childhood. It was her bed, her sink, and her window that had been cruelly sealed. Upon hearing of her jump, I bent over with the pain of her horrible upbringing. I had stared out that same window, and if she had jumped it was because she wanted to die, not escape. Hatred consumed me as I thought of my Mother's life, of Cara's worries, and of being robbed of the answers I needed direly. All of it radiated from the evil harridan only ten feet away.

I wanted her to feel pain. I wanted to rip the wicked harpy into rags. Without contemplating repercussions, I leapt at her.

I wasn't sure who pushed the button, but when I was within an inch of her tiny white neck, pain struck from the collar and blazed its way through my body to my toes. Before I hit the ground a memory took me.

Reaching the roof, I could barely hold on to the broom in my tiny blackened hand. The other chimney sweep boys were yelling bad names at me because I was small. "I can lick you all!!" I yelled. Masters could be heard walking streets and calling for the boys to come down because lightning was near. Crawling on all fours, I made for the edge of the roof. I peeked my head over the edge, "Can I come down too?" The Master snapped at me and said, "Stay there while I talk to the proprietor."

I waited alone as I wished to be with the other boys who had obeyed and were safe on the ground. Pacing and counting, I had just made my twelfth turn when the brightest light I'd ever seen flashed at the far end of the roof, ripping fiery hot light through my body.

I awoke flat on my back staring at the ceiling. My skin felt charred beneath the collar, and my toes and fingers tingled. Knowing she would eventually do it, I thought I was prepared for the shock, but I wasn't prepared to lapse so fully.

Lying there, I noticed the room's quietness and hoped I was alone. When at last I did sit up, I found Granny gone, and Charlie sitting in her place.

"Are you OK?" he asked, choosing to look at his brown work boots instead of me.

"Can't say that I'm OK, but I am alive at least."

Standing up, I walked to the bathroom and rinsed my face with cold water, avoiding the window's view. Thinking of my mother's suicide attempt was not an emotional journey I wanted to take. I half expected Charlie to be gone by the time I got back into the bedroom, but he was still there. "Am I on twenty-four hour surveillance now?"

"No, just wanted to make sure you were OK." They were the most words he had ever said to me, and the slowness of them hinted he wasn't very bright, or perhaps hailed from a part of the country where they spoke in such a way.

I thanked him for his concern, still hoping someday I'd convince him to help me escape. He only seemed saddened by my gratitude, and he stood up and left.

I crawled into the bed and pulled my fork-knife from its hiding place. I thought about using it to remove the collar, but that would be a temporary solution. Granny would only replace it and have the room searched for what I had used to remove it. I hung onto the knife as if my life hinged on it, the only control I had left. If I lapsed every time she hit the button, she'd defeat me mentally as well. I was losing the battle. The thought of never seeing Cara again welled heavy tears.

I wondered how many months or years she would keep me captive. While it was likely I would outlive her if she didn't kill me, I knew a rapidly diminishing number of partially sane days remained. I tried not to think about how every locked up day rotted into one less I would share with my beloved wife.

I sobbed openly. I cried for Cara, my mother, myself, Granddad, my father's violent end, and even found tears for all the horrific memories in my head. I cried until my eyes were swollen shut, salt burned my cheeks, and snot fountained from my nose. When Charlie returned with food hours later, I didn't stop my wails.

I lay paralyzed in that bed for days, finding no strength or will to do anything else. I only got up to eat when Charlie pleaded. Going for broke one day, I begged him to set me free, but he said no.

"Why not Charlie? I know you're a good man."

"Jeremiah would cut my throat and bury me in da yard with all dem other folks."

I wasn't the only one living in fear, and I wondered how many bodies were buried back there.

"But we could leave *together* Charlie. I have a lot of money - *a lot* - and I can help you start a *whole new life*. You don't have to do what Granny and Jeremiah say anymore."

He simply shook his head and left. Alone with my thoughts, I understood why Granny put Charlie in charge of me instead of Jeremiah. She knew from the start I wouldn't have the heart to take his life.

After all of my sorrow spilt into the sheets and soaked the mattress, the only emotions I had left were determination and hatred. When Charlie arrived the next morning with breakfast, I was prepared.

"Charlie, I have an idea. Could you bring me a piece of paper and a pen? Because if you can, I can write a letter to my wife telling her where to find me. She can bring *help*, and when the police show up I will tell them that none of this was your fault. Granny and Jeremiah will be arrested and hauled away to prison forever. What do you think?" I could see him thinking it through as he set my tray down in its normal spot.

"I would go to jail too," he said.

"No, you wouldn't. I could convince them that you were innocent all along." I put my hand on his shoulder, but he shied away from it.

"I done other stuff," he admitted painfully.

"None of that matters anymore. It'll be OK."

He sat down and stared blubbering, "You would hate me if you knew what I done. You would hate me."

"Charlie, I'm not going to hate you. Just tell me. You can tell me."

"I killed your pa. I killed 'im. I'm sorry but dey made me. I was wearing da collar and real hungry, and dey made me do it. He said it was OK though. He said it was OK."

I couldn't help but feel deeply repulsed by his admission. The man was still my father, regardless of my mother's murder and the fact that I had spent the last several years building a wall of hatred for him. I stood there and frowned at the crying man-child, and couldn't help but find empathy for him. He had been trapped like me, and the only one to blame was Granny.

Putting my hand back on his shoulder, I spoke kindly. "I don't hate you Charlie. My father was a very sick man, and it sounds like you gave him the peace he deserved. Nobody can put you in jail for something you were forced to do, and I'll make sure of it."

Recovering a bit, he wiped the tears from his eyes and looked me straight in the face. "I will get da paper." An enormous sigh of relief left me.

Agreeing that he should wait until my normal feeding time to bring the supplies, Charlie departed.

The wait for lunch seemed to last two days, and I paced the floor to pass the time, imagining what I would write. It felt good to envision Cara reading my letter. When at last I heard the lock undone, I rushed to the door and jumped up and down like a kid at Christmas, but the joy was cut short when a loathsome creature appeared. I fumbled back a few steps. Without so much as a grunt, Jeremiah took two steps past the doorway and carelessly dropped a plastic bowl on the ground, spilling half its contents onto the floor. He left and slammed the door behind him.

Tiny waves of tomato soup slipped over the edges of the teetering bowl and I wondered, *Why the change?* I tried to stay optimistic, telling myself Charlie must have had other duties. My darker voice was convinced he had gotten caught with my supplies and I'd never see him again.

I tried to eat the soup, but too many of my relatives had eaten soup when destitute, and their bleak memories sickened any real appetite away. Faced with the potential of being alone in my struggle, I retrieved my fork dagger and slipped it into the waistband of the ill-fitting pants. Knowing I wouldn't see anyone else for hours, I sat on the floor of the bathroom and stared out the window.

I memorized the view. The trees, birds, black gate, and dirt road burned into my skull. Trying not to fixate on my own doomed state or whatever happened to Charlie, I let the part of my mind that controlled the memories relax. Hundreds of them faded in and out in fast waves. They were all based around random images of the outdoors, many of them from hunting trips. The backdrops reshaped from lush greens to rocky prairies and back again, and the experience passed almost enjoyably.

When dinner arrived in the hands of Jeremiah, I barely scoffed at it before returning to my safe haven at the window.

Charlie wasn't coming back. One missed feeding could be explained away, but two meant something more. I hoped Granny had simply banned him from caring for me, but with her I had come to expect the worst. She had left me with only one option. I had to kill Jeremiah. But how?

Plotting and planning all night meant I barely slept. For hours I tried in vain to cut the collar off, but the leather was tough and the wires inside were encased in heavy plastic. Giving up, I lay in the bed and waited. As soon as the room started to lighten, I took my position at the door.

Holding my breath, I could hear his heavy, measured footsteps as he neared. My heart pounded in exact time with his footfalls.

As he opened the lock, I gripped my dagger so hard that the sweat from my palms dripped down my wrist. The door swung open and I plunged forward and stuck the fork handle through his blue shirt into his chest. The surprise force knocked him backwards onto the ground, taking my breakfast tray and me with him. As I scrambled to my feet, I could feel him doing the same. Both of us slipped on the oatmeal puddle, but I found footing first.

I was at the end of a long hallway that led to stairs. Running blindly, I'd made my way to the first stair when the familiar shock coursed through my body, knocking me limp. I started lapsing into the chimney sweep memory again before I hit the stairs.

CHAPTER 27

All hope in me died. I gambled every trick I could think of and failed miserably. Lying on the floor covered in oatmeal and sweat, I curled into a ball and gave up. I knew I was doomed to be my Grandmother's pet until she died. Sunrises and sunsets went by and I let them. With no reason to stop, I dropped my guard and let my relative's memories overtake me. I drifted in and out of the past aimlessly and welcomed the distractions, unsure of who or where I was for days. Insanity felt better than reality.

During my disconnect, I barely moved and ate only when Jeremiah forced food down my throat. Grandmother came and visited a few times, but I could no longer play her games. I sat silent while she screamed callous insults. I tolerated her merciless beatings with the cane. Every visit ended with a brutal shock from my collar, and the pain came as a relief because I would lapse into elsewhere.

My only remaining sense of focus became lapsing, and I nearly perfected forcing it on command. I spent hours conjuring up other people's happy memories and allowed myself to get sucked in like a deep meditation, only coming back out when forced by the jarring clang of the door bolt. In my madness, I had found a way to find false happiness.

During sleep however, I tormented. I couldn't control my dreams. They were always about Cara or Granddad. While I kept myself distracted externally, my inner self desperately missed them. I worried constantly about Cara being alone. Or worse, what if Granny had gone after her? I awoke several times each night screaming Cara's name. I cuddled with my pillow, imagining that if I pretended to be spooning with her somehow she could feel it.

Lost in my strange new pattern of existence, I lost track of days and braved few hours in reality. Many times I shifted from a lapse to find myself in front of the window with my whole body pressed against it. Without too much concern, I wondered if at some point I would manage to jump out and kill myself. Contemplating the pros and cons, something shiny caught my attention out of the window. The sun was bouncing off the rearview mirror of a dark car parked on the road just beyond the gate. It was too far away to discern if there were people inside, but I couldn't let my only opportunity pass me by.

Running over to the bed, I grabbed the torn bed sheet. The memories I had been welcoming were creeping back in, and I struggled to maintain the focus to push them away. Returning to the window, I kicked it out. The breaking glass crashed loudly, and I knew someone would hear it. Large shards sliced my exposed ankles as I pushed the glass through the window onto the ground below. I flung half the sheet out the window and waved it wildly, ignoring the blood seeping into my shoes.

The car sat there, and no one got out. I screamed and waved and screamed and waved, "HELP! OVER HERE! HELP!"

Then I watched as the car forwarded onto the road, leaving a cloud of dusty, useless hope in its wake. I shouted with all my throat in one last attempt, but they either didn't see me or didn't care. It didn't matter. I was left in the same hell, only now with bloody ankles. Granny's powerful contempt of my father had warped her, and she had won. She didn't want to just own me, she wanted me to suffer, and I did.

I cursed her and my father. She may have degenerated into a twisted hand of false justice, but my whole life was painted with the brush my father had held. I went over the list in my head. My genetics were deformed - his fault. My mother was dead - his fault. My wife was suffering - his fault. I would become hopelessly crazy and die alone - his fault. Any love I had still held for my father, I murdered in that moment.

At first I considered cleaning my wounds and making bandages out of the sheet, but my will to live and be healthy had expired. I sat in the pink chair and let my blood spill where it wished. I didn't move when the door opened and Jeremiah entered the room.

"See, I told you he was too gutless to kill himself." Granny tottered into the bathroom to inspect the damage with Jeremiah at her side. I stared at the open door, tempted to run out, but I knew I would only get a few steps into the hallway before the shock. When they turned back into the room, she observed the cuts on my ankles. She began giving Jeremiah instructions on how to care for the wounds when I interrupted.

"Why not just let me die?"

They had become accustomed to my comatose silence, and the sound of my voice surprised them both. Collecting herself and pulling her folds of skin into a smile, she exposed her true, malevolent nature.

"Now what fun would *that* be? And besides, I take care of my possessions, even if they are sniveling little brats." I could feel detest welling up like bitter vomit, except it wasn't collecting in my gut this time. It was in my veins.

"How did my mother ever come out of such a crazy bitch?"

It was a rhetorical question. She answered brutally by administering blow after blow to my ankles with her cane. The tiny chips of glass snagged in the lacerations slashed deeper into my skin. The devastating pain dropped me to the floor, and I could see blood smears on her cane as she hobbled out.

I wasn't sure if I had lapsed or fallen asleep, or both, but I awoke very startled. It was the first time I had heard any sounds from the rest of the house, and I could clearly hear yelling. Unable to stand, I dragged myself to the door and pushed my ear to it.

In a shrill, panicked voice I could clearly hear Grandmother shrieking, "Kill him! Kill him now!" Her order was followed immediately by loud footsteps running toward my room. I pushed my back against the door as I felt Jeremiah struggle against it. He tried ramming it with his shoulder, but I had just enough strength to shove it closed again. He took several steps back to hit the door again and I braced myself.

The sound of a single gunshot rang through the house. At first I thought it was Jeremiah trying to shoot me through the door, but then I heard him fall. My ears filled joyously with the sounds of several people running through the hall towards him.

"Help me!" I cried. "In here! I'm in here!" Seconds later I was being assisted by several policemen.

"Thank you," was all I could choke out as they examined my ankles and tried to keep me still.

"Please don't move, sir. We'll bring a stretcher up here to move you."

"No!! Get me out of this room right now! I'm OK, really I'm OK. Just help me up and get me out of this room right now. Please!"

The officers looked at each other and agreed my desperation trumped protocol. They slid their arms around me and hoisted me into a standing position. They hurriedly carried me down the hallway to the stairs. As we descended, I looked over the banister. On the floor below, officers gathered around the body of my grandmother, a large puddle of crimson on the floor extending to a pistol near her hand. The image hit too similar, and I instantly lapsed into the memory of my mother's death...

When I returned from watching my mother die yet again, I waited to open my eyes, hoping I was really saved and hadn't dreamt it.

"Chamberlain?" asked Cara, and instantly my fears flew away. Opening my eyes, I saw her beautiful face and reached for her, but my arms were strapped down. My eyes bulged in panic a second before I realized we rode in an ambulance. Seeing my efforts, Cara leaned down and nuzzled my cheek with her nose and spoke to me softly, "You're alright now. I'm here with you. Please try and sleep."

I felt myself fuzzily dozing from a sedative, but before my tongue slouched I flubbed, "Dadzin da backyard, maybe Charleee." Allowing the weight of my eyelids to win, I heard Cara say, "Libby, have them check the backyard for bodies."

Pain eventually woke me. My ankles burned and the rest of my body ached like I'd been pressed in a car compactor. Cara sat in a chair next to my hospital bed, asleep with her head cradled on my right arm. I stroked her beautiful black hair and pushed it off her face. A few moments later, she woke up and kissed my arm.

"I'm so sorry I didn't get you out of there sooner." Her tears dripped on my arm.

"Cara my love, don't blame yourself for something you couldn't control. I thought I would never see you again." I leaned over slowly and kissed her cheek. She straightened up and half smiled.

"I know this isn't the most romantic thing to say, but I *really* need to go to the bathroom." I reached down to pull the blankets off my legs when Cara jumped up and stopped me. "I need to get a nurse to help you. You can't put weight on your legs yet." Looking down, I found both legs bandaged from my toes to my calves. Cara pressed the call button on the wall.

"Chamberlain, the damage to your ankles was really bad, and they had to perform surgery to repair some tendons. The doctor said you'd be walking again in no time with rehabilitation." She tried to smile but frowned. "But you lost a lot of blood, and the scars on your neck will be permanent." I reached my hand to my neck. More bandages. Without the collar, my neck felt wholly unfamiliar and completely welcome.

While explaining each detail, guilt coated Cara's voice, which confused me.

After the relatively mild embarrassment of having two female nurses carry me to the bathroom and back, Cara helped me resettle into bed while I asked her exactly what had happened the day I was rescued. "I have to tell you the full story to explain that day. Are you up to it, or do you want to sleep some more?"

"I think I'll sleep better if I know the whole thing."

She nodded and gave me a kiss. The soft push of her lips against mine nearly made me pass out as I relinquished myself to the bliss. She caressed my cheek as she pulled away.

"Well, when you didn't come home, I obviously went looking for you. I couldn't believe your car was still at the prison, and unlocked. Inside, next to your cell phone was a letter. At first I hoped it was a note from you, but when I opened it the first thing I saw was Amber's name at the bottom."

Totally confused, I interrupted.

"You're telling me Amber had something to do with this?"

"I'll get there, just listen. The letter was from Amber, and in it she wrote that she couldn't live with what you had done to her, and that you needed to die. She said her brothers agreed to help her and that we would never see you again. Naturally, I freaked out and called the cops. So, they showed up and fingerprinted your car, questioned everyone around, and even pulled the surveillance video from the parking lot. The video was grainy, but plainly showed you being taken by a woman and two men.

"That's when the search for both you *and* Amber began. It took days before the police were able to figure out that either Amber wasn't a real person, or the person pretending to be Amber was using a fake name. Then they were out of leads and had no idea how to even begin looking for you, but I couldn't shake the feeling that this had more to do with your father than anyone realized.

"I went to the only person who knew everything that was going on, Libby.

My eyebrows popped up.

"It wasn't pleasant, but I would have done anything to save you."

I laughed softly as I pictured the two of them working together, but Cara kept talking. "And now I'm glad I did because, well, it worked. I told Libby about Amber not being a real person, and she demanded we go straight to the prison. When we got there, she forced them to give her a list of all the guards and officials who worked at the prison when your father was there. We cross-referenced it with those still employed at the facility and ended up with only three names. Libby insisted that we be given contact info for all of them, but she had to bribe two guards heavily to get it. After a lot of money and some really sketchy meetings, we found one taker.

"The man is named Dale Harkins, and he is a total slimeball. We had to pay him ten thousand dollars and fly him out of the country to get him to give us the truth, and it still was like pulling teeth. *He* was the guard who took money from your Grandmother years ago in exchange for your father, and everything was cool until you started searching for him. When Libby started showing up at the prison, Dale got nervous. He knew your grandmother intended to kill your father, and he didn't want to get in trouble for releasing him and destroying his records, so Dale went back to her for help.

"Your Grandmother had devised a devilish plan. It so happened that Dale had a niece with drug problems who was always looking for money. Her name was Courtney, but we knew her as Amber. Your Grandmother hired her to seduce you and then scapegoat her for your disappearance."

"That's horrible. Where is she now?"

"Nobody knows. They can't find her...

"Anyways, I was so terrified that they had already killed you, but Libby kept telling me that if they wanted you dead, they would have done it in the parking lot. So when we went to the cops, I expected them to jump in their cars and go after you, but they wouldn't. We didn't have any proof that you were in the house Dale told us about, and he was gone. Without proof all they could do was go to the house and ask if they had seen you. Of course they did that and were told nothing, so I decided to go myself... You probably don't want to hear all of this do you?"

"No, I mean, yes. Yes, please tell me. It's just that...Wow. What happened?" I wanted to listen. I needed to. But my concentration flitted away in a deluge of terrorizing memories.

"I went to the house, and I snuck in through an open window on the first floor. I searched most of the rooms, but got caught in the kitchen by one of her goons."

"The big mean one or the slow nice one?" I asked, remembering my promises to Charlie.

Cara tilted her head, confused I would refer to one of my captors as nice."He was the nice guy, because he kept apologizing the whole time."

I exhaled somewhat reassured that it had to be Charlie. Maybe he was still alive.

"He grabbed me by the wrists and took me outside and tied me up in the car, and then he drove me to the police station and made me tell them I broke into his house. The police asked if he wanted to press charges, but he just kept saying, 'I want a piece of paper to keep her away from the house.'" Cara made a mopey face like Charlie's while she said it."I'd already been annoying the cops obsessively for weeks, so they kicked me out and threatened me with jail time if I didn't stay off the property."

"Right away Libby and I bought some binoculars and a big camera with a telephoto lens and a tripod and everything. And... I'll admit... It wasn't so bad hanging out with her, because I had come to realize we were both there because we both loved you so much. Which was good because we spent *days* watching the house together. We were there for so long I thought it was the wrong place. But something told me to keep looking, like I could *feel* you in there.

I remembered replacing her with a pillow all those lonely nights.

"There was only one side of the house we couldn't see from our hiding places in the woods, and that was the side nearest the road. So one day we decided to park there as long as we could taking pictures until someone came out, and that's when we saw you break the window out and wave that towel - the timing was perfect! We took the pictures right to the cops and that was that."

She smiled like a magician finishing a trick, kissed me eagerly and cried."I wanted to jump out of the car so bad that day, but Libby pulled me back because it was too dangerous and, and... I missed you sooo much." I wanted little else but to fall back asleep in her arms, but questions dogged my numbness.

"Did Grandmother kill herself?"

Cara wiped her face. "Yes, she did. She shot herself when they stormed the house. But they were able to arrest that one guy. That's going to be one hell of a strange trial."

I winced."What about the bodies in the backyard?"

"I still haven't heard anything, but I've been here for two days. I told the police I'd call them when you were awake. But they can wait if you want to go back to sleep."

"Go ahead and call them. But I need to tell you something before they get here."

"Sure," said Cara a little scared.

"When I was locked up in there, I tried everything I could to escape. But when it all seemed helpless, I forced my brain to lapse. It was my only way of handling it. I used it like a drug Cara, and now I'm scared I won't be able to stop the memories anymore. I've been fighting them off ever since I woke up." I had sped up the curse and there was no turning back.

"It's OK Chamberlain. We can get through this together. If that's what you needed to do to survive, I'm glad you did it. Whatever happened to you, we can fix with a little time... and, oh! That reminds me, I have a gift." She jumped to a leather bag sitting in a chair by the window. She retrieved a thickly bound, black notebook, and rubber banded to it was a smaller one. The large one I recognized immediately as my father's.

"Where did you get that?" I asked in amazement as I reached for it.

"Well, Libby wanted proof from Dale before we gave him the money. He had this stashed in case he needed to blackmail your Grandmother at some point. The police said it was all circumstantial because it's just a bunch of stories in a book, but there's some pretty horrible stuff about her in there. Looks like we both failed epically in the grandmother department." Cara wouldn't look me in the face as she talked. She had yet to ask what they had done to me, and I hoped she never would. I never wanted to subject her to the details.

I traced the hard cover with my fingers. "I hope you don't mind that I read them. After we found out who had you, I *had* to search it for information." I barely heard Cara. Holding the book, I realized I would never be able to question my father about my mother's death. I hoped an answer could be found in its pages.

"What's the little one?" I inquired.

"When they locked him up, they took away his big book, but he kept writing every day in this small one."

I set the smaller book on the bed, and opened my father's journal to read the first page. Written in Granddad's handwriting was his transcription of a tale told from the perspective of my four-year-old father. The faded ink told of chasing a toad around puddles under a sky of fluffy white clouds. I saw the day through my father's eyes, and lapsed.

The fat, warty toad wouldn't hold still. It was amazing something so fat could jump so fast. "Dad, you have to see this! Come here little froggy. Heeeere froggy. Please come here Mr. Toad, I won't hurt you."

I awoke with a pinging head on the cold hospital floor. Cara stood with her back against the door like she was guarding it. She hustled over to help me limp back into bed.

"I lapsed, didn't I?" She shook her head yes, tucking the blankets around my legs.

"I told you it's gotten worse," I faltered dejectedly. Cara started giggling. I looked at her sternly, thinking perhaps she was losing her mind too.

"I know what it means," she grinned, "and I'm glad no one else was around to see it, but... Never mind, it's inappropriate."

"What?"

She hesitated and then said quietly, "It was *so cute*. You were crawling around saying, '*Here, froggy froggy*' in a sweet little boy's voice." I couldn't help but laugh too, realizing that if we were going to deal with this damn curse the rest of our lives, the only way we'd survive would be by making light of what we could.

Picking up my father's journal again, I started flipping through the pages to find the night of my mother's death, but Cara put her hand on mine and stopped me. "You should wait until we're alone, just in case. The doctor said you could go home in just a couple of days." I didn't want to wait another second, but I had to admit Cara was right. The chances of me lapsing on my own were high enough, and retracing the worst night of my life guaranteed to fry my brain.

Pleased I had taken her advice, Cara went about inspecting my ankles, unraveling the wraps. "Just making sure you didn't rip out any stitches while you were frog hunting."

My ankles resembled puffy patchwork quilts sewn with numerous rows of blue stitches. "They look good," said Cara. "Are you ready to go back to sleep, or maybe eat something?" Feeling Cara hover over me like a mother hen, I noticed how tired, pale, and thin she looked.

"When's the last time *you* slept or ate?" I asked, reversing the role of mother hen. She tried to tell me she was fine, but I knew better. "Alright love, I have a plan. Why don't you call the police and let them know I'm awake, and then as soon they leave we'll do nothing but sleep and eat for the next month. How's that sound?" She kissed the top of my head and pulled her cell phone from her pocket.

CHAPTER 28

It didn't take long for two detectives to arrive, and the first thing they did was piss off Cara. She already held serious animosity towards them for not listening to her leads, so when they asked her to leave the room, I thought she'd go raging into beast attack mode. I interjected before her transformation took place.

"I'll only speak to you if she's allowed to stay."

They nodded in unison, and Cara sat in the chair with her red face and clenched fists.

I didn't know for sure how involved the two men had been, but their stiff faces and jittery movements illustrated they were well aware of Cara's involvement. I just wanted to be done with the whole mess, so instead of yelling at them like they seemed to be expecting, I smiled, "Thanks for coming." I could hear Cara grinding her teeth.

They had come to me for answers, but I had questions of my own. I asked them where I had been held captive, if they had caught Amber, and most importantly how many bodies they found in the backyard. Between the two men, one was the mouthpiece and the other recorder. Taking his time and choosing his words carefully, the mouthpiece explained, "You were being held in a little mountain town called Rye, only an hour away from the prison. We think we know where the girl is, and we're working on bringing her into custody."

Before he would answer my last and most important question, he asked, "How did you know there were bodies buried in the backyard?"

"My Granny told me she buried my father back there. And the man who was going to help me escape said he'd end up there if he got caught. I need to know if he's OK. As I spoke, the recorder scribbled furiously on his pad, appearing to catch every word.

I waited for the mouthpiece to mull over the new information. I could see conflict in him as he squinted his eyes, stretching long wrinkles across the expanse of his forehead. He clearly did not want to tell me everything he knew, but then he realized holding it back might delay him from finding more answers.

"Dr. Shay, I am sorry for your ordeal, and to answer your question, yes, we have found *four* bodies. Two appear to have been there a very long time, and one of those is a small child. The third body matches your father's description, but we can't be sure until we have DNA done."

He paused, and I thought I was going to throw up.

"The last body is an unknown male that was buried very recently."

Knowing that I was responsible for Charlie's death landed a burden I was not ready to heft. The room began to spin as layers of memories of guilt and pain forced their way into my mind. I faded elsewhere as I looked over at Cara desperately. She said, "He needs his rest. I think you two should leave *right now*."

I opened my eyes and I was still in the bed. Cara had her whole body draped over mine. Puddles of tears gathered in the creases of my neck, and I had fresh scratches on my arms. I had no idea which memory had taken me, or worse, if I had played the whole thing out in front of the detectives.

"Did they see?" At the sound of my voice, Cara sat up and crawled off the bed, holding firmly onto my arm. "Not really, you just started sobbing and yelling that it was your fault. I got them out of here pretty quickly, but they're still in the waiting room. I hope I didn't hurt you, but while you were lapsing you started to scratch really hard at your arm, so I held you down as best I could."

"I'm alright, I think. Thank you for protecting me." She smiled, but I could see a new pain in her eyes, one she couldn't hide. Cara was starting to understand how much I had deteriorated, and it frightened her. Seeing that look and thinking about Charlie made me wonder why I didn't just jump to my death when I had the chance. I grabbed her, and holding on as tight as I could I whispered, "I love you" over and over again. She stopped me, "Chamberlain, none of this is your fault."

While the detectives waited, we pulled ourselves together just enough to invite them back in, knowing that once they were done with me, we could focus on us. Shaken from witnessing a small bit of my breakdown, this time their tones differed. Where they offered only a small portion before, compassion now spilt out of them in gushes.

Their questions forced me to talk about my search for my father, and to explain exactly what happened while I was under Granny's roof. Cara stayed at my side this time, ready to kick them out at any hint of a lapse. When my recounting neared closer and closer to the physical pains I endured, my answers stumbled hesitant. I never wanted Cara to know how much pain I experienced, but for both of our sakes I couldn't chance being in the room alone with them either.

I tried to be honest, downplaying what I could. With grandmother dead and Charlie's death on Jeremiah's hands, there wasn't any reason to hurt Cara needlessly. When I had to explain the shock collar and the numerous canings, Cara made little whimpers, and her tears fell regularly.

I didn't have answers for many of their questions. I had no real idea who Jeremiah and Charlie were, or how they found themselves under Granny's sinister thumb. I also couldn't tell them the identity of the other two bodies in the yard, but I had guesses. I explained that no one knew anything of the whereabouts of my maternal grandfather. Then I told them of the abuses perpetrated on my mother, suggesting they check if the child belonged to Granny. It seemed sadly logical that if she abused her daughter and grandchild so brutally like she had, then perhaps at one point she had gone too far.

Taking my suggestions seriously, their questions ran dry. Before leaving, they asked if I had any more inquiries. I thought about it for a half minute, and while I felt the swirl of hundreds, I said no. They couldn't answer my deepest questions. No one could explain the cruelty of the old crone who shot herself. I did have one request of the detectives.

"If you find out more information on Charlie, would you please let me know? I'd like to arrange to pay his funeral expenses." Cara squeezed my arm in agreement as the mouthpiece said he would do what he could to make it happen. They left as I promised again to contact them if I remembered anything else.

With the exception of visits from doctors and nurses, the rest of the stay at the hospital passed in splendid quietude. Cara had extra blankets brought into the room so she could sleep in the chair, and she never left my side. I slept most of the time, and with great effort and focus I was able to ward off most of the lapses, although they continued to engage me willy-nilly without triggers. The only disruption from the outside world arrived in card form, sent by Marisa, accompanied by a gift dropped off the morning of my release.

A thin nurse walked in with a stunning clay pot, bursting with the same flowers from our wedding, undoubtedly from Briggy. I asked Cara to read me the card. "*Chamberlain, I hope you are feeling better. Come back to school immediately, we have much to discuss. If you don't, I will come to you. Take care, Professor Briggs.*"

We both chuckled, and as Cara helped me out of the hospital gown and into real clothes, something occurred to me. "How does Briggy know I am here?" At first Cara seemed not to hear me, but catching her reticent expression, it became clear she just didn't want to answer me, so I asked again.

"The press likes to write about you, and this was *one helluva story*. When I went to the cafeteria yesterday, your agent called and asked if he should send any of the condolence letters from fans." First I felt angry that once again my private life had risen into the public parade, but the annoyance faded as I hoped to eventually use the attention to proclaim Charlie a hero.

Cara pulled away from the hospital, and I reached for my father's notebook. I knew I couldn't read it in the car - too dangerous - but I wanted to be ready as soon as I set foot inside the door. Cara noticed I was impatiently fidgeting, and she tried to fill the hour-long drive with conversation.

"I really need to thank Libby for everything she's done."

Cara let out a hearty laugh. "Aren't you a little curious as to where we are going?" Looking out the window, the scenery confused me. I had assumed we were headed for our little apartment, but the cedars and spacious pastures told me otherwise. I asked Cara to explain.

"Nope. It's a surprise."

After a few turns and ten minutes more it dawned on me.

"The new house?" I asked, and Cara nodded, grinning hugely like she might implode.

"How is that possible? We haven't even made an offer or signed any paperwork or anything."

She explained it all in one word: "Libby."

"I don't think she's human," Cara said as if she were a scientist. "Because humans require sleep, and that girl never stops." I smiled a real smile and couldn't wait to thank her personally.

"Maybe it's the tepid lattes?"

Cara's half serious glare proved that while they once worked together for me, they shared no lasting love between them.

It wasn't much longer before we pulled up to our new home, with Libby's blue Volvo parked in the driveway. Unaccustomed to using crutches, it took a while for me to get out of the car, and Libby came out to greet us. With her arms crossed in front of her chest, she waited for us on the porch.

"Hello Libby," I smiled as we approached, and as she responded "Hello" rather stiffly, she held open the front door. "I didn't have a lot of time, so this will have to do." Dazed by my new home, it became clear that a lot of time or just a little didn't change the quality of Libby's work.

She had not only taken care of purchasing the house with free use of my bank account, but also found the time to have it completely furnished with both new items and all the remaining items from our storage units. Decorated in a rustic, wood cabin style, Libby had matched my wishes for the place without a hint of input. Cara seemed to feel the same, praising every item she touched. I wanted to explore the entire place, but the pain in my ankles stopped me. I helped myself to the large reclining chair facing the hearth fireplace.

"So, what do you think?" Libby asked.

"I think you are incredible, and I will never be able to thank you enough for everything you've done, including help save my life." Her weasel smile lit up her face, but she answered in her typical cool style, "Oh please, what was I going to do, let you die? And besides, if you died, how would I get that glowing letter of recommendation? Consider what I've done here as my going away present."

"Wait, what? You're leaving? Where are you going?"

"I always thought solving the great mysteries of history would make me happy, but as I worked on them it felt stupid. I now see they are pointless things that don't really make a difference to anyone." I wanted to interrupt and defend the work of myself and all other historians, but I knew exactly what she meant. I bit my lip. "But when I worked on finding you, I felt like I was doing something important -something for *today's* history. So I decided I'm going to change degrees and become a criminal investigator."

Without a doubt I knew right away the law enforcement sector fit Libby perfectly.

"I'm very happy for you Libby, and I'm willing to bet you'll be the most formidable detective on the squad. Thank you so much for everything you have done for my family and me. My life would have been so much harder - hell, my life wouldn't even exist if it weren't for you."

While I spoke she swelled up with pride, pulling at the bottom of her blouse as she tried to maintain her professional tact. For a split second I saw something else leak through. It was sadness, and I couldn't help but wonder if losing me to Cara still caused her grief. I hoped not.

After filling us in on all the details of the house purchase and showing Cara all the paperwork, Libby announced it was time for her to go. Standing up on my crutches, I extended my hand to her. She shook it hard like a man. She turned to Cara.

"Take care of him White Trash."

"I will, and thanks again Tepid Low Fat," Cara quipped.

The sound of her high heels disappeared out the door as she called out, "I'll keep in touch."

With the house quiet, Cara went to the car and retrieved my father's books. She sat on the arm of the chair and kissed me. "I'm going to make some lunch while you start reading."

Adrenaline pulsed through me as I opened the book. At last I would find out which memory caused my father to kill my mom, and hopefully why he never tried to contact me after he fled. At last I would know the truth.

It was pointless to read the first two thirds for what I wanted, as all of the memories he had made during that time were already in my head. Only the facts after my conception interested me. I flipped through the pages until I found the time period I wanted and eagerly began.

CHAPTER 29

I selfishly needed two full weeks to read it, not because of particularly long or hard to decipher content, but heavy lapses kept cutting in, and I'd lose hours each day flailing in the swamps of other people's lives. I set a fire to the front room floor. I hid in closets. I ranted incessantly. One day I believed Cara turned into a naughty toddler, and I spanked her and force-fed her pickle relish. The Shay bloodline brimmed with derangement.

When I first started reading the book, I assumed I'd find insight into the workings of my father's mind. I was mostly wrong. His book revolved around my mother.

Father worried about her. After becoming pregnant with me, she obsessed. Her every moment and thought centered on being The Perfect Mother. At first he wasn't sure if she modeled the normal, overly cautious behavior of a new mother, or if she desperately fought her fear of becoming one.

After I was born, Father changed. While he still loved his wife very much, his center of the universe shifted to me. His description of the first time he held me read more beautifully than any words I'd ever seen, and made me feel intensely loved.

The serenity of that day didn't last long. My father was mired in worry about Mother. Every day she became more and more obsessed with perfection, and to her that meant making sure I never felt *any* physical pain.

Father wrote a vivid description of the day I was supposed to go to the doctor's office for vaccinations. She fought him for hours, begging and pleading that I didn't need the shots. He insisted it was for my own good, and she violently threw a plate at him and it shattered on the wall. She wouldn't change her mind.

One day he snuck me to the doctor's office using the pretense we were headed to the park for a play date.

Slowly, passage by passage, he elucidated her snowballing irrational fears. Every time I cried she'd panic, convinced something fatally serious loomed. Brand new baby clothes were thrown out because Mom claimed they scratched me. Windows were shielded by heavy drapes because she thought the sun hurt my eyes. With each new day, more issues arose. Father somehow found superhuman patience, and when he wasn't working, he spent every waking hour trying to relieve her fears, ensuring her decaying sanity wasn't affecting me too much.

As years went by, my father suffered immense conflict in loving both his wife and his son. He knew she couldn't continue her overbearing behavior without negatively affecting me long term, so he laid down an ultimatum. Either she would go to a therapist, or he would leave and take me with him.

He described giving her that choice as the most difficult thing he had ever done, and admitted later he scarcely managed to front the veiled threat. He earnestly did not believe he had the strength to leave her.

Luckily a nonissue, she took him seriously and sought help, and for a few years it alleviated most issues. Thanks to weekly hours on a couch and prescribed sedatives, Mother relaxed enough to give me a life not so much normal, but not harmful. During those good years Father unfortunately began experiencing problems with the curse, or as he called it, "the affliction."

Mother had always been very understanding about his condition, but with me around she grew more and more concerned he might unknowingly hurt me during an episode. He doubly shared her concerns, and did what he could to never be alone with me.

At the end of the good times came a revelation. In a very long and painful excerpt, Father described the day he figured out I had the affliction.

Knowing our history, he always worried about it being passed to me, but his optimism kept him believing it would skip a generation. His hope died the day I drew a picture of a house that had burned down two hundred years before I was born. Devastated, father's guilt crippled him for burdening another living soul with the hell he knew inevitable. For months he mourned what he had done, never telling my mother what he had learned. As I grew and started to articulate extraordinary extracts of history, he knew he had to tell her.

Father decided to take her out to dinner to share the dismal news. Not knowing how badly she'd react, he chose a very busy restaurant. A terrifying night for him, Dad didn't know if she would flip out and leave forever, kill herself, kill him, or be the sweet person he knew her to be.

He seemed very confused by her reaction. Once he told her, she did not respond. He gave her a few minutes to process what he had said, but she dumbfounded him by changing the subject to the new carpet she wanted. When he tried again to bring it up, she dismissed him like he wasn't talking at all. After much pondering, Dad eventually came to the conclusion her brain just couldn't handle it, so she blocked it out. Unfortunately, he was wrong.

Three years passed before he found out what she really thought that night, until the night of my ninth birthday. The day started like all others. He kissed his lovely wife and son goodbye before leaving for work. When he returned home, an ideal birthday cake graced the table, and everyone warmed the room with good spirits under the candlelight. He plucked out my smoking birthday candles and reached for the trash when everything fell apart.

In the trashcan sat several boxes of rat poison, resting casually on top of an empty box of cake mix. Chilled by the horror, my father knew why she kept so quiet that night, and acted so aloof and at ease the last few years. She had a plan all along.

He never described the physical struggle between them, or how she ultimately died. I believed those details were too painful for him to put into words. Fearful of what would happen to me, in its place he wrote about the disbelief he felt when he saw her despicable plan take shape. He admitted over and over he would have eaten the cake if it had just been the two of them. With me in the picture, he had no choice but to survive. Deep down, he loved me more than her. He swore he loved me more than himself, and loving his soul mate less than his child stung a difficult epiphany within.

When I finished reading what actually occurred, I remembered Granddad. For years I fought with him to take a stance against my father, and now I understood why he held his ground. Although difficult to swallow at first, I admired Granddad's honor. It would have been so easy for him to tell me the truth, but in doing so he would have tarnished my feelings for my mother. Father was the martyr of my love for her, and myself as well. I finally understood all too well the words Granddad passed on the night he died:

"Haven't you learned by now that memories don't tell a full story?"

My memory of Mom's terrible death, which I had clung to for years, told me only a facet of history, a limited truth I had chosen to believe.

After Cara and I discussed what had occurred between my parents, she asked if it changed my opinion of my mom.

"It might have, if I hadn't met Granny. I think if I'd found out all this years ago, I would have just flipped the blame from Dad to her. Now, thanks to Granny, I realize neither is to blame. I spent just a short amount of time in the nightmare my mother coped with for *years*. I understand why she acted the way she did. I don't believe what she did was right by any means, but I understand her actions. She had to feel permanently debased and messed up from Granny's abuse. In her sick mind she spared her child from a life of pain. I only wish she could have trusted my dad more. Perhaps together they could've worked through the fears before they turned deadly."

"That all makes sense, but you have to at least blame your Grandmother, right?" asked Cara.

"I don't. She was evil and disturbed, don't get me wrong, but she also had a choice to turn into the monster she became, and for that I do blame her. But we will never know what caused those abusive traits to begin in the first place. It doesn't really matter, they're all dead, and blame won't bring them back or distribute any justice."

"You're right," Cara agreed, "but I won't be forgiving that haggardly old bitch anytime soon."

"Me either babe, but I have to try. Blame and forgiveness are petals on the same flower."

Reading the rest of Dad's book hurt. I always assumed he'd knowingly run from his incarceration, but he simply fled from what happened that night. He wandered aimlessly until he got caught shortly after. Only one entry offered clarity, explaining he left me with Granddad because his last name had been changed to James, so my grandmother would hopefully never find me. He could've never guessed I would be the one contacting her in my pursuit of him.

The smaller red notebook he kept while in prison read very differently than the other. He no longer filled the pages with the occurrences of his days. If I hadn't been told he wrote it while locked up, I would have never known.

Each entry revealed daily messages to me. He repeatedly apologized and wrote constantly about how much he loved Mom and me. The pages were filled with all of his hopes for my life, wishing me to find love, happiness, and fulfillment. Each new section started with "*To my son,*" and each ended with, "*Survive in honor and learn from what has passed. I love you Champ.*" To my surprise, the little red book required more weeks to read than the black journal.

After weeks of heart-wrenching discoveries, I fell ill and gave in to guilt and depression. I had despised and hated my dad for so long that each line of sacrifice and love he wrote about cut deeper than the one before. Cara's presence unwittingly amplified my agony. Each day, as she watched me rot mentally and self-destruct emotionally, I watched fragments of her die. Many times she begged me to talk to her about how I felt, or about what I needed her to do, but I knew the truth would kill her.

The uncanny pestle of my life had ground me down and left me hopeless. I didn't blame my relatives, but I constantly felt terrified of being Cara's object of blame. The spawn of an abused homicidal mother and a diseased father, I felt nothing good enough inside me to make a life with her anymore.

In a desperate attempt to cheer me up, she called Marisa to stay with us a while. Genuinely happy to see her in the first few minutes of her visit, the conversation too quickly turned to Granddad, pushing me back into my hole.

Marisa stayed for two days, and then left after watching me lapse. She couldn't take it. She crumbled under immeasurable sorrow when she realized I was doomed by the same illness she had carried Granddad through.

At her wit's end, Cara cracked and finally unburdened herself.

"When you were locked up, I know you fought to live. Why are you giving up now? We don't have much time together. Why are you wasting it on mourning people who are dead, and torturing yourself over circumstances you can't change? I signed up to love *you*, not this self-pitying shadow you have chosen to be. If you don't stop, you will end up killing us both."

Her words punched me in the face. It took me a second to process them and clear the fog, and before I could respond, she straddled me in my chair and kissed me urgently. We both softened in the long overdue pleasure of touching sensually.

Her kiss made me feel more alive. For a brief moment, I forgot the emotional scars I picked daily. I kissed her back harder, trying to match her energy and will it into my weakness. She threw her shirt on the ground and used both hands to undo my belt and pants. Forced by desire, I melted under the basic instinct to live and thrive. No time to think about the fact that sex was a temporary fix. I needed it.

Standing from the chair, I lifted her with me. Cara wrapped her legs around my waist and I hastened to our bed. We collapsed on the bed in an irresistible trance when a clumsy knock on the front door and a timid "*Hello?*" stopped me.

CHAPTER 30

Irate, I flung open the door and yelled, "What the hell do you want?!"

Poor Briggy nearly dropped the enormously awkward box he held. Before he could say anything, I reached out to help steady the thin but heavy rectangle he juggled.

"I'm so sorry Briggy. I didn't know it was you."

He reached into his unusually normal looking overcoat, and pulled out a handkerchief to wipe the sweat from his brow. "I was *worried* about you," he said emphatically. "I *told you* to come back to the school *soon*. Anyways, that mean blonde girl said she didn't know when you'd be back, and I have something important for you."

"I can see that. What is it?"

"Oh, this?" he asked, motioning to the big, thin box, "This isn't important. Well I guess it is. It all depends, I guess." I couldn't believe how refreshing complete befuddlement made me feel. I was happy to see Briggy, but I would have been much happier if he would have arrived an hour later, or called first.

Cara appeared in the doorway, clothed and blushing, adjusting her hair. After greeting Briggy, she invited him inside, and they followed me as I tried to find a good place to set down the box. Cara asked what was in it, but Briggy goaded, "It's a surprise and you have to wait."

Leaving the two of them to exchange pleasantries, I went to find a knife to open the heavily taped box. By the time I returned, Briggy spoke loudly in the kitchen, admiring how well Cara had cared for the plant he'd sent to the hospital. I listened as I worked through the excellent packing job, and called them when it was almost open. Side by side they stood and watched as I peeled back a thick cardboard panel and pulled out my cherished painting of Lamarck.

"Holy restoration Batman!" Cara exclaimed. "He really did a great job."

Running my hands over the frame, I agreed, but as I scrutinized the painting further, I knew it was wrong. The clothing Lamarck wore didn't match my painting, but they matched a different outfit I remembered him wearing in real life.

"Briggy, is this the same painting we sent out to be fixed?"

"Oh heavens no! That one was beyond repair, the blonde girl told me so. I still can't believe someone could destroy such an amazing piece of history. No manners, that's what's wrong. Students these days don't have them, and my cacti have been behaving the same way. Just this morning a young succulent I transplanted refused to get along with its pot-mate. Can you imagine?"

"Briggy, where did this painting come from?" I asked.

"From my house. I thought you might..."

I didn't hear the rest. The painting struck too close to the real thing, and I lapsed.

The sun no longer shone through the living room windows. I came to hours later, standing on my recliner, and near me Briggy and Cara sat drinking tea. As I watched their blurred visages focus into sight, I marveled at how relaxed they both appeared. I had been giving a speech about something, but it seemed I was invisible to them. While I climbed from the chair, I caught bits of their conversation about tea plants.

"Cara, can I speak with you in the kitchen for a second?" I asked.

"Sure, but if it's about your episode, Briggy said not to worry about it. Would you like some tea?" I told her yes and she causally walked into the kitchen.

Unsure why Briggy wasn't the least bit astonished by my behavior, I looked around the room for the Lamarck painting. They had moved it somewhere else, and I asked Briggy how he came to own it.

"Ohhh, it's been in my family for a long time, and since you were so very sad when that insane girl ruined yours, I thought you might like it. I know how much he means to you."

"Are you sure you want to give it to me? I know for a fact it's worth thousands of dollars."

"Absolutely! The old thing has just been sitting in the house with only my plants there to admire it, and they're not very interested in art."

"Thanks Briggy, it means a lot."

"You're very welcome, but I can't say I am not upset. I have been trying to talk to you about something important. Why have you been avoiding me?"

"I'm sorry. I haven't done it on purpose. I've been in a bad way for some time now. I haven't been a very worthy friend to anyone I'm afraid."

I didn't want to admit I couldn't go out in public for fear of lapsing. I steeled myself against competing memories, hoping I could finish his visit without another incident.

"You're forgiven of course, but the reason I needed to speak to you concerns our research. I came here today to give you the fruits of our labors." He stood while speaking, and I could tell he meant to make a formal attempt at a speech. Each far too scientific phrase followed another I didn't comprehend, and when he pinnacled his denouement, he reached into his coat pocket and produced a medicine bottle containing a thick, milky white substance.

Falling back into our old ways, I congratulated him on completing it, even though I didn't know what it was. It tickled me that he thought of his research and its success as ours.

"Don't you want the specifics?" he poked, a little miffed I didn't ask for details. Trying to save face, I nodded, and he called Cara into the room. She came in carrying a white teacup, and after handing it to me, she sat next to Briggy.

"This neurotoxin is capable of neutralizing specific prefrontal cortex synapses. It has taken me years to isolate them, and while I believe it will work, there is no guarantee that they won't *all* be wiped out. Many fine plants gave their lives to create it, so I hope you appreciate it." Finishing his explanation, he pulled his handkerchief from his pocket and swiped invisible sweat from his brow.

"Briggy, could you use some smaller words to explain it to us non-geniuses?"

"Speak for yourself," Cara said, smacking me on the arm.

"You know what he's talking about?" I asked indignantly.

"Not a clue. I just didn't want Briggy to know that."

I laughed. It felt good to laugh. "Briggy, explain it in small words for me."

He begged with his eyes, "You really don't know what I am saying?" He frowned and shook his head. "I am indeed sorry, I do this all the time apparently. I was in a restaurant the other day trying to order a salad, but I must have used too much Latin because the poor waiter brought me soup. Anyhow, what I'm trying to explain is that I have finally finished the cure for your illness."

I nearly dropped my teacup. Cara looked like she had stopped breathing.

"Back up, Briggy. What are you saying? A cure for *what* exactly?"

"Your problems with soft inheritance of course, your memory issues. Now I wasn't able to test it on people for obvious reasons, but it worked on the rats, and none of them died, so it should be safe. I'm not sure the extent of it though. You might lose your memory completely."

I felt paralyzed. My mouth fell open and I thought perhaps I was imagining it all, but in case I wasn't, I asked, "How did you know I needed a cure?"

He peered at me like I had already lost all my memory. "Did you really not know what we were working on all this time?" I almost answered truthfully no, but I asked a more Briggy-appropriate question.

"Who do you mean when you say 'we' have been working?"

"My family of course, we've been working on a cure for the Shay affliction since we first met in the French Royal Gardens."

Finally grasping the depth of my ignorance, Briggy started at the beginning.

"Lamarck made the introduction between our families. He thought that if anyone would be interested in the genetic implications of your heritage it would be us, and he was right. My family was fascinated by it. Though try as we might, we still can't replicate the necessary juxtaposition in the nucleic acids. Anyhow, at first we just wanted to study you to see where it could apply to plants. After observing your family for years, we began to notice how many issues your evolution caused. It was hard to watch as so many of them wasted away in asylums, and by my research those were horrible places."

I was starting to lapse. I could feel the restraints on my wrists and ankles. The drone of an electroshock machine permeated the room. I could taste the mouth guard still crusted with the lasts patient's saliva. "Cara, help. I'm slipping."

She jumped to me and pushed up my sleeve. She spoke in my ear, "Look at your arm. That's your birthday tattoo. You are Chamberlain, my husband. Say it with me, CHAM-BER-LAIN." I repeated my name several times and focused on her voice. It helped. Slowly, I could move my arms, and the bitterness in my mouth retreated. When I recovered enough, I wanted to finish speaking to Briggy before another episode took over.

"I'm sorry friend. My great grandfather was committed as a child and his memory got me. Please go on, just don't mention hospitals anymore."

"Most certainly. Now where did I leave off? Oh, yes, we felt bad for you. We changed our plans and decided to find a cure. When my father retired, I followed his notes, and the notes of my grandfather."

I couldn't believe I had no memories of a family that had been stalking us for several generations.

"Briggy, what was your relative's first name?" I asked.

"I don't know his real name. I only know that everyone called him Fleurs."

"Flowers! I remember him. We did see him sometimes with Lamarck, but I don't remember anyone talking to him or the rest of your family."

"Well, we do have our own long history of social ineptitude. I am the only one to have mastered the art of social interaction."

"Why didn't any of you tell us what you were doing?" I asked.

"I don't know what you mean. I told you the first day we met, and several times since, but I guess you didn't understand what I said. Maybe that happened with them too."

"Briggy, did you have something to do with the school begging to hire me?"

He adjusted his hair and tapped his feet like a thumping hare. "You are a fantastic professor, and any school would have been lucky to have you. I merely brought your skills to their attention."

I didn't ask further. Briggy was the reason the university kept me around after Amber's sexual harassment complaint, the freak out, and my extended absences. All that time I had an inflated ego, assuming my fame had kept them groveling after me.

I stood up, walked over to him and bent down to his eye level. "Are you saying you can cure me?"

"Yes, but I will warn you again, there is a small chance you may lose all of your memory."

"How small of a chance are we talking here Briggy?"

"We're not entirely sure, but some estimates are as high as... thirty percent."

Wrapping my arms around him, I hugged Briggy so hard he couldn't breathe.

"My friend, you have saved my life!"

"Both of our lives," Cara added.

"I can never repay you for the thankless work your family has done all these years." His cheeks flushed bright red, and tears filled his eyes, which he quickly wiped away with his handkerchief.

"You are my best friend Chamberlain. No one has ever been as kind to me as you. I hear how people laugh at me and I see them mock me and roll their eyes, but never you. If it would have taken the rest of my life, I would have found a way to help you." He laughed and laughed like he'd been holding it in too long. "And to think all this time you never even knew what I was doing."

Briggy placed the cold glass vial in my hand as Cara attacked him with her own suffocating hug. I rolled it in my palms and held it to the light. So small, it held the potential of my entire future. I could be free of the memories, and all the unknown dangers. Cara and I could raise children, and give them the cure when needed. I could grow old, and stay in my own head.

On the surface, it appeared to be the perfect solution, but as I thought of it more, I understood the curse inside the cure.

I always feared the affliction would turn me into someone else, but I realized the cure could do that as well. I wasn't sure if I would still be me in the absence of the memories. Living with them was all I had ever known. Even if my brain still operated in the same manner, and my personality and tastes remained the same, I could still lose all the people I loved - the people who formed who I would always be. Every moment with Granddad, my first night with Cara, and the sound of my parents' voices could be lost forever. I tried not to think of these things as Briggy stood near me. Only a fool could deny the wonderfulness of his gift, and I didn't want to even hint at my hesitation in putting it to use.

When Briggy said he needed to leave, Cara and I begged him to stay.

"I would love to, but plants can't water themselves, yet. I am still working on that though. Besides, I know you both have a lot to discuss. Please keep in mind, you don't have to take the cure if you don't want. It won't hurt my feelings at all. It's *your* decision. I just wanted, sorry, *we* just wanted to give you the option. I wish I could tell you for certain how many memories you will retain, but I guess I'll have to leave that up to my son to figure out."

He started walking to the door, but I stopped him. "You never told me you had a family." I felt awful such an important matter had never come up in conversation.

"I don't. But there is a wonderful gal at the garden supply store who smells like gardenias, and she has a terrific grasp of the turgor pressure in the *Mimosa pudica.* Martha is her name, and she is going to tour the greenhouse with me tomorrow."

"Briggy that's great. I can't wait to meet her." His first mention of Martha or any woman, I wondered if he had put his whole life on hold while he worked on helping me. The thought made me melancholy, but also poured a gallon more gratitude into my overflowing tank.

"Thanks again my friend. I will call you tomorrow." I shook his hand and watched as he walked to his car, not in a straight line, but in the haphazard zigzag only Briggy could manage.

The End

ACKNOWLEDGMENTS

Soft Inheritance is a novel and Chamberlain is a figment of my imagination, but the bones of this story are based around the theory of genetics developed by the brilliant Jean-Baptiste Pierre Antoine de Monet, Chevalier de Lamarck, whose theory of inheritance of acquired characteristics, has in many ways inspired the current transgenerational epigenetics field, which sadly many still debate his contribution. Regardless, I personally owe Lamarck my gratitude for being my muse.

Many of the settings and memories in *Soft Inheritance* are loosely based on actual historical events. I am grateful to the men and women who lived these lives, for the good and the bad, and their contributions to the collective history of mankind.

I owe an immeasurable thank you to my husband, Connell, who has spent the last four years sleeping with the glare of a computer screen in his eyes. His faith and love encouraged me to never let my dream die. He is my rock and train, keeping me grounded and moving forward. Thank you Hubby!

My family is my root and core. Without Mom, Dad, Martha, James, Charles, Naomi, Brandon, Zack, Lily and Fiona my stories would still be locked in my head and my characters would be rotting into ghosts. I love you guys!

Thank you Amanda Lay who loved this story and sweetly guided it into a better version of itself. Her advice and confidence kept me pushing when this novel seemed destine for the drawer. The fingerprints of her advice are visible on each page.

To the slayer of the "Was" Anthony DiMatteo. Thank you. Your diligence, quick eye, passion, extensive knowledge, patience, and brilliance brought this novel into realms I never knew it could reach. As an editor you're the best and any story would be lucky to have you whip it into shape.

My deepest gratitude to Robert Dwight Brown. Not only for your expert knowledge in the field of publishing and design, but for your friendship and sage advice. Your help was priceless and I am lucky to have you in the family. Thank you!

To everyone else who helped bring this novel together, my beta readers, the ladies in the book club, my Fly Shop family and all of my literature, history, and science teachers and professors... THANK YOU!

CPSIA information can be obtained
at www.ICGtesting.com
Printed in the USA
FSOW01n1012131216
28522FS

9 780692 741184